East or West

A collection of twenty-two eclectic stories

Sudhir Jain

 FriesenPress

Suite 300 - 990 Fort St
Victoria, BC, V8V 3K2
Canada

www.friesenpress.com

Copyright © 2017 by Sudhir Jain
First Edition — 2017

Author is grateful to Brigid Stewart for encouragement and advice and Susan Scott for proof reading and many suggestions to improve the stories.

ISBN
978-1-5255-0277-4 (Hardcover)
978-1-5255-0278-1 (Paperback)
978-1-5255-0279-8 (eBook)

1. FICTION, SHORT STORIES (SINGLE AUTHOR)

Distributed to the trade by The Ingram Book Company

The book is dedicated to my wife Evelyn.
Without her encouragement, I would not have published a word.

Heartfelt gratitude to Susan Scott, Brigid Stewart, Pat Kover and Kamini Jain for editing and encouragement.

Table of Contents

East or West

1. Mysterious Move of God

I

They say that the extroverts have all the fun. We introverts know that it is not true. Only our idea of fun is different. Getting drunk, being boisterous without knowing why and cheering in a sports stadium till we are hoarse is not our game. We enjoy intense discussions on serious topics plaguing mankind with or without an agreement at the end. The idea of fun is one where the twains – introverts and extroverts – shall never meet.

The discussions are usually held over lunch. The topic of discussion is set in advance. We read all we can get hold of on the subject, mull over the material, come to some conclusions and prepare arguments to support them. The debate is often heated, certainly hotter than the tepid stew served in the 'always open' modest diner where we meet. In younger days I had a large number of friends and such meetings were frequent. In later years, retirement claimed many of them and I was lucky if I could find a guest once a month. In one way it was good. It helped me lose weight as I grew older and lost height.

I remember the time with great fondness when I regularly locked horns with Ravi. We first met thirty-five years ago when he moved a few doors away from where I lived in one of the communities of middle class young professionals and hopeful business managers that were springing up in and around Calgary. His wife was a pleasant young lady who got along well with mine, perhaps because both of them were from the Shetland Islands and had periods of acute homesickness. Each family had two girls of similar ages who played well together. I worked then, as I do now, with two other architects specializing in renovations. Not much has changed, not in my professional life anyway. Ravi, on the other hand, had a remarkable career. He was lured into coming to Canada by a small service company with big plans. He designed innovative software to help in the exploration of oil and gas. Ravi had big ideas for himself too. For a change from my other stories this one is not about me. This is about the remarkable careers of Ravi.

We had our last meeting some fifteen years ago. Unlike other meetings there was no give and take that day. We agreed that the great rally on stock market would continue because there was nothing on the horizon to slow the economic growth rate. When I asked him if he had come across something interesting, he propounded his theory of 'Quantum of Energy' as if he really believed in it. He may have, I never found out. It is an interesting concept and I will describe it from memory in my own words.

According to Hindu scriptures, every soul carries with it a quantum of energy to the new body it is moving into. The size of the quantum depends on the deeds in the former life – better karma means bigger quantum. As the body uses energy in the normal course of living, the quantum shrinks. When it is used up, the soul departs to be born again with a new quantum. It is in our interest, if we want a long life, to conserve the energy and not to waste it unnecessarily in endeavors like jogging and other physical exertions. True to his professed belief, Ravi was never seen doing anything hard physically. How he stayed fit remains a mystery to me. I scoffed at the idea and forgot all about it. Then an acquaintance had a heart attack while jogging and Ravi's theory started to make sense. It also explained why Hindu armies of previous centuries always lost to the invaders and Indian athletes do not win many medals in international events – they can't reduce the quantum by wasting precious energy in physical training.

1. Mysterious Move of God

We were heading to our vehicles after that lunch when Ravi looked at my truck and asked whether I could help him move his desk and chair from his office to the basement of his home. I agreed without the slightest hesitation and we set the date and time convenient to both of us. This unexpected request drove the quantum theory out of my mind and on my way back to work the parabolic trajectory of his business life occupied my thoughts.

Much happened to Ravi over the years and I watched it with some amazement. A couple of years after we had met, he came over to visit one weekend morning. When we had made ourselves comfortable in the den with mugs of steaming Kona coffee in our hands, he looked straight at my face and said, his dark eyes glowing in excitement, "You won't believe what I have done."

"I don't know whether I will or not. You have to tell me first."

"I have resigned from my job. I am starting a consulting business in oil industry."

"No I don't believe it. You can't do something so foolish. You couldn't have considered it fully. Brenda may have been a doctor once, she is a full-time homemaker now. You have two little girls in elementary school, you have just moved into an expensive home. I guess you have a big mortgage."

"You are right on the details. To add to this we have very little in the bank."

"Not only that, you have been in the country only two years and I don't imagine you have all that many business contacts. You don't seem to be the type to have a mentor. Your being brown does not help in this country either."

"You are bang on with the negatives. Mind you, there are a few positives too."

"Tell me. I am all ears."

"I have worked in five countries and my broad international experience is an asset. Unlike most consultants in business I have studied and worked in all aspects of oil exploration. I have presented

5

papers in meetings of professional societies and this has given me some exposure."

"That is all fine. Do you have anything lined up to put food on the table next month? You are always welcome here of course."

"I hope it won't come to that. My former employers in Denver have offered a lucrative, though short, assignment. I will use this time to drum up some local work."

"What does Brenda think of it?"

"I explained all this to her. She listened very patiently and agreed. She thought it was worth a try if I wanted to do it so bad."

"You have a gem of a wife. I know many women who would kill their husbands for less."

"I know Brenda is a treasure."

2

Brenda suggested that Ravi work out of home office to begin with. He brushed it aside and subleased a small office space on the ninth floor of a building downtown. It had two rooms, one for him and another for a helper if, and when, he could afford one. "Farsighted guy, he will go far," I thought when he told me this. As it turned out, he needed a technical assistant a few months later and I recommended a good candidate who had applied to our firm. The business expanded rapidly. Four years later I renovated two thousand square feet for his eight employees: five professionals and three support staff. One evening I saw a marvellous view of sunset over the Rockies from his seventeenth floor corner office. I felt sorry for my friend because I did not believe that he had either time or inclination to appreciate such niceties. He occupied that space for five years.

A gas station in our community went out of business. It was an attractive building on a large lot. One evening over beer on his patio, Ravi asked whether the gas station could be converted into an office space of four thousand square feet within a budget such that the mortgage payment would be about the same as the rent he was paying for his downtown office. A month later I presented the plans and the cost estimates. I could use the existing facilities almost as they were and add two floors of office space where the gas tank had been. Ravi was delighted and the construction started soon after. He moved into the converted gas station the following year. A year later I built for him another building on the lot where Brenda opened her medical practice with two colleagues. Two physicians and a small lab rented the upstairs floor. Ravi and Brenda had the only 'His' and 'Hers' pair of buildings in town. At this point, his consulting operation had seven professionals, three technicians and an office manager. His reputation in the industry was such that the size, revenue and profitability of his business stayed at this level for several years with only minor fluctuations in spite of notorious ups and downs in the oil industry. Unbeknown to either of us this was the crest in the trajectory of his business career. Then the gods turned against him and made him proud.

3

Muslims make their way to the mosque every Friday afternoon, listen to the Imam and pray. Christians do the same on Sunday and Hindus on Tuesday. Atheism, the fastest growing belief system, if you can call it that, has no holy day. In fact, you will not find the word holy in their book. Maybe you would, if they had a book. Let me call a spade a spade, there is no room for 'holy' in their lives. I do have some sympathy for them. They have nowhere to go to strengthen their wavering faith, no guidebook to help them through the vicissitudes of their humdrum lives. They have to survive by their own wits, no divine guidance for them.

Atheists of the world, take note. Help is now available. No more stewing in your own juice. Swami Dharyanand - a man whose only pleasure is selfless service - has felt the misery of his fellow atheists and devised a solution. It is so elegant yet so simple that you would wonder why no one else thought of it. Could it be divine inspiration? Of course one would not expect Swami to credit divinity. But inspiration it was, and he has spared no effort in making its realization possible.

Swami has set up an ashram in one of the most picturesque places in the world. An ashram you say! Is not an ashram where Hindu devotees of a saint go to seek peace and tranquility in his august presence? Well, it is. Only the Swami calls his abode a Nastic Ashram, a sanctuary for atheists, if you insist on the English equivalent. His idea is that the atheists who need support in any form, except financial of course, can visit him, spend time at the ashram, under his guidance resolve the issues bothering them and return rejuvenated to their normal lives, further fortified by Swami's blessings, bestowed after a donation appropriate for the severity of their problem with scant regard for what they can afford.

What took so long for such a crying need to be addressed? Atheists are generally self-assured, individualistic persons who hate to seek help however much they may need it. Dharyanand was no different till six calamities struck his immediate family. If they had struck simultaneously, he could have borne them; with a lot of suffering, still nothing he could not endure. Statistically improbable though it was, they struck him sequentially, and without a break! Each misfortune weakened his resistance and by the time last one struck he had reached the end of his tether. Fortunately for all other atheists, he was able to garner new internal resources and survive what would have been a fatal stroke to most ordinary humans. It did lay him low, though. He spent several months recuperating in the padded cell of a mental hospital. Dharyanand, made of different stuff than most of us, spent this time considering what to do with the rest of his life now that all he valued had been snatched away, not feeling sorry for himself as we would have. The enlightenment came with the last bump of his head on a patch of the wall where the padding had worn off a little. As he is fond of saying, its source was from within, not from above. There was no invisible finger pointing towards him sending a spark. It was an idea crashing into his sore head and causing a rather ugly bump. Being a man of action he planned to put the idea into practice as soon as the opportunity presented itself.

On his release a few days later, Dharyanand was greeted by his trusty accountant in the lobby of the asylum. For once, the old bean counter was the bearer of good news: the investments his late wife had left to him had grown substantially. Of course the news came with suggestions on what he should do with his life now that he was free. Dharyanand waved these aside without hiding his contempt. After thanking the kind gentleman perfunctorily he took a cab home. He was pleased to note that everything there was just as he had left it except for a thin layer of dust.

Dharyanand phoned a realtor he had known since they worked for the sanitation department. The ex-colleague had just what he needed: a buyer for his home with all its furniture. He sold his other possessions and acquired a farm near the town of Rishikesh on the bank of the holy river Ganges. Within a few months the site boasted a building with modest private quarters for Dharyanand, a meeting room to accommodate fifty people, separate dormitories with washrooms for men and women, a row of cubby holes to serve as meditation rooms, a suitably equipped kitchen and a dining area. A small unassuming sign went up at the entrance, "Swami Dharyanand ka Nastic Ashram" in Hindi vernacular and "Swami Dharyanand's Atheist Retreat" in English. Not many people passed the rustic dirt road and there were no curious visitors. No one questioned the origin of Swami or what the ashram was about.

The road did not remain quiet for long, however. A quarter page ad appeared in a spiritual magazine announcing the opening of the Nastic Ashram in remote foothills of the Himalayas. "A sanctuary for those who feel uncomfortable in religious gathering places because of their personal beliefs and who need to commune with like-minded individuals. Visit www.nasticashram.com" for details. The hits of the website over the next two days set new records. Before the magazine bearing the ad had dropped in the newly minted Swami's mailbox, arriving flights to nearby airports were filled and all available ground transportation booked for months. Dharyanand was thrilled at the reception of his idea in faraway lands. He could wait for more local colour he would have liked among his disciples. Fortune favoured him in another way. A young lady visitor from Europe recovering from a personal tragedy lost her heart to him. Dharyanand knew that he needed help in managing the ashram and before long the ashram had a swamini walking three steps behind the swami and ahead of every one else.

4

I forgot all about Ravi till I helped in his move. After we had set up the desk and chairs and hooked up his computer system, Brenda asked whether I had time for a slice of pecan pie she had baked that morning. "Only if it comes with plenty of whipped cream and a cup of Tetley's tea," I cheekily replied. Ravi and I sat across the desk waiting for refreshments when he told me some things about his career I had not known before. These filled the holes in the story I had in my mind. It is a long tale. I will spare you the details and only touch the salient points.

Ravi had set up a registered retirement savings plan soon after his arrival in Canada to take advantage of the deferred tax on contributions to the plan. At first, his investment activities were restricted to this, "if only because that was the only money I had," he told me. Call it beginner's luck, his investments did well. A few years later he was buying shares with the money left over from business operations. In spite of a few grand failures, these investments were productive too. Then came a point at which the investment income was comparable to that from his consulting operations. I now quote him because I can not bring myself to believe it, "This is when business sense left me and vanity took over. I began to believe that I could do no wrong and it was time to diversify the operations into fields I only had superficial knowledge of." He acquired exploration rights for two large areas, one for oil and gas and the other for iron ore. I remember his excitement at that time and him telling in excruciating detail anybody who would listen all the technical reasons for expecting huge deposits. On my wife's insistence I kept the cheque book in the drawer, though a few of his other friends with gambling in their blood put some of their retirement funds into the so-called high risk/high reward, in my opinion all risk/no reward, projects. Years later Ravi had this to tell me: "While the ventures were sheer folly they were nothing compared to my decision to give up the lucrative consulting business. With no flow of spare funds from this business the cash eventually ran out. After several years of hard work and an expenditure of considerable amount of money, both ventures had to be folded. Not only did I lose money, I lost face as well, although the generous partners stayed on congenial terms."

When the consulting business was put to bed, the building was too large for the remaining operations. A developer made a reasonable offer for the property which, after much heartache, Ravi accepted. He first leased a two-thousand square-foot space with five offices for five years, then moved to twelve hundred square feet with three offices for two years and relocated again to eight hundred square feet with two offices for four years shedding employees at each stage. Let me use his words once more for the final stroke of fortune, "The recent stock market meltdown heaped the ultimate ignominy on me. The account with the money leftover in both our corporations was entirely wiped out. I laid off my last employee, the long term office manager, and now I have had to move my desk and computer to the basement of our home."

I should have been more understanding of the weight of melancholy my dear friend was under. Instead I was inwardly gloating about the wisdom of staying in the same cubicle doing the same job till my days were done. "How does it feel to fall from the high point in the trajectory to the prospect of working on retirement funds in the basement?" I asked.

"Even though I will not miss the grind of the daily commute, I can not get rid of the sense of failure. If any of my operations had succeeded and I had retired to the basement after handing the business over to a successor, I would have an upbeat sense of having created something which outlasted me. Now when I look in the mirror I see a man who thought he was great only to discover that greatness is not assumed, it is bestowed by proven success."

"This is all so sad. I am really sorry for you."

A smile lit up Ravi's face, "No need to be sorry dear friend. The sense of failure is ephemeral. In spite of everything I have love and respect of a wife and two daughters, high achievers all, and of that I am most proud."

5

Ravi settled in his new office and the couple worked out an arrangement for each to get their work done without getting under the other's feet. Then calamity struck. Brenda was diagnosed with breast cancer in a fairly advanced stage. She had to go through a double mastectomy, chemotherapy and radiation treatment. The treatment sapped all her vitality. It took several months for her to get back to normal. However, she was only a shadow of her formal vibrant self. She tried to pick up her practice from where she had left eighteen months ago. However, medicine is a demanding profession and she no longer had the strength to look after the needs of the ailing. She looked at her situation from all angles and gave up the career which had meant more to her than anything else except her daughters.

A few months later Brenda and Ravi moved to Montreal to be near their girls and I lost contact with him.

6

Two years went by. My wife Monica and teenage son Billy, a late addition to the family and the only child left at home, decided to have a bash to celebrate my sixtieth birthday. They told me about it because they knew I don't like surprise celebrations. I was allowed to make suggestions on the guest list and to help with the arrangements. Dinner was to be catered and served on the lawn of our modest bungalow. Fifty guests were invited and most accepted. Three days before the party, Monica said to me, "I have a surprise guest coming on your birthday."

"Who is it? Someone I know!" I asked with some anxiety.

"Don't worry; it is not any of your former girl friends. Yes, you know him. No more questions please. Let us keep it a surprise." Monica put a tight lid on the issue and to please her I agreed to let her have her way for once.

The day arrived in its own time. Sun had risen hours before we opened our eyes, scattered white clouds sparkled against the bright blue sky; and a gentle breeze promised to keep the heat at bay. The forecast for a pleasantly warm sunny day seemed to hold again. Monica prepared a sumptuous breakfast of pancakes, scrambled eggs and bacon. The cards that I opened first tried to convince me how wonderful I was and then the presents; a pure wool cardigan from Monica and a book by Pastor John of our church from Billy. Monica and Billy hung Happy Birthday balloons in green, red, blue and purple in the front porch. To humour me on my special day, my dear wife and son played games of Scrabble and Monopoly with me. In between the games we arranged tables and chairs for the guests, one long table for the caterer to set up and serve the food and another for drinks to be served by Billy. I was instructed to let them do all the entertaining. I was to enjoy the adulation of the guests for having survived the rigours of life of a low profile architect. If the surprise guest was on my mind it was far back and no one mentioned him.

After six, guests started arriving in twos and fours. Half an hour later when most people were on their second drink and Monica was beginning to look nervous the door bell rang. Monica's face lit up and she rushed to welcome the guest. A few moments later I heard a familiar voice and then saw the face of my long lost friend who had launched a thousand debates.

To say that I was surprised to see him standing there is an understatement of the magnitude only I can make. I looked at him with my mouth wide open. It was not that his looks had changed much in two years. Not one of his long hairs had turned grey, it was the same light brown complexion, and there was not a pound more on the slim figure, short by Canadian standards but still impressive. The odd element was his dress, white loin cloth and a long cotton tunic in pale orange. He looked like a monk on the bank of River Ganges I had seen on TV. I, on the other hand, had lost most of my hair and quite a few teeth, gained twenty pounds and stooped a little. I was dressed in blue jeans, jean jacket, calf length boots and a cowboy hat for the Stampede season. It took a pat on the back by Billy to bring me back to Earth and to move forward to greet my friend.

As we shook hands vigorously and then hugged, the other guests cheered. Somehow they had known about the surprise. He asked what I was up to and I told him of my good fortune in Monica and Billy and of a job that still paid enough for us to live in some comfort. I asked him about his unusual dress. "We will talk about it later," he answered.

The party was a great success. Ravi was a hit. When people asked him how Montreal was he told them interesting tales of confusion caused by his beginner's French. Now that I think of it, he said only the minimum about himself. He asked everyone about their families and interesting events in their lives, listened attentively and paid due compliments. I noticed that he drank only water and avoided meat. Every one had good words for my old friend. I basked in the reflected glory with delight.

7

After the other guests had left, Ravi and I headed for the den. While refusing the offer of brandy, he encouraged me to have one. After some small talk, I asked him again what was behind his monkish appearance. Here is what he said, as well as I can remember it.

"Life was good till we moved to live near our daughters and the grandchildren. Then the house collapsed as if it was made of cards. Perhaps it was. I loved Brenda and took her frequent tantrums in stride. I suspect chemotherapy did something to her. Her moods became much more intense. When she was happy she was blissful as if in communion with some higher spirit. When she was upset all hell broke loose. She screamed at me for two or three hours non stop outlining in great detail every act of mine that had harmed her, and, believe me, her list was accurate. Top of the list was, no surprise, my losing all that money and she told me how she could not forgive me for that. My bossing her about was intolerable. She wanted to get away from me so she could start all over again as her own person. She was exhausted at the end of the outburst and went to sleep for ten hours or more. She woke up and behaved as if nothing had happened.

"I would have weathered the tantrums. What disturbed me were her snappy retorts, derogatory comments and unfair fault-finding throughout the day. Most of the time I took it with a smile although it was impossible not be tormented by a simmering resentment. Outwardly I kept calm yet I was shattered inside. I was never an emotional person, won't say I really knew what loving a human being was. Friends said my Emotional Quotient was zero and that is why I was such a success in the profession. The girls were occupied with their families and sided with their mother anyway. Brenda was the person I most cared for in this world. Now she told me every so often that she wanted no part in my life.

"One time I lost my cool completely. I did the only thing I could think of at that moment of utter distress. I went to a cliff not far from our home and jumped off. The cliff was not high enough and after a few months in hospital my bones were as good as they were before the fall. The crazy attempt moved Brenda and she became very kind to me. She looked after me during the recovery with amazing devotion and was very calm throughout. However, as soon as I was walking again she moved out and filed for divorce. After we had agreed on the terms she did something for which I will always be grateful.

"She found out from some article in a San Francisco publication about the ashram - what they call a retreat here - of Swami Dharyanand near Rishikesh, not far from where I grew up. Rishikesh is a beautiful little town in North India located in the foothills of Himalayas on the Ganges before it is polluted by the discharge from the millions who live in the cities along the river and its tributaries. This swami is unique; he is an atheist and his ashram is for atheists who are suffering emotional distress. The cost of living is low in India and the ashram did not cost much more than I would have needed here anyway, so the money was not an issue. I spent six months at the ashram. There were thirty disciples, as they were called. Every month a few of them left and were replaced by the new ones. Those six months with Swami changed my life and I can not thank him enough.

"The disciples were of all ages – from late teens to sixties, from all walks of life and from all over the world. We lived in dormitories, one for men and one for the ladies. Intermingling of sexes was encouraged and there were a couple of private rooms available to couples for their occasional rendezvous. We had two things in common, we did not believe in omnipotent God and all of us were emotionally distressed. Our lives were quite regimented. The diet was strictly vegetarian, alcohol was not permitted and consumption of coffee and tea was limited to two 8 oz cups a day. We were out of bed with the sun rise and had half an hour to prepare ourselves for the day. After a breakfast of oatmeal and milk, we worked in the garden for an hour. Then we headed for the morning discourse.

"The discourse was the best part of the day. Swami and Swamini, his partner, sat cross-legged on the carpet on a raised platform. We sat on the bare floor facing them, ladies on the left, men on the right. Swami spoke in heavily accented English and often asked Swamini for appropriate English words. He set the ball rolling by wishing every one a good day and asking if there were any questions on previous discussions, or suggestions on topics we would like to study. There were many questions from the floor, mostly of a personal nature and some suggestions based on what had been bothering the individuals. Swami responded with patience and answered in detail. Once in a while Swamini nudged him and he allowed her to say her piece.

"The sermon came next. There was no mention of any superpower, not even Darwin, or of any holy book. He talked for an hour or more on how a human being should live and the principles that should guide him or her. Most of his sermons have now receded to the back of my memory except one principle he enunciated that stands out. For me, this was the foundation of all the other principles and I vowed to practise it for the rest of my life. I knew there would be times I would fail and every failure would need to be followed by greater effort. Among much I am grateful to the swami for, it was his illumination of this simple rule, which all religions preach and all saints have practised, is what transformed my life from a stressed to the breaking point existence to a succession of peaceful and harmonious days."

He stopped to take a few sips from the glass of water. It broke the reverie I was in and I picked up my snifter of brandy and a handful of salted cashew nuts. Our smiles reflected our renewed affection for each other. We enjoyed a few moments of silence. Then I asked him to tell me all about the teaching that guides him now. He continued from where he had left off.

"It is something so obvious I have often wondered why I had to return to my birth place and go to a swami to learn it. Let us face it; Hindu swamis have the image of self-serving, money-grabbing individuals that educated Indians despise. Yet here I was under a swami's wing, an atheist rather than a Hindu, yet a swami all the same. After being accustomed to the comforts of Canadian homes, it was tough, particularly for the first few weeks. Yet, something there gave me an inner peace I had never known. Swami and Swamini talked in soothing tones, never raised their voice and answered even the stupidest queries gently although a faint smile could sometimes be noted by a careful observer. Hard physical labor in the fields before and after the morning session must have contributed too, as did the lack of stimulants in the diet. As you may have noticed, I have continued Swami's diet regimen although I sleep longer and work on the computer rather than on a farm. I have managed to retain the peace swami helped me acquire and stresses, whether from the downturn on the stock market or the kids' and grandkids' demands, last no longer than a few minutes. In any event, I have kept away from the cliff and any inclination to go there has been fleeting."

Monica came into the den to check we were still awake and asked if we needed a snack. Instead of answering her query I suggested, "Come and join us. Ravi is telling me what changed him from a stressed to the hilt yuppie to a man at peace with his inner self. He spent six months in an atheist retreat in India and he is just getting to the point of telling me his swami's key teaching."

"It won't mean much to me without the context. I will go and finish putting the house back in order. You can tell me all about it later," Monica said tactfully leaving old friends on their own.

Ravi picked up the thread, "As I was saying I stay away from the dreadful cliff. The only time, and it is only momentary, I feel that way is when word gets to me of Brenda telling our common friends of my numerous shortcomings, particularly how deficient I was in bed. She never forgave me and also invented some new blemishes in my personality. How much of it is due to my actions and how much due to her being alone is hard to tell. It is all so odd because she had always been so supportive. Regardless, I am completely focused on observing the principle and the failures, when they occur, make me try harder.

1. Mysterious Move of God

"Okay, I have kept you in suspense long enough. The new principle in my life, and you will be surprised to hear it because it is diametrically opposite to what I followed when I was in business, is amazingly simple to state and immensely difficult to practise. Just trying to do it washes away the accumulating dirt in my soul; it makes me feel good all over. It is nothing new; sages have said it in different words for millennia. It is the wisdom accumulated by the human race in a few words. Here it is: 'Love fellow human beings with all your heart irrespective of who they are and what they believe. Show your love in the only way you can: Work to make each instant better than it is for everyone around you. To do this, make each person you come in contact with feel happier than he or she did before meeting you.' It comes naturally to some lucky individuals, it is hard for me. I have to constantly remind myself. I am getting better at it though."

Ravi stopped and looked at me waiting for a reaction. I was a little confused by his short statement after such a lengthy introduction. Words were expected of me and this is what I mumbled, "You are right; it is simple to say and hard to do. In our own ways we all try to do it without really realizing it. Our ego gets in the way. The problem is equally simple to state and just as hard to solve: how do we put the other before self?"

Ravi replied, "Swami Dharyanand devoted several mornings to this problem. Sages have emphasized humility as the most important characteristic in a noble human being. Humility means being aware of our shortcomings as well as the goodness in others. It means living for others; putting self after the person you are with. It means relieving the suffering of others and replacing it with joy. It means providing a source of strength to the down and out individual whatever the cost. It means letting go of the ego. It is hard, very hard. I fail more often than I succeed. I have to constantly remind myself of my vow to the Swami. That is why I wear the simple apparel of a disciple – to remind me of my primary responsibility. Even if it might sound phony I get great satisfaction in trying."

"How do you control your natural reaction to fire back when some one near and dear to you is harshly critical of you on a regular basis?"

"Swami covered that too in one of his sermons. Difficult maybe, it is by no means impossible. One has to realize that getting upset does not improve the situation. I would look at my recent actions and try to identify the one that may have prompted the criticism. There is no smoke without fire. If one finds the fire and puts it out, the smoke disappears."

"One more question. You may have answered it already but I will ask anyway. How do you stop people taking advantage of you?"

"If you are humble enough to have your only purpose in life to make others feel better in your presence, you are only here on this planet to serve in any capacity you can. You are here for others to benefit from you; to take advantage of you. A true disciple of Swami will be glad to have been provided an opportunity to serve."

This reply didn't satisfy me. So I asked a similar question, "What would the swami have to say about dealing with people like me who have an elephantine memory for perceived and real injuries done to them and no recollection of favours, and therefore have frequent out-bursts for no apparent reason?"

Ravi stayed calm even though he saw through my query. He said, "Many disciples had similar problems with their close friends and the Swami discussed it in detail. We have to be tolerant; it is not for us, in spite of what proud advocates of Atheism like Christopher Hitchens spout, to teach our fellow beings except by setting an example. Swami added a line which I will never forget, 'Toleration of injustice is the cross we must bear with all the grace we can muster.'"

The clock on the wall struck twice. Ravi stood up, "Time to say goodbye. It was kind of Monica to think of me and it was a joy to renew the old friendship. I am sorry if I bored you with my monologue. I do get carried away. Please convey my thanks to your charming wife and best wishes to your delightful son. I will write to you when I am back in Montreal."

We walked to his rented car and shook hands firmly before he slid into the driver's seat. I turned back towards the front door with moist eyes wondering where an atheist gets the strength from to take such a vow and to work so hard to keep it. Monica was awake when I crept into bed. I told her my dear friend's strange story. In spite of the late hour, she listened to it without falling asleep and did not interrupt me once. When I finished she looked at the ceiling, perhaps through it, and mumbled, "God moves in a mysterious way."

8

Ravi sent me an email message a few days after returning to Montreal and a pack of six cans of maple syrup to Monica. After that we corresponded on a regular basis. I am grateful that he found time to keep me informed of unexpected developments in his life. It brought some excitement in the humdrum world of this fixer of collapsing structures. I haven't asked his permission because I am certain the request will be denied. Therefore, I am sharing the bewildering story of his new career with you in confidence.

The ashram of Swami Dharyanand attracted notice of the media in California where the saints from India have been revered for more than a century. Several television and web personalities broadcast glowing reports of the ashram on their stations after travelling to Rishikesh to interview the Swami. Thanks to the publicity, not desired by the Swami though not discouraged either, the trickle of disciples from California became a torrent. Swami could not attend to the vast numbers at his door step and he had to consider the establishment of another ashram. After months of serious consideration of their pros and cons, and discussions with the prospective sponsors, he put into operation a plan to open an 'ashram' in the Bay Area of California where Swami Vivekanand had set up a Hindu ashram in the nineteenth century, atheists being rather scarce in those days. It would take three years to set it up, the time required to select and train a disciple in the code of Atheism as well as in managing an ashram with the efficiency Swami's disciples were entitled to expect. Swamini took on the responsibility of finding the right disciple who had the attributes necessary to be a Swami or Swamini so far from Rishikesh, and of designing an appropriate training program for the chosen one. The selection was critical for another reason: he or she would take over from the Swami when swami's quantum of energy was depleted.

Swamini was nothing if not thorough. She drew up a list of qualifications, those a prospect must have, those he/she should have and those it would be nice if she/he had. The 'must' included being a convinced atheist – agnostics wouldn't do, thorough knowledge of the Vedas and other Hindu and Buddhist scriptures, the Bible and the Quran to be able to counter the attacks of religious fanatics and pretend Western atheists. Also the candidate had to be a successful businessperson, or a professional, so she/he did not need a salary. 'Desirable' included being an Indian living in North America. 'Nice to have' had only one entry – spouse who was a devoted atheist and suited to the hard life of the second in command. No one knew how hard this life was better than the Swamini.

Swamini went through the file of disciples on her computer. Most of them were easily eliminated because they knew little about the scriptures. Of those few who were conversant in the scriptures of major religions, all except one could be dropped on the grounds of uncertainty about their faith in atheism. The person left standing was my dear friend Ravi. Although he did not have a devoted wife, not then anyway, it was much better than having a wife who was devoted to some faith, as indeed Brenda had been. One could hope that one of the new disciples would break open the tightly shut door to his heart before the new ashram became fully established. After approval of the Swami and checks with major contributors Swamini emailed Ravi the offer of the position of swami-in-training.

1.   Mysterious Move of God

Ravi saw the email and pinched himself. He went on a walk around the block in spite of sub-zero temperature and checked the message again. It was still there in black and white, 16-point, italicized, bold font the Swamini favoured. He pinched himself again, really hard. Yes, it was true. He was the chosen one. He replied in a humble 10-point, regular font his acceptance of the great honour being bestowed on him. First thing the next morning he told the broker to sell everything in his portfolio turning down the suggestion to reconsider his 'obscenely hasty' decision. "Opportunity to serve in this way comes once in many life times and I am blessed to be given it. I must focus on it with all my faculties and give it all I have," Ravi told him. He sold all his possessions and gave away what he couldn't sell. A week later he was in Rishikesh rubbing the dust off the sole of Swami's right foot onto his forehead.

Swamini already had the training sessions planned and booked. During the two-day orientation Ravi learnt that his training was divided into three parts, each lasting nine months and devoted to the study of Islam, Hinduism and Christianity. Six months of each period were to be spent in a refresher course to become intimately familiar with the concepts of the religion being studied followed by three months of meditation. The idea behind the religious studies was not to convert the faithful of other faiths - Swami firmly believed from his own experience that life was difficult for most folks and whatever made it tolerable for them, even a belief in something he did not agree with, was fine and no one had any right to try to change it – it was to prepare the arguments to counter that faith and to develop techniques to bring round his future wavering faithful to save them from an uncertain future. After completing the religious training Ravi was to spend six months in a premier business school in Bangaluru to learn the A,B,Cs as well as the X,Y,Zs of managing the retreat as a business. He was to spend his final three months of training as swami's second in command to gain first hand experience. Thus prepared, he would be ordained as a swami in a ceremony to be held in Rishikesh with the simplicity the occasion deserved although it would be broadcast via internet to the atheists of the world.

9

In view of the increasing importance of fundamentalist Islamic groups in the region of the next ashram, Ravi's first training assignment was at the celebrated Jamait - academy - in Deoband, four hours by bus from Rishikesh. Most of the renowned fundamentalists whose sermons had inspired Muslims all over the world to frightening acts in promotion of Jihad were trained here. He enrolled under an assumed name, Muharavi, so he would receive the same training as Muslim students. He expected the teachers to be firebrands who shot poisoned arrows at other religions and extolled the virtues of the holy Quran at the tops of their voices with amplifiers set at the maximum. In this he was disappointed. The poison-tipped arrows were from foreign students and were aimed poorly. Jamait's emphasis was on teachings of the Quran as interpreted by the scholars through centuries. Muharavi was so impressed that he would have converted to Islam except for timely reminders from Rishikesh of the purpose of his study. It took all of the allotted three months for him to marshal counters to all the convincing arguments he had heard over and over during the term. His report on the first stage of his training ran into hundreds of pages. Although Swami preferred concise reports, he was impressed by Ravi's explanation of the theology of Islam and delighted with his clever demolition of the arguments presented by his tutors.

'Ravindra' set off for the ashram of the holy among the holies, the most revered Sant - saint - Mahacharya in the holy city of Varanasi to spend six months learning all that the saint had to teach about ancient Hindu scriptures. The ashram consisted of four mud huts with straw roofs, located on the bank of Ganges, the same river that flowed past the ashram in Rishikesh five hundred kilometers upstream, the river where one dip cleanses the sins of a whole life and prepares devoted

Hindus for eternity in Heaven. Although the atheist in Ravindra was horrified by the floating carcasses and other filth in the river and nauseated by the foul smell, such was his determination to prove his worth to the Sant that he rose with sunrise and bathed in the river every morning. The Sant taught Ravindra all he had learnt from the scriptures in his long life devoted to study. There was so much to learn that the brain of the devoted disciple was full every few days and the learning had to be consolidated, as it is on a computer memory, to create space for new knowledge. It is a miracle that Ravindra survived the term without his head exploding with the pressure of all the Sant had forced in it. What may have helped the lucky disciple, without him realizing it till later when he was working on the counter arguments, was the inconsistencies which had crept into the creed developed over five thousand years under many contradictory influences. It was these inconsistencies that neutralized the impact on the overworked neurons in his brain.

'Ravid' arrived in Kochi on the southern tip of India after travelling by train and bus for two days. He noticed immediately that he was in a different environment from Rishikesh, Deoband and Varanasi. There were no day and night chants from devotees or calls from muezzins. The religion was a low key affair in this part of India where Christianity had arrived before it found a foothold in Europe. It was generally believed that Bishop David Maharaj was descended from the first converts two thousand years ago. His knowledge of the old and new testaments was vast and his sermons had been so popular that they had attracted visitors of all faiths from all over the country. Compilations of his sermons were translated into twenty Indian and thirty foreign languages and sold tens of millions of copies. He donated the royalties to the church with one proviso: the proceeds were to be spent on the education of the poor. Much to the regret of his followers he had retired a few years ago due to ill health. It speaks volumes of the powers of persuasion of Swamini that he agreed to take Ravid for the whole duration of his training.

Bishop David set up a routine which Ravid followed every day of the week except Sunday. Ravid woke up early, walked over to the beach to watch the sun rise and do yoga exercises. He had a bowl of idli for breakfast and arrived at the door of Bishop's home at nine sharp. They sat cross-legged on the floor of the prayer room facing each other with a small desk in between them. Ravid read a chapter from the copy of the Bible he had brought with him, beginning at the beginning. The Bishop asked him to describe what it meant to him. When Ravid had finished there was a discussion which lasted till it was time for lunch. The discussion took the form of the Bishop asking him short pointed questions when he felt Ravid's understanding was somewhat vague, then providing his own explanation. In the style of ashrams of the golden age of religions in India, Ravid was not permitted to make any written notes and had to listen attentively to every word from the mouth of the holy man. Ravid was free to ask the Bishop to clarify his explanation and the Bishop did so with a smile. At one in the afternoon, Ravid walked to his digs for a simple lunch. After a short siesta, he made detailed notes of the morning session. In the evening he went to the beach for a swim. Before calling it a day, he read the chapter which was to be discussed the following day. On Sundays, after attending the service at the church, he played tourist visiting places of interest in and around Kochi.

When six months were up, Ravid expressed his deep gratitude to the Bishop for sharing his vast knowledge with him and the Bishop, in turn, thanked him for helping him understand the Bible better. Both of them had enjoyed the time, although the Bishop was beginning to feel some strain towards the end due to his age.

Ravi worked really hard over next three months absorbing all he had learnt under the Bishop's tutelage and preparing his answers to all the queries a swami might face from ex-Christians in his ashram. He expected pressure from his fellow atheists and also from fundamentalist right-wing Christians who controlled vital parts of the media and were very vocal in their opposition to other faiths as well as the faithless. For the last one month he worked closely with the Swami and the Swamini, particularly the later who drew on her background as a lapsed devout Christian in her native Belgium, to prepare acceptable arguments against the waverers of her former faith. The dissertation that he prepared for the Swami delighted him so much that they agreed to publish it, albeit under assumed names to protect the ashram from rowdy protesters.

After the grind of tuition in three religions, the management school was a cake walk. He had attended a number of management courses in his former life and the same principles of marketing for revenue enhancement and cost control for maximizing the profits were recommended for ashram management. After the course ended, it was a relaxed, smiling Ravi who walked through the gates of the ashram in Rishikesh, very different from the exhausted man who had crawled up the path on earlier occasions.

The final training sessions with the Swami were much more hands on than his similar experiences with his superiors in the companies he had previously worked. At first, the Swami let him answer disciples' queries. Later in private, they discussed in minute detail the answers, both his technique and what he said. Swami offered suggestions stating frequently that it was for Ravi to consider them and to adopt them only if it suited his personality. In the second month, Ravi was asked to deliver the sermons on mutually agreed topics. Swamini was so pleased with his way of presenting his thoughts and his brilliant delivery honed by giving award-winning research papers that she unwittingly embarrassed her husband by stating in his presence that they were better than any she had ever heard, either in a church or in the ashram. In his last few weeks he delivered the sermon every morning while the Swami edited Ravi's dissertation on Christianity to prepare it for publication.

IO

On the morning of the consecration ceremony, Ravi had a bath in the water from river Satlaj rather than in the holy Ganges nearby. Swamini had the water trucked from two hundred miles away to highlight the integrity of his atheistic beliefs. He put on the simple garb of a swami, long saffron kurta - a knee-length tunic - and white loin cloth which barely reached his knee, both handspun cotton woven in the ashram and stitched by the expert hands of the Swamini. He combed his lustrous black hair with a parting in the middle; disciples trimmed his nails. The plastic thongs on his feet were the only concession to modernity and these were discarded on the door of the hall crowded with the present and past residents of the ashram.

The ordination was a grand yet simple affair. Cameras were set at critical points for broadcast around the world on television and the web. Although much to Ravi's disappointment his tutors had not responded to the invitation, social, political and industrial leaders, who had been to the ashram in their time of need, arrived with little fanfare. The only way to separate them from ordinary disciples or to judge their importance in the world outside was to count the number of uniformed and discretely armed security guards accompanying them. Every one turned to face him as Ravi entered the hall with the Swami on his left and the Swamini on his right. They shouted 'Greetings, New Swami' in unison as if they were a well rehearsed choir. Ravi responded by "Thank you. May joy be with you." The three made their way to the raised platform. Here the simplest of all investitures was performed. A noted Bollywood actor, who had rehearsed them with a renowned Hollywood director, read excerpts from The Origin of Species especially selected by the Swami. Swami held both Ravi's hands in his and said in a loud and clear tone, "Ravi was picked from all past and present disciples based on his outstanding qualifications for the job. He proved himself worthy of our confidence in the exhaustive training process set up for him and in his practical performance in this ashram over last three months. Therefore, I appoint Ravi the Swami of our ashram in America and charge him with all responsibilities, from setting it up to daily operations. Henceforth he shall be called Swami Suryanand and serve the atheists of America selflessly with all his strength. I also anoint him my successor if I am incapacitated to perform my duties as the head of all our ashrams." Swami raised Ravi's hands as the audience cheered. Then the Swamini presented a rolled sheet of paper, the franchise contract for the new ashram, which both swamis - old and newly minted - signed with a flourish.

Swami Suryanand gave a short interview to a TV personality whose show was broadcast all over the world. He extolled the virtues of Swami Dharyanand, thanked him for establishing the ashram where he and Swamini so humbly and ably serve the distressed atheists with nowhere else to turn, he expressed the hope that his ashram would be able to achieve a fraction of such results and appealed to disciples to open their wallets a little wider. In the meantime, volunteers brought carafes of mango and lemon juice, bowls of fruit, plates of samosas and Indian sweets prepared in the kitchen of the ashram. The new Swami mingled with the crowd, answering their queries with good humour. When the visitors from Silicon Valley introduced themselves, he thanked them for their past support and encouraged them to set up foundations to finance the building and the operation of new ashrams. Swamini watched him with pride when he encountered female disciples and became convinced that a worthy co-leader for the new ashram was not far off.

II

Swamini's hopes did not materialise. Her chosen disciple never forgot the kindness of Brenda even after their divorce, and the ashram had to manage with only one guide. This deficiency notwithstanding, my friend demonstrated unusual business acumen and his ashram became the first of fifty seven ashrams in North America, a billion dollar enterprise with foundations supporting education, health services and poverty eradication in communities where the ashrams were located. Yet, serving the fellow atheists in distress remained the central aim. I have an inkling that my dear friend was often nominated for major honours which he humbly, and firmly, directed towards his Guru in Rishikesh.

His messages became rare soon after the investiture and stopped altogether a couple of years ago. I assumed that he was much too busy to think of his old friend whom he had seen only once in a decade. I did hear a few months ago in a roundabout way the shocking news of cancer coming back and claiming Brenda. Then the events took a strange turn. I was visiting Santa Maria last month to visit Billy. On a walk to the beach I saw a road marker with an arrow pointing to "Swami Dharyanand's Ashram." I followed the sign and was soon talking to a gentleman clad identically to Ravi when he visited us. He told me in a distinct local accent the strange story of Swami Suryanand's disappearance. On his way to Rishikesh a few months ago he is known to have landed in Delhi and has not been heard of since. The young version of Ravi told me of several rumours, many bizarre beyond belief.

I have no idea what Ravi could be doing and whether Brenda's death played any part in it. Knowing what little I know of human nature, it does not seem impossible to me that he eventually realized that his focus had unwittingly shifted to building an empire than in helping the helpless. This began to agitate him and he decided to live truly for others in one of the many beautiful small towns located in the foothills of Himalayas. On the other hand, it would not surprise me either, if the great success he achieved seemed an illusion to him now. He may have felt that he had to change the course of his life to use to maximum effect the shrunken quantum, if he still believed in it, or in the few remaining years of good health, if he had been joking. This may have prompted him to follow an ancient Indian tradition to become a sanyasi. If this is indeed the case, my dear friend is now dressed in nothing more than a white loin cloth and is wandering in bare feet with a staff in one hand and a bowl in the other, from one village to the next, helping the troubled folk of all faiths feel better than they did before meeting him by advising them on how to cope with whatever is troubling them.

2. FLIP OF THE COIN

I

I am excited. And with a good reason. I have a date. First date in months. Such a fine lady too. Met her by coincidence. The concert was sold out. I had a spare ticket, she was looking for one. The stars were aligned. We hit it off during our chat in the intermission. After a rather exciting second half, I asked her if she was free for dinner some evening. "You set the evening, I will set the menu," I said giving her my card with my email address. No sooner had I given up hope, the message arrived setting today's date. I spent the week finalizing the menu and the right wine and picked the fresh produce in the farmers' market this morning.

I am a man of simple tastes and limited talent, particularly when I put on the chef's apron complete with a drawing of flames shooting out of a saucepan. Accordingly, the menu is pretty run of the mill – start with cold zucchini soup, an entrée of chicken cordon bleu with broccoli, baby carrots and baked potatoes, sherry trifle for the dessert. Two bottles of 1985 vintage Pinot Noir will help the food glide down the palate and fifty year old Port, saved for such an occasion will follow Turkish coffee. The trifle with exactly one and a quarter cup of vintage dry sherry and the soup were prepared in the afternoon to the tunes of Carmen being broadcast on the radio. The vegetables are chopped, chicken, ham and goat cheese ready to go in the pan. It is still an hour before her arrival; enough time for a gin and tonic.

It is funny how gin sends me back to those days in India when I was young and foolish, though didn't know it then. Having graduated from an elite business school in Bangaluru where I had secured admission due to family connections, I found a job as an assistant to the vice president of a company partially owned by an American multi-national. I was beginning to get my feet wet when Boston told us that they were sending an expert to train us in modern management techniques. On a beautiful morning in November Amanda Graves arrived in our office fresh as a daisy. She showed no signs of fourteen-hours travel on three planes, or the time difference of ten hours. We looked at her and wondered when she had learnt all she was going to teach us – she looked barely out of her teens. Still taught us she did, a lot, for the whole week till even the keen ones couldn't absorb any more. There was a farewell dinner for her at the president's palatial apartment. I had the great fortune of being seated next to her.

It is a short story, no point making it long. During the couple of hours we shared at the table, love was kindled in our hearts. I offered to drive her to the airport for her flight a little before dawn and she accepted with alacrity – which I found very flattering coming from an American woman of the world although would have regarded unseemly in an Indian girl. On the airport when I was carrying her bag to the check in, she asked if I would like to be transferred to Boston. It took a second to flip a coin in my mind – it was 'servants' versus 'dollars.' 'Dollars' won and I said it would be wonderful. Within a year I was in Boston. To keep her parents happy, I lived in a modest hotel for three months before we were married and then moved into her condominium.

2

Problems began as soon as we returned from the honeymoon. We woke up at a reasonable hour. There was time to relax and read the paper before breakfast and drive to work. Amanda suggested that I made a pot of coffee. No one had ever expected me to do anything at home, let alone make coffee. I had no idea what the women did in the kitchen to make coffee, or anything else for that matter. I was shocked. I gulped and asked, "What do I have to do to make coffee? Never made it before."

Now it was Amanda's turn to be shocked. She sat up with a jolt that almost tossed me out of bed, "What do you mean you never made coffee before? You have coffee in India, don't you? What do you drink when you get up?"

"We drink coffee of course. The servant makes it. My mother would have fainted if she saw me in the kitchen."

"Oh God!" exclaimed the self-proclaimed atheist, "What have I got into?" She went to the kitchen, made the coffee and thrust a mug into my grateful hands with scant grace.

When we returned home from work she looked at the floor and remarked, "Two weeks away is a long time. The floor needs vacuuming."

"What is vacuuming?" I asked innocently.

There was an explosion matching the one in the morning. "What do you do to clean the floor at home? Lick it!"

I disregarded the insult remembering our wonderful honeymoon. "One of the servants uses the broom and mop every morning after breakfast. No man of my class would be seen dead holding a broom."

"One of us will be dead soon if the floor is not vacuumed before dinner. And you better vacuum it, if you want anything to eat. Go to the cupboard in the hallway, find the vacuum and work out how to use it. I want the whole apartment finished before I serve the meal." She issued the order and disappeared in the kitchen. Fortunately, I worked out how to plug in the machine and use it to pick up the dust. I was amazed how easy the work was, though not as easy as it would have been to watch someone else do it. Amanda examined the floors, pointed a few corners I had missed and after I had done them and put away the machine, we had dinner. The food tasted plain to my palate, I enjoyed it all the same. After we had finished eating, she showed me how to make coffee and told me that making coffee in the morning and evening was my job.

We sat down and watched the news on TV. It was doom and gloom as usual. We had become used to it and neither of us was depressed. Amanda dropped another bombshell after the news, "I have to prepare for a meeting tomorrow. Will you do the dishes and clean the kitchen?"

"Dishes, what dishes? I have never even dreamed of doing the dishes. I do not know how to do the dishes? We always had servants to do the dishes and clean the kitchen."

"Well, you don't have a servant here. You do have a wife who is your superior at work. Every thing you need is under the sink. Surely you can work out what you need to do. You have a college degree, albeit from an Indian college."

I swallowed this insult too and worked out the nitty-gritty of the job. First time everything was hard and my hands were sore. After a few days I worked out a system and the job became easy, although there were times Amanda sarcastically showed me dried food on the pans which I had to scrub again. Over the months, the dried food problem faded and many others arose.

A couple of days later Amanda saw the dirty pile of clothes, looked me in the eye and asked, "What do you do with dirty clothes in India?"

"Dhobi picks them up every Monday and Friday and brings them back all clean and ironed," I replied.

"Well, there is no dhobi here. You can take them to the cleaners and pay big bucks. We use a washing machine here."

"Washing machine! Is there something you don't have a machine for?"

"Let us not worry about other things at this time. I will show you how to do it once. Then you are on your own. If you pay attention, you won't have to pay for my dresses or woolens that you spoil."

The threat drove home. I listened carefully to the instructions, memorized them as if they were delivered at her management course and only had to pay for two dresses and four sweaters over the next three years.

It was a cold Saturday morning a few weeks later. We had a leisurely breakfast of pancakes and finished the newspaper. Taking the last sip of coffee, by now quite presentable, Amanda remembered something I wish she hadn't. "The maintenance of green spaces is shared by the condo owners. It is our turn to do the lawn. I will attend to the flowers if you cut the grass," she said looking out of the window at the yard.

"Cut the grass? How do I cut the grass? Never done it before."

There was no explosion, only the witty repartee, "Of course gardeners did it at home. What a shame I didn't get immigration papers for them too. You should have reminded me. Now that you didn't, better get down to work."

Amanda showed me where the lawn mower was, how to fill the gas, check the oil, hook the bag for clippings and start the engine. I did the job to her apparent satisfaction except when the engine stopped and I didn't know why. She pointed out that the bag was full. Then I asked the silly question, "What do I do with the clippings?" She answered, "Dump it in the compost, what else? And don't just throw it on the top, mix it in with what is already there." For some reason I couldn't fathom, she sounded exasperated.

3

Now that I could clean the apartment, do the dishes, wash the clothes and cut the grass, life became easy. I shopped for groceries according to Amanda's detailed list and she did the cooking and general home management. Life became a comfortable routine. If every one knows what is expected there are no arguments and days, weeks, months pass by pleasantly. This pleasant routine must have started boring Amanda. One dinner time she said, "You should learn to cook. It is not fair that I do everything in the house even though I have a more stressful job."

"My mother will turn in her grave if she knew that I was cooking my own meals?" I said rather tamely.

"Your mother is not in a grave. She was cremated, wasn't she?"

"Indeed she was. I have no talent in culinary arts. I will need detailed instruction."

"No problem. I am a trained instructor," she reminded me as if I could ever forget it.

It started with washing and chopping vegetables, moved up to boiling, steaming, baking and frying them. Then it was grilling or frying chicken, pork and beef. In between there were lessons on boiling, poaching and scrambling eggs. It took a couple of years before I could serve an edible meal. I must admit to a sense of achievement when I cooked my first meal from scratch. I was disappointed, though, when Amanda left the table after coffee to prepare for a meeting and I had to do the dishes as usual.

4

Amanda was the boss at work and the example she set in the office had to be followed at home. However, I could now do everything an Indian man of my social background marries a woman for and began resenting her rigid rules. This is when I ran into my old boss from Bangaluru. He had started his own software business that had prospered. He was making plans for an American subsidiary and asked if I would like to run it. There was a problem though - he wanted the business to be located in Silicon Valley. Again I flipped the proverbial coin in my head, 'be bossed' or 'to boss.' It came with 'to boss' on top and I accepted the offer then and there. When I told Amanda she blew up. "I am not leaving a great job and going to the wretched West Coast. My ancestors have lived in Boston for six generations. My whole family and all my friends are here. Why would I leave behind every one I know to go to the boonies and live among strangers?"

2. Flip of the Coin

Well, Amanda stayed behind and I moved on. I returned once a week at first, then once a month and then not for six months. Not interested in much else, I spent the evenings improving my culinary skills and developed a taste for wines. For someone who couldn't tell a Shiraz from Merlot not so long ago I became quite an expert. Of course I shared this expertise with Amanda when we were together. However, she was not impressed. One evening I received papers from her lawyer. Our days as a couple were over. In due course the divorce was finalized and a relationship of convenience initiated by the flip of a virtual coin came to an end. Thankfully, there were no children to suffer from the break up.

Even if you are a man who regards modesty as the greatest virtue, and some may say I have a lot to be modest about, there comes a time when ego takes over and one wants to show off a newly acquired skill. This is why musicians perform on stage, authors publish thick books, athletes climb on the podium. What can chefs do? They can open a restaurant. But not if they run a company in Silicon Valley. They cook for some one special. That is what I am doing - cooking a special dinner to persuade someone to become someone special to me.

3. DEBBIE GOES TO PESHAWAR

I

It must have been late September of 1966. I was very young then, in the second year of my nursing course and had recently moved in the only international student's hostel in Liverpool, England. It was open to both men and women, very unusual in those days. It was popular because the location was convenient for the university and the city centre. There were many cultural facilities within walking distance.

The buzz among the girls in the residence was pretty close to deafening. All of us were talking about Noob, the only son of a warlord in Pakistan. He was rumoured to be a little more than twenty, tall and handsome, so fair could pass for a Brit, even had blue eyes we were told. Lived in a fortress in Peshawar, had more servants than Prince Charles. Needed to be trained in how to put on his clothes and to use the cutlery before leaving for 'Vilayat' - overseas. His mothers and sisters cried for days when the warlord decided his heir needed education at a British university. Who told us all these stories? I for one can't tell who told me first. We told each other, not once, not twice, dozens of times. It was exciting and the excitement just kept growing. I am sure every girl was planning ways to corner him. I even went and bought two skirts and a dress like those Twiggy was modeling; skirts barely covered the underwear and you had to watch out when sitting down.

I missed the alarm, must have been dreaming of my Noob from Peshawar, and had to rush for breakfast. I took the only space available, next to a stranger, a short young man who could be anyone of the hundreds of students from the Indian subcontinent. He stared straight at his empty plate and looked distinctly uncomfortable when I sat down. I felt an urge to make this new arrival comfortable. "I am Debbie, studying to be a nurse," I said offering my hand for a handshake.

He shivered and pulled as far away as he could without paying attention to my hand that still had a faint odour of soap. "I am Ahmed. I have just arrived from Peshawar. The male followers of Muhammad are not permitted to talk to women who are not their relations." With that he started buttering a slice of toast. I rubbed my left cheek and picked up the knife and fork. "So this is the Noob all the excitement was about. The handsome prince turned out to be a frog. What a shame," I said to myself.

A few weeks went by. I was in the laundry room one morning loading clothes in the dryer when Ahmed walked in, his eyes admiring his toes peeping through the sandals. He was carrying a bag overflowing with clothes. He looked at the washing machine as if it had just dropped from the moon. I took pity on this "short, rude, crude and ugly to boot brownie" as the disappointed girls called him and asked, "Do you want me to show you how to work it?"

"Yes please, if you don't mind," he muttered, his eyes still focused on his toes.

"Look, don't think I am being rude. You have come all this way to live and learn with us. You will have to stop being silly. Start treating women with some respect. They won't eat you. They might help you in many ways that will make your life a bit easier without your principles or your religion being compromised. Think over it. Now this is where ...." And I showed him how to wash his clothes. He said, "Thank you very much," almost in a whisper, still staring at his toes. I gave him up as a lost cause and stalked out.

3.   Debbie goes to Peshawar

It was later that week that I received the shock of my life. I was lining up for dinner when Ahmed came over to me. He was not staring at his toes and not facing me either. "I am sorry for my rude behaviour. The Quran tells us to respect women and specifically forbids rudeness. I have been rude. If you will forgive me and forget the past, I will make amends, I promise you."

I could not believe my ears. Neurons in my brain picked up speed. Wonder how he intends to make amends. Perhaps he will ask me for a date. I have never dated a shorter man. So what? Here is my chance to make a foreigner feel comfortable in a strange land.

The storm subsided and I said, I hope the right thing, "Oh! Don't worry. It is very difficult to move into a different culture and know what to do. I would be just as awkward, if not more, if I went to Pakistan." With that I offered my hand for a handshake. He gently took my hand in his and held on till I pulled it away. "Oh God, how can a man have such soft hands," I said to myself.

Now that the rumours about his appearance had turned out to be false, I took the opportunity to check those about his royal status. Over dinner I asked him about his life in Peshawar and he confirmed many of the stories. He was the only son of a tribal leader, he had two male servants to bathe and dress him, his wish was the command, not only for dozens of servants meekly serving the family and for the constant stream of visitors as well as for his mother and three sisters who insisted he spent a lot of time with them in the janana, the part of the house reserved for females and where a male could enter only when invited. In public, even at home when male guests were present, the women covered their faces with something like a loose tea cozy, only it had a strip of netting around the eyes so they could see others without others seeing them. This imprisonment of women annoyed me.

"How can you justify this system? It is enslavement of women."

"Oh no, just the contrary. It protects women from male ogling and misbehaviour. The holy Quran instructs us males to protect the females. This is the method sages devised and we have been practising it for centuries," Ahmed responded with a straight face.

"How can a woman do any work with face covered like that? Surely most women have to earn a living and do chores at home? Not everyone can have servants. What about female servants?"

"They get accustomed to the burqa and find it quite convenient. The separation of male and female spheres is very strict. Women don't cover their faces when men are not around."

"It is a way to keep women in permanent bondage. I would like to learn about the religion that treats half of its followers so abominably."

"Well, I will be happy to explain to you the key elements of Islam. It will take between thirty minutes and an hour. Perhaps we could do it next Saturday. Tell me the time and I will get my room ready."

"That is great. I will ask Liz if she will join me. She is interested in religion. We will come to your room after lunch."

2

It didn't take long for Saturday to arrive. As I had anticipated, Liz was delighted to join me. We lingered over coffee to allow time for Ahmed to get organized. An elevator jerkily took us to the top floor and Liz knocked on the door of the corner room. We had heard that this was the biggest and most expensive room in the hostel and we were looking forward to the views of the city and the University from windows on two sides. "Come in," we heard Ahmed's voice on the speaker. Liz opened the door and our mouths fell open.

There was a bed sheet hanging in the middle of the room, a make-shift curtain dividing the room in two. On our side were two chairs facing the sheet and we could see the silhouette of Ahmed on the other side. We heard his voice, "I had to do this because the Quran prohibits males and females who are not closely related from being in the same private room. Please make yourself comfortable and we can start our discussion. Is there any particular topic you want to start with?"

3.   Debbie goes to Peshawar

Liz was quite frank, "It is hard to be comfortable with a sheet separating us from you. Maybe you can start with the reasons the Quran has for treating women as untouchables and why they are still valid?"

I do not recollect the details of the discussion. I do remember that, thanks to aggressive queries from Liz, it lasted for over two hours. We agreed to disagree on social issues that Liz raised and Ahmed answered clearly though unconvincingly. We did learn a lot about the history of Islam and the principles preached by the Prophet. Leaving Ahmed to rearrange the room Liz and I walked to the nearby park. We complimented each other on our good fortune that we were not born into an Islamic culture and could interact with the whole of humanity, not just our half. It would be a miserable life without boyfriends, and even worse, having to marry at puberty.

At dinner time the administrator announced that two complimentary tickets were available to the residents for a concert of twentieth century classical music, courtesy of the Rotary Club. Foreigners were to be given preference. The diners were struck dumb when Ahmed raised his hand. No one expected Ahmed to go to any musical event, let alone one of modern classical music. He couldn't have known what he was asking for. Most residents thought he deserved what he would get. The administrator managed to suppress her smile as she handed him the tickets and the problem of finding someone to go with him.

He found a sucker. It was me. He cornered me after dinner. "Will you be kind enough to accompany me; you can explain what the music means."

I was no fan of classical music, leave alone Stravinsky and Schonberg. I could tolerate three Bs, and three Ms under duress, that was it. Trying to find a way out without hurting his feelings, why I cared I can not fathom to this day, I asked, "How is it that a follower of your faith cannot discuss its teachings with women without a sheet in between them, and can go out on a date with them?"

"It is not a date, just an innocent outing to a cultural event. The Quran does not say anything about such visits. In fact it encourages the interactions between a teacher and a student."

I did not believe a word of what he said. He was twisting some stray saying for his own purpose. Still, I was not doing anything important that evening, "OK, I will take the ticket. Don't expect lessons from me though. My music education is Grade 5 piano. I have perhaps heard the music. Forget understanding it, I don't even like this modern stuff."

It must have been amusing to see a tall, platinum-blonde of seemingly bleached skin in a miniskirt and high heels with a short dark-skinned, young man with oily black hair parted perfectly in the middle and dressed in tight white pajamas with hundreds of horizontal folds and black Sherwani, long, body-hugging coat reaching the knees. It was just as well that he was chatty and oblivious to the strange and sometimes hostile glances directed at us. It occurred to me that his loneliness may have been getting to him and that he was using a rare opportunity to exercise his vocal muscles. Therefore, I did not have to say much about the music, or anything else. Fortunately, most of the concert was Mahler's Seventh Symphony which is not bad compared to most of the music of that kind. I have no idea what the other noise was. All told, it turned out to be a reasonable evening; I learnt what the loneliness in a strange country does to the cultural aspects of faith. Ahmed must have enjoyed it too. He thanked me profusely when we returned to the hostel. I do remember my dreams having a little romantic tinge that night.

Ahmed seemed to have developed an unquenchable thirst for Western culture. He invited me to accompany him to some or the other show once or twice every week. We went to tragic and comic theatre, opera, concerts, ballet, you name it. He avoided pop music performances like a pork chop; perhaps that was compromising his faith too much. He thanked me after every show and we separated without so much as a handshake.

Christmas was on the horizon and students were planning for the holidays. I was going home for a week. Walking back from a performance of The Flying Dutchman, I asked Ahmed what he was doing over the holidays. "Oh, I will catch up with my studies. We do call Christmas the Big Day, do not celebrate it though."

"Well, you can come with me to Nefyn. It is a little village on the coast about three hours bus ride from here. I am sure my parents will be happy to meet a future nawab."

"Don't give them such ideas. My father is a tribal chieftain, not a nawab. Nawabs disappeared with the British. If your parents can stand a stranger for a week I will accept your invitation. Just make sure I am not served bacon at breakfast. Fried eggs will do with toasts buttered on both sides."

That is how we ended up riding on a bus on a cold, sunny afternoon to the seaside home of my parents. Ahmed was careful to avoid the physical contact and apologized, a little hypocritically I thought, every time a bump or a bend on the road pushed us against each other.

Ahmed was heartily welcomed by my parents. It surprised me somewhat because he was perhaps the first foreigner to cross the threshold of that house. After tea and digestive biscuits mum showed him his room in the attic. He expressed admiration for the view and gratitude for her hospitality. Mom seemed pleased by his courteous manners and pleasant personality. This impression lasted only till bed time. I was lying in my bed comfortably tucked in, with mum sitting on it. We were talking about my days away from home in general terms when she became serious, "You need to watch out that you do not become serious with this friend of yours."

"Why mum? He is a nice young man; his father is a big shot in Pakistan. Although a bit short, he is nice company and a brilliant student. He has not made any serious advances, not even a peck on the cheeks. Says we do not date, we go on innocent outings."

"I am glad to hear that. Dad and I would worry if you two became serious. It is not only our only child going to Pakistan and living with

47

those strange people and us rarely getting to see our grandchildren. Who knows? He may already have a wife at home. They do marry early you know."

"Mum, you don't have to worry about his wife at home. First, in Pakistan he is allowed four wives. Second, the youngest wife has all the privileges."

Mum stood up and left without a word. I heard her muffled sobs from the parents' room on the other side of the wall, where a large framed photograph of a young couple with a few days old baby had pride of place.

3

The week in Nefyn changed Ahmed. On our way back he held my hand and when I pulled his hand over my shoulder he moved to establish a close contact. This was the first realization on our part that the acquaintance had romantic undertones. In a few weeks we acknowledged to ourselves, and to each other, that we were in love. Ahmed wrote to his father in May about this young white girl he was 'fond' of. The alarm bells rang in Peshawar. The girl had to be approved by the family before his fondness broke the bounds of propriety. "Will she be allowed to travel to Peshawar by her parents?" he was asked.

After shedding enough tears to flood the living room, mum agreed to let me go 'on a fact finding visit' so long as we promised, my hand on the Bible and Ahmed's on the Quran, that we will be gone only for three weeks. To make sure, as far as dad could, the return ticket had a short time limit.

Our problems had only begun. Ahmed started to behave like a Pakistani husband even though we were not even engaged yet. One day, he showed me a long head to toe dress – yes, head to toe not shoulder to toe. "You will have to wear it when you go out in Peshawar or when men are around at home. Maybe you should practise a little so you can walk without stumbling."

I looked at the tent with a slit near the top. "Tents are to live in when you are camping, not to wear. If you think I will wear that monstrosity, you are sadly mistaken. I would die before I am seen in one of those."

"You will not be seen. That is the whole idea. You don't want all those strangers leering at you, do you?"

"Why not? Looks don't hurt. I would rather be admired for my looks than go around hiding in a tent."

"What do you want? Go around Peshawar half naked?"

"You don't have a problem with me going around half-naked in Liverpool. Why should it bother you in Peshawar?"

"Because men in Peshawar are not used to girls going around without any clothes on. You don't want trouble with rogues any more than me or my family."

"I was half-naked a second ago. Now I have no clothes on at all. If you want me go all naked in Peshawar, I will do it for you. No way will I wear a tent. Not for you, not for your family. That is final."

"I can't take you to Peshawar in a miniskirt. Let us cancel the trip. I will write to tell my family that the whole thing is off. Their sigh of relief will travel half way round the world and you will hear it."

"Cancel the damn trip if that is what you want. Don't throw empty threats at me. I have no shortage of men wanting to court me. You are the one who can't do without me. Think it over before you burn your bridges."

"There is nothing to think over. Miniskirts and Pakistan don't match. Will you agree to wear salwar kameez with a dupatta?"

"I don't know what you are talking about. If you tell me what they are I can tell you whether you should waste your money on them, or not."

"Salwar is baggy cotton pants, kameez is a loose full sleeved modest shirt from neck to the knees. Dupatta is a long cotton shawl that goes around your breasts and one end is used to cover the head when older relations are present."

"I will die of heat wearing all those clothes. I will not wear them. I will not cover my head. I have beautiful hair and I like showing it off. I like men turning around to admire my looks. I will tell you what I will do as a special favour to your family. I will get some skirts which cover the knees and that are not tight even though I like clothes that show my figure. I will get a couple of half sleeve loose T-shirts. That is as far as I will go."

"We are getting somewhere. If you get skirts which go to your ankle we could manage it."

"No way. I can't walk in full length skirts, never could, never will. I will see if Blackler's has calf length skirts or dresses. Men in Peshawar will have to imagine rest of me from my calves."

"It is not the men I worry about; it is the women. All the complaints will come from women. We will face the music when it starts playing."

Ahmed came shopping with me and was very helpful with colours and fit that could pass muster in his homeland. I had helped to acculturate him, now he was returning the compliment.

4

I changed from my comfy miniskirt and form fitting blouse into a cumbersome midi dress before the plane landed at dawn in Lahore. Abba, as Ahmed called his father and I was to call him, was to meet us at the airport and we were to drive 500 kms to Peshawar the same day in a caravan of three cars. An official formally greeted Ahmed on the tarmac as we stepped off the plane and escorted us past the immigration and customs to Abba. When he saw him Ahmed rushed to his father and they hugged each other for a long while. When Abba let him out of his clutches Ahmed turned to face me and said, "Abba, this is my friend from Liverpool, Debbie." I paid my tribute as Ahmed and I had rehearsed on the plane by bowing deeply with folded hands and uttering words emphasizing my humble status, "aadaab arj." However, Abba did not wish to, perhaps could not, hide his discomfort with looking at a female face. We had three meals at roadside restaurants and ten hours in the car. Not a word was exchanged between Abba and me. Poor Ahmed, he did not know what to do. Maybe I should not have been hurt, I was though and wished I had not changed into this inconvenient outfit just to please a man who would not be pleased anyway.

It was pitch dark when we arrived at the family home about half an hour beyond Peshawar. Again Ahmed was welcomed joyously by his mother Amma, sisters and the husbands of two of them and I looked on awkwardly feeling like an intruder. At last Ahmed introduced me to the female relatives one by one. They greeted me coldly, almost as if I had arrived from Mars to devour them. The language barrier was not the problem; hostility seemed to ooze out of their pores. I was glad when Ahmed showed me the room I was to occupy. When I asked him why every one was being rude to me, he brushed it off, "They are excited at my homecoming, that's all. You are being overly sensitive."

"Leave me alone, I need some sleep," I huffed and started taking the cumbersome clothes off.

Next morning a maid brought me tea in a metal tumbler. The tumbler was hot and the maid gave me a towel to hold it. The tea was very creamy and spicy, quite pleasant in its own way. "I will have to get used to their tea, just like their spicy food and haughtiness," I thought. Two maids showed up in a while to help me through the toilette. My clothes stumped them and they left me to dress myself.

Ahmed came in to show me his family's "humble abode" as he called it. There was a huge courtyard with rooms on three sides. The fourth side had a large kitchen and storage room for food supplies, milk and water. There was a large and heavy wooden door with large cracks which, Ahmed told me, separated the janana, women's quarters, from the men's domain and the outside world. Before entering the janana, men sent a maid to warn the occupants to cover themselves. Women had to be properly attired in a burqa to go outside. When I asked to see the male's side of the house, Ahmed told me it was similar to the janana except that instead of kitchen and pantry there were two large rooms where Abba met the visitors and conducted his business. There was a large, open area in front of the building for the cars, tractors, ox carts, cattle and horses, and the compound was surrounded by thick stone walls with a large gate for gentry and a small one for servants. Both were manned by armed security guards day and night.

Ahmed left and I joined the women for breakfast. Two married sisters, Satlaj and Chamba, could manage some English and they explained what was served and showed how to eat it with the fingers. Amma did not say a word to me directly, confirming the impression that the hostility was not just my imagination.

After the breakfast Amma gave Satlaj something that looked like a black mask. She told me it was for me to wear when going out or when men visited the janana. As a demonstration she put it over her head. It covered her face and shoulders with an opening for the eyes. Then she took it off her head and put it on mine. It needed a lot of adjusting for the eyehole to match the eyes and did not reach the shoulder. That did not seem to bother Amma and all four women looked very pleased. "You look great in it," Chamba said.

"What of me looks great?" I wondered.

A maid arrived to warn us that the young women's husbands were coming to take them for a visit to their own parents. Satlaj asked me to put the mask on. I looked dumb and did nothing. Men came in, looked at me and smiled. I had the impression that they liked what they saw and wouldn't have minded seeing more. I expect Amma received the same massage and expressed her fury to the girls. They translated to me. I shrugged my shoulders, stood up and left to have a little walk around the courtyard.

Ahmed came in a little later and received an earful from his irate mother. His attempts to pacify her failed miserably. He took me aside and tried to persuade me to wear the mask for his sake. I reminded him of our agreement and repeated my statement, "Over my dead body." He went back to his mother and they had a long discussion in hushed voices as if I could decipher their conversation in Pashto. It must have worked because Amma smiled when we sat down for lunch. Later in the day when the hot sun had gone behind the mountains, I asked Ahmed to show me the village. He asked me, very humbly I must say, to put on the mask to make his life tolerable, I could take it off once we were safely beyond the gate. I had had my argument for the day, so I covered my face and asked "How do I look?

"Just great, now no one has to look at the ground when talking to you," he replied.

"Anything to keep your peace with the family," I countered.

Soon after crossing the main gate I took off the mask and breathed easily once more. There was not much to the village: a few stalls, one with a variety of guns openly on display, an artisan weaving a carpet, a carpenter repairing a plough, a boy making local sweets in a huge wok full of fat. It was all new to me, therefore interesting. Everyone stopped whatever they were doing to look at my face or my legs. Wherever the eyes went first there they stayed. I was amused. "Will their eyes pop out of their sockets if I had a miniskirt on?" I asked Ahmed. There was no response.

On our return, Ahmed helped me with the mask when the entrance came into sight. However, the word had already reached its destination. Abba and Amma were sitting on a string bed in the court-yard of the janana with furious looks on their faces. Amma started screaming as soon as she saw us. Abba quietly slipped out and I hid in my room leaving Ahmed to face the music. It must have been an hour later when Ahmed knocked and asked if we could discuss the situation calmly.

"Several people told my parents that they had seen a half-naked Firangee woman with their son. Firangee is the local term for a detestable foreigner. I was wrong to think that the people will not dare to report on me. Any how, my parents have decided that they don't mind what you wear in the janana. When you go out you have to be in a burqa. Amma thinks the family honour is at stake and Abba worries he could have a rebellion on his hands 'if you are not controlled,'" Ahmed said in a hushed guilty voice.

"I am sorry you are in such a pickle. I care for your family's honour and I do not want a rebellion. I do believe though that I have nothing to hide, not my face, not my legs, not my hair. If people are uncomfortable looking at them, let them turn the other way. I am not wearing a burqa. And I am not staying locked up in the janana when there are so many interesting things to see in this beautiful country. In fact, I have a good mind to go out in my miniskirt and tight blouse that I wore on the plane just to show your family how annoyed I am with their rudeness and lack of concern for their guest's convenience."

"Debbie, be reasonable. You have come to this god-forsaken place to win my parents' approval. The way it is going, we can forget approval. They might boot you out. Then what?"

"Look future Nawab of Peshawar. No one threatens Debbie. If they boot me out and you stay here to lick the soles of their feet and claim your title, good luck to you. I have my ticket and enough money to get to Lahore. Don't worry about me. I can look after myself. I am not a helpless woman in a tent for the dress."

"Debbie, no one is threatening you and no one thinks you are helpless. My only interest is to mend relations between you and the family. My parents treasure their only son and wherever we live, I have to treat them with respect. It behooves all of us to get on reasonably well together."

"If you believe what you say then go and tell your parents to be hospitable, let me find out about their culture, their country. They need to check me out, sure. I need to check them and their surroundings too. I am not a chattel being given to your family to do with me what they please. I am a human with the same rights as you and them. Find out if I am welcome on these terms. If not, get me a taxi to Lahore. I have time to catch a flight tomorrow."

"My parents are devout Muslims. Only way they know is their traditional way. They are not going to change, even if it kills them. The decision is not theirs or yours. It is mine. I must chose between them and you, between East and West, between past and future. More than anything my choice is between tradition and love. The most important lesson I have learnt from you is that love overcomes all hurdles and life without love is like a pitcher without water. Let us pack. We have to hurry to make the next flight."

Tears were freely shed and no one had the will to turn the tide.

4. Wretchedness Shared

1

Earth spins on its axis during summer and winter. Night and day even out over the year. Joy and grief take turns and even out over a life time. Perhaps they do for many. They did not for me.

2

The year was 1950. The year of joy and sorrow. Joy because our son was on his way to a brilliant career that would bring fame and fortune to the family of this lowly civil servant in the government of the newly minted Republic of India. Ramesh had graduated with a medical degree from the elite medical school in Lucknow and had won a prestigious scholarship to go to America to specialize as an oncologist. Sorrow because our only child was going away for who knows how long. Joti was in tears most of the day. Her delight was going so far away, a letter took ten days to get there. When would she hear the voice that made her body shiver in excitement from head to toe? I promised her to pull strings and get a telephone. She was still disconsolate. "It will cost a bundle for even the shortest call across seven seas," she said. Ramesh could not understand her mother's grief. He told her again and again that he was coming back in two years. He promised to work hard and finish the course earlier if at all possible. He vowed to write a long letter every Saturday. Joti's grief was not assuaged. It was as if she had a premonition of disaster. Still, she pulled herself together as the day of departure approached. When Ramesh touched her feet at the station before boarding the train for Bombay, she blessed him, "May goddess Saraswati help you with studies, goddess Lakshmi look after your worldly needs and goddess Kali protect you from enemies. May Lord Ganesh fulfill all your wishes." I pulled Ramesh up as he bent down to touch my feet, embraced him and held back the tear which would have given away my feelings.

We received letters from him every week for the first few months. Joti gave the mailman a rupee whenever he knocked to hand over a letter from 'Amrika.' There were at least three people now eagerly waiting for a letter with the bald eagle stamp. However, the income of the poor mailman started dwindling after the New Year and had dropped to an occasional rupee a year later. Joti worried all the time about her son's health; what he was eating, who was washing his clothes, cleaning his room and if he had started drinking alcohol and eating meat. Her biggest worry was American girls and she was certain that every one of them between the age of fifteen and fifty was out to get him. Her relief after every letter could be sensed from across the street.

Two years were nearly up. Joti bought a new bed, pillows, sheets and a Kashmir wool blanket and redecorated his old room. She made me promise that we would go to Bombay to see him get off the boat. However, his letters, full of news about the acclaim he was receiving from professors and fellow students, made no mention of any travel plans. On the second anniversary of his departure, Joti insisted that I call him on the phone and find out the details of his return trip. It took several tries to get him on the line and, when I did get him, the line was poor and it was difficult to understand what he said. One thing did become clear. Instead of reserving a place on the ship home, he was planning to stay there for a while longer to get some practical training. He would not be specific on how long his training would be. He did promised to write us a detailed letter explaining his situation.

It took a month for the letter to arrive. "From my enquiries I have learnt that there are no hospitals in India where my expertise could be useful. My contacts in the profession at home tell me that the people suffering from fatal diseases like cancer go for Ayurvedic treatment, or have holy men pray for them, rather than call a doctor or go to the hospital even when they can afford to. They also confirm my suspicion that the government has no money to properly equip existing hospitals, let alone building new ones. You will not want your America trained son to come back and work as an ordinary doctor. Therefore, I will work here till things improve in India. I can earn more in a year here than I would earn in a long life time in India. I promise that I will come on a holiday next year and every year after that to be with you. Please give me your blessings as you have done at every major step I have taken."

Joti would have liked nothing better than to have her only son in town, as a lowly medical orderly if need be. Her disappointment took a new turn. Now she took her frustration out on me, "You wanted Ramesh to be a big success. You spent all my dowry to send him to the doctor school. Now we don't have a son. We don't have anybody to look after us in our old age. It is all your doing – you wanted your son to be what you didn't have the brains to be." This would be followed by two days in bed with headache and a mild fever.

Ramesh came home for two weeks the next year. Several relatives had lined up prospective matches from great families for our boy with prospects of six-figure dowries. Joti was too weak for us to travel to Bombay and I could not leave her alone with the servants. Ramesh was shocked to see how thin his mother had become and cancelled plans to travel to Lucknow to renew acquaintance with his old professors. He spent most of his time near her and refused to see any of the girls we wanted him to choose from. He assured us that there was no one in America he was involved with, just that he was not ready to settle down. It broke Joti's heart. She became convinced that she had lost her son for good. The smile that had returned to her face when she greeted her son was replaced by a look of deep sorrow. She took to bed the day before Ramesh left and did not get up to see him off at the door.

3

My grief at the turn of events was no less than Joti's but I had to put on a brave face to help her. We had long discussions, she in tears and I the consoling voice. She told all our visitors that her son had turned his face away from parents who had done so much for him. The expressed opinions divided along gender lines. The women agreed with her without exception and some even suggested that he "was in the clutches of a shameless white witch." Gradually Joti also started believing it. Men, on the other hand, irrespective of what they really believed, told Joti that Ramesh had always been a good son and she should trust him. Her reply was always the same, "You men don't have a heart, you cannot feel and therefore you are taken in by the sweet talk. I can see behind the words of my son. He is in the clutches of the devil. He is not going to come back on his own."

A renowned sadhu was visiting our town. I approached the organizers of the event and persuaded them to have a prayer ceremony, yagya, "to free Ramesh from the devil." The yagya was held on the holy day of Dussehera in the month of October. We set cross legged on the carpeted floor in the front row facing the sadhu who was clad in a saffron dhoti with his upper body covered in ash. He recited in a singsong voice Sanskrit shlokas which were mostly incomprehensible to us, and probably to him too. Without interrupting the recital, he threw spoonfuls of ghee into the fire, the flames shooting up dangerously as the offerings were accepted. The pot of concentrated butter lasted till the last shloka was pronounced after an hour. "Hare Ram, Hare Hare, Agni Mata ki jai," shouted the sadhu as he stood up and folded his hands in reverence before the flames. We raised ourselves on our feet with some difficulty, touched the sadhu's feet and he gave us his blessing, "May all your wishes be fulfilled." Joti looked as if a big load had been lifted off her back. Faith in our son had returned and we now jumped for the good news every time the phone rang, or the mailman announced a letter from 'Amrika.'

Another year went by. After several perfunctory letters we had one with some news, though not what we had been anticipating. "I will arrive there on November 24 and I have a surprise for you. I am sure you will love it." We were in suspense. What surprise could he bring? We lost several strands of hair scratching our heads yet could not guess what it could be. Joti had a suspicion that it wasn't anything good. "Trust your son, he has never disappointed you," I replied every time, though with a little less conviction with each passing day.

4

Joti was not well enough to go to Bombay this time either. It was unusually cold that day and we splashed to rent a motor car for the evening and drove to the railway station in good time. As is often the case when you are early, the train was late and our suspense built up to an almost unbearable point. What surprise did our son have in store for us? Was it good, as I had hoped, or evil as his mother was certain? I must admit that by now I was secretly beginning to agree with Joti. Her suspicions were always well-founded and were proven true with only rare exceptions. Here we were, Joti sitting on a bench looking straight ahead with unseeing eyes, I walking up and down the platform, and the coolie, a frail elderly man in tattered clothes and bare feet, standing next to Joti fidgeting a little. Suddenly Joti stood up and walked to the edge of the platform. She had heard the whistle of the engine. We looked along the railway track and saw the black smoke from the engine darkening the sky as it lumbered uphill pulling carriages loaded with hundreds of passengers.

The train stopped and I heard the shout of "Pitaji" from the window of a first class compartment fifty feet away. We walked towards him, the coolie following close behind. Ramesh jumped out, ran to us and bent down to touch his mother's feet as she tried to hold back her tears. When he straightened up I asked him to show the coolie the luggage. He went back and pointed out what the old man was to carry. After jumping onto the platform he turned around and held out his hand. What I saw set me shivering as if I was suffering from malaria. There was a tall slender white woman with very short red hair in a clumsily put on sari, ill-fitting blouse and men's shoes cautiously stepping down the two steps to the platform. I looked at Joti. Her eyes were blank, her face as white as that of the young woman leaning on our son's shoulder to regain her balance. I held Joti to stop her from collapsing on the platform and whispered, "Have courage, Lord Ram will look after us."

Ramesh and the girl walked towards us holding hands. She bent down and touched Joti's feet and then mine before being erect again with head modestly bent. Our son now delivered the final blow of his surprise, "Amma, Pitaji, meet your bahu. Sally and I were married last month. I am sure you will love her." So we now had an American daughter-in-law right out of the blue. The thought in my mind was, "Bhagwan ki jai, we don't have a daughter. Who would have married her?" Joti, I am sure, was thinking, "He will never come back. I have lost my only son."

The couple spent a month with us. Sally had not learnt any Hindi and Ramesh acted as a translator. Bit by bit Sally won us over. The night before they were to leave, after the lights had been turned off and Joti was sure that Ramesh and Sally had gone to sleep, she turned to me, "Are you awake?"

"Yes. How can I sleep when my son is going away again, who knows for how long?"

"He will never come back. We have to get used to our lonely lives. We will never see our grandchildren. Our only consolation is that Sally is a good girl. She will look after our Ramesh."

"Yes, it is better than it could be. He could have married a woman who treated him like a brownie slave."

"We should thank Bhagwan for sending Sally to look after him if He was going to keep him there. Only He knows what He has in mind for them."

Joti's words calmed my fears and we fell asleep, in each other's arms.

5

Joti put up a brave face although she was feeling empty inside. As my luck would have it, a flu epidemic spread all over India the following spring. People were dying like flies everywhere. It was the time of Holi festival when people splash everyone in sight with coloured water. Joti had more than her share and was drenched. She brushed off my advice to change her clothes straightaway, she was having too much fun to pay me attention. In the evening, she started to shiver. During the night her throat became sore and she was feverish. The doctor's visit in the morning did no good because the pharmacies had run out of the medicines he prescribed. For a week I endured the cries of physical pain and tears of emotional suffering of my beloved wife of thirty years before Lord Ram called her to His side. My grief was made infinitely more unbearable by the absence of Ramesh at the cremation ceremonies.

After Joti's loss I felt all alone. Every so often, at work or at home, a vision of what life could be and wasn't would float in front of me; my eyes would become wet, my body, drained of all energy, would shake like a banana leaf in a storm. I would ask myself why I was alive. Then the apparition would pass, I would pick up what I was doing and carry on with a heavy heart. Must have been the good deeds in a former life, I kept my sanity through that difficult period.

My son and daughter-in-law visited twice over the next ten years, for one month each time. The first time they had a baby boy and the second time, two boys, one an energetic six year old and the other a bouncy toddler. I retired from my job just before their second visit. I loved my grandchildren. I took them to the playground where other nicely tanned children looked enviously at their fair complexion. We went to the circus that was visiting town and swam in the river Jamuna, a walking distance from home. It was the happiest time of my life since Ramesh was a boy.

Those were the days when air travel was gaining ground. I looked into fares and found that if I managed with just Mohan to cook and clean, let the other servants go, and rented out a room in the house, I could save enough in three years to visit my American family. I set up a savings account and started putting every extra rupee in it. As the time passed I could see my savings grow. At long last I could write to Ramesh to ask what would be a good time to visit. Although his reply might have offended many parents, I was too pleased with myself to notice. "Christmas is best for us, a month with us will be enough time," the letter said.

I spent the whole month in Boston indoors because it was freezing outside. The house was comfortable and I did not need clothing warmer than a sweater. The boys were twelve and nine now. The family was out during the day at their jobs and schools. In the evenings, the kids had homework and Ramesh and Sally their social engagements. I spent the time reading the local newspaper and watching TV. There was never any news of what was happening outside Boston and the TV was annoying because just when the story became interesting it was interrupted by the ads for things you don't need. I enjoyed being near the family all the same and was sorry to leave when the month was over.

6

The letters from America were few and short. I assumed that no news is good news and did not worry about them. I woke up with the sun, went for long walks and swam every day in the river. The rest of the day was spent reading the scriptures and praying at home and in the temple. I looked and felt younger than my seventy years. Then the disaster struck. On my way home from the swim, a horse sprang loose from a cart and ran amok towards me. Looking back I was fortunate that it was content with just one kick. It did not kill me though it caused serious injuries in the abdomen. The doctor recommended that I hire a nurse. Jaya, a widow my age, looked after me, tenderly replacing the bandages and washing and changing me when necessary.

I became very fond of Jaya and we continued to meet after I had completely recovered. I looked forward to being with her. When I prayed for wisdom from Goddess Saraswati it was Jaya's image that would appear in front of me. The loneliness that had been my constant companion since Joti left was replaced by a longing to be with Jaya. I now wanted to live and make her a part of what little was left of my life.

When we met for our walk one morning I asked Jaya to sit with me on a rock on the bank of the river. It was a beautiful sunrise, glowing clouds tinged with red and purple and a huge red disk slowly emerging from the bottomless emptiness beyond the horizon. I nervously expressed to Jaya my feelings towards her while throwing pebbles in the water. The silence that followed lasted an eternity. When she spoke I could barely hear her.

"I do not know what you see in me, a poor widow who has to work to make ends meet even at my age. More important, I am not as strong as I look. I had breast cancer ten years ago. Fortunately, it was detected early, the tumor was small and I did not need an operation. The shock of my disease is what killed my husband; the poor man had always thought I was indestructible. Cancer is never cured for good. It returns after a few years and the older body often gives in to the disease. I am sorry my response to your affection has encouraged your feelings to become so deep. I was lonely and selfish and did not have the courage to stop when I should have. Also, the dictum of Tolstoy from our school book - Wretchedness shared makes one doubly

wretched - is never far from my mind and it added to my reluctance
to share my misery. You want to share what little of our lives is left. I
do too. Only I know how miniscule it could be and how much grief it
could cause you. I have killed one husband. That is enough."

"I am sorry to learn of your sorrow. I can handle my grief now
that I have been forewarned. I will not give up on you. Why don't
we arrange for an oncologist to examine you and discuss the issue
after his verdict? We have to die one day, whether it is tomorrow or
in ten years. I am prepared to take my chances. In any event, my suggested course will make you feel better and we should proceed with it
without delay."

"All right, I will arrange the medical appointments and we will
discuss it when the results are in. In the meantime please do not take
my response as yes. I have several emotional issues to resolve. At our
age we carry a lot of baggage on our backs and we need to work out
how to reduce its weight. Maybe men are different, they can consider
the future without being bothered by the past. I am a woman, frail one,
and my past haunts me. Please understand my dilemma. I will be able
to express myself better when I have thought a little more about it."

"I understand. We will not talk about it any more till you are ready.
You know what will make me happy; but only if you are happy too.
Martyrdom in the affairs of heart does not behoove people, young
or old."

We were silent for rest of the walk. Dark clouds were gathering
when we turned on her street.

7

I lay in bed that night considering what could be done to raise
Jaya's spirits. My mind kept returning to the idea of whisking her far
away from the daily grind for a few weeks. I wrote to Ramesh the next
day. I told him about her and asked whether we could spend a while
with them and if he could give his professional opinion on her future

prospects. It was a couple of weeks before I received his reply. "Sally and I don't think it will be a good idea to bring a cancer patient to the U.S. She won't have any insurance and the treatment costs the earth here. Of course, you are most welcome any time that suits you. Kids love you and miss you. It is about time they renewed bond with their Indian grandpa."

I was disappointed. While it would be good for me and the kids, the purpose of the whole exercise was defeated by my going alone. I did want to see my family but I did not want to be away from Jaya either, not after what she had told me about her apprehension of recurrence of cancer. I could not decide what to do. Ramesh did raise a valid point; it would have been horrible to watch Jaya suffer and not be able to get her treatment. After tossing and turning in bed for several nights I was feeling quite run down. Jaya noticed it and asked, "You are looking thin and tired. What is worrying you?"

"Oh, it is nothing. Can't sleep at night; maybe the heat."

"It has been quite cool of late. You are hiding something from me. You can tell me. Maybe I can help you."

"My son and his wife want me to visit them. They don't think it will be wise for you to travel with your health concerns. It puts me in a bind. How can I see my family and not be away from you for so long?"

"You are being silly. We are not teenagers; let us not behave like them. I will be all right. I will get checked up when you are away and the good news will be waiting for you on your return. You must go. As you said yourself, we are getting old. We don't know how much time we have before our bodies give out. You have to go. I won't have it any other way."

It took a month to organize the papers and book the seat on the plane. We spent as much time as we could together. Jaya was able to make the appointments for her examination and the tests during the period of my absence. I was not comfortable with the plan although Jaya did not seem in the least bit perturbed. She was waving a green scarf cheerfully when the train for Delhi took off. I could barely hold back my tears.

It was autumn and the trees were laden with glorious golden leaves. Ramesh and Sally had more time for me than on previous visits and showed me around the attractions of the area. The grandsons were now fully grown up, both taller than Sally, let alone Ramesh and me. We played chess and ping pong, and went for walks along the sea. The month in Boston flew by and soon it was time to leave. I was a bundle of mixed up emotions; sorry to be leaving my family, at the same time excited about being with Jaya again. For the last night in Boston and during the naps on the plane I dreamed of her smiling face greeting me at the station and her blabbering in excitement all the good results of the tests.

8

The sun was at the highest point of its trajectory when the train crept towards the station. Storm clouds, if any, were invisible from the train. I felt lively even after twenty four hours on planes and at airports and twelve hours on the train as I peeped out of the window looking for Jaya in the milling crowd on the platform. "There couldn't be confusion about the dates. Maybe I can't see her in the crowd. Maybe she is held up in the traffic." I stepped out, hired a coolie for my suitcase and waited near the exit for half an hour. The train left and arriving passengers made their way to their destinations. I was the only passenger left on the platform. The coolie was getting impatient, "Sahib, I need to be ready for the next train in five minutes." I gave in and followed him to a rickshaw to take me home.

Mohan took the suitcase inside and I carried on to Jaya's house in the rickshaw. The house was locked. I knocked on the neighbour's door. A kindly middle-aged woman opened the door, looked at me, turned sombre and before I could open my mouth said, "Jaya had an excruciating pain in the chest yesterday morning. She is in the hospital."

"What kind of pain? How did they treat her? How is she feeling?"

"I don't know. My husband called the ambulance that took her to the hospital. Visitors were not allowed to see her yesterday. We hope to see her in the evening."

I thanked her and ran to the rickshaw. In spite of my constant urging to go faster, it took for ever to get to the hospital. The rickshaw wallah knew that I did not have time to bargain and asked for fifty rupees instead of the normal twenty. I gave him some ten rupee notes without counting and rushed to the reception desk. The receptionist was chatting on the phone and took her own sweet time to give me the directions to Jaya's room. I ran to the ward shoving doctors, nurses, visitors and patients aside. The attending nurse looked blankly when I reached the nursing station. After many entreaties, she condescended to take me to Jaya. On our way to the room I learnt that Jaya had a double mastectomy last night, the operation had gone well although they were not sure all the affected parts were removed. She told me to be gentle and not to cause any excitement. If I behaved, I could have fifteen minutes with the patient.

At first glance Jaya looked as if she were asleep. When we were closer she heard our steps and opened her eyes. Obviously in pain, she managed to force a smile when she saw me. I sat down on a stool next to her and held her hand. She opened her mouth as if to say something. I had to put my ear almost on her mouth to hear her whisper "You see I was right. I am not here for long."

"Don't be so despondent. It will be all right. Nurse told me that the operation was a success. You will be recovered enough to come home with me in a week. In a month, we will be able to go for walks along the river. I will take care of you."

I don't know how much of this registered with her. She waved to me and I leaned my ear over her, "Promise me you will find some one to love soon after I am gone. Remember what you said about us not having long to live."

"We have, both you and me, many years yet. These will be good years. We will make a list of things we always wanted to do and do them together. You can't give up. I am not going to let you leave me."

"It is not in our hands. Whatever happens you have to live with it. I am so sorry our happiness was cut short like this."

"Jaya, listen to me. You will be well again soon. We will be happy together. Think positively. It is all these painkillers that are making you downhearted. When I come tomorrow I want to see the smile that makes my heart jump with joy."

The nurse returned with a tray of medication. My time was up. I gave her my address and requested her to promptly let me know if I could be useful. My head bowed, I made my way back home. I took my shoes off and lay down on the bed. I heard Mohan ask what I would like for dinner. I turned the other way without answering and sobbed till sleep took me out of my misery, albeit temporarily.

9

It was still dark when Mohan woke me up. "Sahib, a letter," and handed me an envelope. I looked at the sender's address and jumped out of bed. It was from the hospital. I tore open the envelope. The message was short, "Jaya Malini passed away in her sleep. The cause of her death is being investigated."

The sun did not rise that morning. Nor on any morning thereafter.

5. Atheist for a Day

Jainism is one of the sects which shelter under the vast umbrella of Hindu religion. It began, as all sects do, in the form of a reform movement and stayed under the umbrella unlike Buddhism which disappeared from India altogether and acquired its own persona in China and Japan. Bhagwan Mahavir, a contemporary of Buddha, preached self abnegation of an extreme variety as the only way to break out of the cycle of birth and death. His doctrine included not eating anything which moves or anything that grows below the ground. Some extremists, my parents among them, also believe that wearing clothes is a luxury which prolongs the cycle and delays the union of atma with Paramatma – the soul with the Prime Soul.

When I reached the rebellious teen years I refused to go to school in my birthday suit. Instead, with the help of other like-minded teens I acquired the jeans of latest fashion, matching plaid shirts and stylish jackets frayed at the right places. I even developed a taste for animals, killed and cooked by someone else of course. My parents tolerated the clothes. However, the dam broke when Amma, my mother, found out about the nefarious taste buds I had developed. The flow of her tears stopped only after Pitaji, my dear father, intervened. He bade me sit down on the floor, stood towering over me and shouted, "Who taught you all these things to ruin all the good deeds of your older generations?"

"Nobody sir. Everyone in the school does them. They tease me for not being like them," I whimpered.

"Do you think they don't tease your brother and sister? Of course they do. They stand up to them because they are brave, not cowards like you. We are devotees of Bhagwan Mahavir, not any ordinary Hindu. Do you understand?"

"I do sir. I am not brave sir. I can not stand up to them. Blame my deeds in former lives sir, I was born a coward and a coward I will always be."

"I have no room in my family for cowards who are not prepared to amend their former deeds. Do you want to live here or not?"

"I am sorry sir, I can not face the world on your terms," I replied. I tried to touch his feet, he pushed me away. He told Amma to put all my books and other belongings in a paper bag. She left, tears in her eyes, face puffy with grief. She returned in a few minutes. Pitaji had a determined expression on his face which made me tremble. He snatched the bulging bag from Amma's hand and gruffly handed it to me. He pointed to the world beyond the open door, "Go, live with your foul soul mates. I can't let you destroy the credit we have earned by our deeds."

My siblings had been watching the scene unfold. They cheered, I did not care whether with delight or to encourage me, when I started my journey to the vast unknown. I passed the gate without the slightest idea of where I was going. In spite of my admission to Pitaji, there must have been some nobility in the deed of my former lives that pointed out the direction. I turned left when I reached the main thoroughfare. After an hour of walking in the blowing dust and sweltering heat of the Indian summer at its height I reached the outskirts of town and found what seemed to me my salvation. A small sign on the gatepost said Swami Dhunyanand's Nastic Ashram – Retreat for Atheists. I had no idea who atheists were, what they did, or what they believed or didn't believe in and Dhunyanand – joy in wealth – seemed a strange name for a swami. Retreat is what attracted me. It is what my exhausted body, perhaps soul as well, needed. I opened the gate and trudged the small narrow walkway to the door of a small rather dilapidated bungalow. The door was open and there was no sign of activity inside. "Hello, is anyone in?" I said, in a soft voice so as not to disturb someone in meditation and to attract the notice of anyone who wasn't.

After a few moments of suspense I heard some steps. An elderly lady dressed in a green cotton sari, her grey hair streaming behind her, appeared. "What can I do for you?"

"I have just been thrown out by my parents because I did not follow the basic tenets of our religion. I am looking for shelter in return for my labour," I replied

"You have come to the right place. This is a home for people who do not believe in God and who do not practise any formal religion. You are welcome to join us and become a part of our crusade. Make this humble cottage your home. We are one big family who share all the joys and sorrows, comforts and hardships like brothers and sisters. Most important, we share the goal of relieving the world of the blinkers of religion. It is a tough task and the progress is slow in spite of the dynamic leadership of Swami Dhunyanand."

"I am so relieved I found you. I do hope I can help you in achieving this laudable goal. Please count me as a disciple of Swamiji," I said while bowing down to touch her feet.

"No, no, no," she said stepping back. She added, I felt with unnecessary vehemence, "The only person you touch the feet of is Swamiji, to pick some specks of dust to rub on your forehead so some of his wisdom can pass on to you."

She led me to a large room in the back with wooden bunk beds at two levels. I guessed the room had twenty beds. Each bed had a thin mattress and a thinner blanket. Every thing in the room, walls, ceiling, beds, mattresses, blankets, was green. The floor was concrete which was cracking in places. Most of the beds looked as if they had never been used. I put my paper bag on the one nearest to the entrance. "Let me introduce you to Swamiji now," the lady said walking towards a side door. I followed the regulation three steps behind.

We entered a spacious bright room with an open window on my left. With the exception of a bright green door in the corner on the right, the other two walls had floor-to-ceiling shelves filled with books. With a few exceptions, the books looked as if they had not been opened for centuries. The room did have a musty smell, now that I think of it. Again, the ceiling and the exposed walls were painted bright green and the floor was concrete. There was a large mahogany desk in the middle of the room with a high-backed chair placed precisely in the middle on the other side. On my side of the table were two low stools, presumably for visitors.

"Wait a minute here," the lady said before disappearing through the back door. I moved closer to examine the desk. There was a telephone on one side, a heap of files on the other. I was moving towards a bookshelf when the door opened and a handsome young man in a green long cotton shirt, green baggy pants and bare feet entered briskly. He was no more than twenty five, perhaps five feet six, slender with lustrous dark hair parted in the middle and a clean-shaven face, more beige than brown. He stopped a few feet from me and stood erect waiting for me to make a move. The response of the lady when I greeted her crossed my mind. I bent down, touched his feet with the fingers of both hands and then rubbed them on my forehead. A heavenly smile flitted across the angelic face. He pointed to the stools and moved towards his chair.

He leaned back in the chair, his dark eyes penetrating through the skull to read my innermost thoughts. After a long pause which unnerved me not a little, he said his first words to me in a soft, sing song voice, "You wish to join our ashram. That is good. We are always in need of followers in our fight to contain the spread of various religions. Younger the new converts the better. They have more energy and are more persuasive in discussions when they are in their teens and twenties. Tell me something about yourself."

This was the first time in my life a stranger had asked me that. I hesitated for a long moment before venturing, "My name is Rajesh, sir. I am just finishing grade 8. My parents are strict Jains and they expect me to be a strict vegetarian and to go naked even in the winter. When I refused they booted me out of the house, in a manner of speaking sir. They do not really wear boots, only cloth slippers. I now want to work with you to save other kids from the rigours of such religions. All I need is food and shelter and I will devote all my energies to your, sorry sir, our cause."

Swamiji's eyes had not wavered for a moment. The pause was longer than the earlier one and I was beginning to feel uncomfortable. My eyes were focused on the table as if I were counting the shining particles on its surface. At long last his soft voice played pleasantly on my ear drums, "I will accept you as a disciple although you are much too young to spread the Word by yourself. You will be in training for the next two years. During this period you will help the staff in the maintenance of the ashram. If you pass the test at the end of two years, you will become a deputy to the Junior Assistant Preacher."

"Thank you very much, sir. What will be my responsibilities as the deputy to the junior assistant preacher, sir?"

"You will do what the JAP tells you to do. You might carry the bag of brochures in a backpack and hand him one when someone opens the door on his rounds. You may prompt him if he needs it during his spiel. You will do whatever helps him and whatever he asks you to do. When he determines that you are ready to preach, he will make that recommendation to the assistant preacher who will send it to the preacher with his comments. Eventually, it will arrive at this desk for the final approval. If I am having a good day, you will win the promotion."

I was impressed by the orderly process. I did have a slight problem though, "The place is very quiet, sir. Where is everybody?"

"They are all out in the field converting the God fearing into blessed heathens. They should be back by the dinner time. Unless you have some serious questions, run along and help Sita Ma. She is in the garden."

I made my way to the garden where Sita Ma was pulling carrots out of the ground. She showed me where the potatoes were and told me to dig a handful. Apples and pears were picked next. I helped her carry two buckets of produce to the kitchen. "The dinner will be ready in an hour. You can use this time to study the teachings of Swami Dhunyanand," she said pointing to a thick binder on a side table in the dining room. My tummy was protesting a little too much for me to read anything, let alone something as important as Swamiji's teachings. "Do you mind if I take a walk in the garden first?" I asked looking greedily at the fruit trees. "That is okay. Just watch the monkeys," Sita Ma replied in a kindly voice.

I had barely munched through an apple and a pear when I heard some excited voices from the kitchen. I suppressed my inclination to join them; I could hear the conversation while eating another perfectly ripe pear and no one would be interested in the opinion of a raw recruit anyway. I could see Sita Ma in the kitchen listening attentively to two men and two women dressed in, you guessed it, green apparel. If I heard it correctly, and there is no reason to believe otherwise, one member of the group had had an epiphany when they were passing a church, they did not say of what denomination. This individual stood in front of the Cross attached to the building as if in a trance. Then shook his head gently from side to side and said, "Friends, I just heard from God. My place is with the Believers – those who believe in Father who is in Heaven. God has given me yet another opportunity to take my place in the pew. I pray you too, my friends, will see the light one day. Till then, goodbye." With that he ran into the church and for all they knew the repentant erstwhile atheist collapsed in front of Christ on the Cross, stream of tears making a mess of the dirt floor.

Sita Ma introduced me to other disciples. They showed little interest in me, perhaps they were starving too. The dinner was even more plain than any served by my mother on the days she was feeling particularly devout. The only spice used was a touch of rock salt. The minimum amount of butter was used and the chapattis were served dry – that is without a dollop of butter as my mother did. The conversation was all about the deserter, the assistant preacher who was Swamiji's favourite disciple. When I remarked on Swamiji's absence, Sita Ma told me that he cooked his own meals and had them by himself so that his meditations were not interrupted and the disciples could have uninhibited conversation. I had my own suspicion which I kept to myself.

Life at the ashram came to an abrupt end the next day. A short, thin man appeared early in the morning followed by four hefty men who could have been members of the national heavy weight wrestling team. The man was the owner of the building who had not been paid rent for several months. He had obtained an evacuation order and had brought enough muscle to enforce it.

I picked up my paper bag and retraced the steps of the previous day. As a sign of reconciliation I took off the clothes I was wearing before entering the house. Amma rubbed her eyes before screaming with delight when she saw me. Her eyes welled up; she hugged me, gently pushed me back to make sure it was me, hugged me again. My brother and sister rushed in when they heard the scream. I noticed a smirk on their faces when they saw me. Pitaji stayed in the next room saying that he knew it won't be long before I learnt my lesson. I couldn't care less about small put downs; I was drinking mango juice and eating buttered chapattis with spiced curries; a bowl of assorted sweets within reach.

6. QUIRKS OF FATE

I

One never knows how the quirks of fate will work out. It was a wonderful change and I felt fully rejuvenated. Two weeks in London after so many years. Nothing had changed since I left for good. Lush green parks, an amazing variety of flowers blooming in neat little gardens of pocket-sized homes, charming manners of beautiful people dressed to please; it was just too much to leave behind with no regrets. However, the meetings were over. It was time to return to dull and dreary Edmonton and to an even duller husband.

I met Ronald thirty years ago when he had just immigrated to Britain from Jamaica. We hit it straight off. He took me dancing several nights a week even though I didn't dance well, played cricket on Sundays, loved the Beetles and the Rolling stones and told me funny stories from his childhood. His tall, elegant frame with shiny ebony face and tight curly hair, his open laughter and the ability to resolve thorny problems won me over and I married him in spite of the dire predictions of family and friends about living with a man of different race and the ugly children I would bring in to this beautiful world. A year later, we moved to Edmonton when his old friend Sabu invited him to work with him. After a few years, Ronald set up his own business which prospered. The business affairs kept him very busy. First went cricket on Sundays, then dancing on Fridays. He stayed at work late and never took a day off. His laughter became restrained. The solitary life started getting on my nerves when all my complaining got me nowhere. As soon as our two sons were old enough, I went back to school and obtained a business management diploma. A growing company hired me in their human resources department and promoted me to replace the retiring manager the next year.

Soon after I went to work, Ronald received an offer he could not refuse and sold his company. Now he had time at his disposal. Twenty-five years of work, work and more work had permanently changed him. He did not get back his old spark and remained quite taciturn. Although I knew of his changed personality, it must have surprised him. He could not return to his old hobbies. He was too old for calypso, too wise for open laughter, too organized for his own good and too proud to be friendly with anyone who was not a CEO. Other than attending concerts and opera, I can't stand either and he went alone, he spent all his time puttering around the house. He had lost all interest in social events and, if we ever went out together, his sullen mood and sarcastic remarks ruined my evening. I could have stood it if he had done something useful. Like cooked dinner, fixed a broken tile in the bathroom, cleaned the floor, or even replaced the toilet roll when empty. No, it was too much to expect. I gave up and engaged a maid whose husband did the minor repairs.

When I first noticed the changes in Ronald, I tried to help him get out of his depression and suggested counselling. When my efforts failed, I began planning my own rest and recreation. Now I go to the plays and movies with Carmilla who is lively and takes a serious interest in theatre. We enjoy in-depth discussions over rum and coke after lively performances and often meet other friends with whom I can laugh without fearing one of Ronald's put-downs. I go hiking and cycling with bright young colleagues with whom I can discuss and sometimes resolve the nagging problems at work. Ronald is happy left alone to read every line of the newspaper twice and to listen to the melancholic symphonies of Mahler and Vaughan Williams. It doesn't worry me any more to leave him to his own devices. He may not even notice if I stayed the night with one of my male friends. I suspect he knows that I am too much of a prude to break my marriage vows and I remain faithful in spite of almost irresistible temptations.

The hostess breaks my reverie with the offer of a last drink before the plane lands. After eight hours of being pampered with fancy drinks and fabulous meals, it is time to put papers back in the briefcase and to prepare physically and mentally for the routines of normal life. The plane comes to a stop and as a privileged business class passenger I am among the first passengers to get off. After "Welcome to Canada" by a charming immigration officer, I collect my suitcase and wheel it past customs without declaring the expensive toys and gifts I acquired on Oxford Street for the grandchildren and friends. I look for Ronald and feel annoyed that he is late. Then the tall, turbaned figure of Sabu comes forward from behind the crowd, "Greetings, Ronald's mother is very sick, he had to go to Jamaica to be with her in her last moments. He asked me to pick you up and drive you home."

I am surprised to hear this and say, "I talked to Ronald only two days ago; there was no mention of the sick mother, let alone a dying one. His mother is a healthy woman who has power walked ten kilometers every day since she retired twelve years ago."

We get into Sabu's sporty Mustang. On the way I ask Sabu, "Has Ronald given you the key? I did not take one with me."

"Ronald is organized if nothing else. Indeed, he gave me the key." Sabu put my fear at rest.

In the drive way, like the true gentleman that he is, he opens the door of the car for me, gets the suitcase out of the trunk and goes ahead to open the front door. He shudders as the door opens, closes it, leads me back to the car and gently advises me to stay there till he has investigated the foul smell. I do not know what he is talking about. I would have known had I paid attention to very faint music that was in the air.

2

Sabu goes inside the house and leaves the door open to let the smell out. Now the music I barely heard earlier is clearly audible. It is the dreaded Mahler's Ninth Symphony, a manic-depressive composer's reconciliation with death. "Why is the CD player on if Ronald is in Jamaica? Something doesn't jibe here," I think. I run out of the car and rush in the house. Sabu is on the phone. He turns to me and says, "Please wait a second till I finish this call." He hears the other side, puts the phone down and leads me to the dining room. Neat stacks of papers on the dining table catch my eye. From the table my eyes go to the floor and I gasp. Lying on the floor covered by stale vomit with his head under a chair is Ronald. An empty bottle of Tylenol 3 is lying beside him. My head goes in a whirl and as I am about to collapse Sabu grabs me, takes me to a settee, helps me lie down and gets a glass of cold water. He whispers, "I called 911, the police are on the way."

It does not take long for the police to arrive. The sergeant looks at the body and pronounces it dead; dead for a day or more. I tell him that I have just returned from England and when I talked to Ronald two days ago he seemed perfectly normal. Sabu tells him his story. The officer picks up the empty bottle with gloved hands and tells me, "There is little possibility of foul play and it is almost certainly a suicide. Still, formalities have to be gone through. I will arrange for the body to be picked up. Madam, I am very sorry and please accept my heartfelt sympathies. I strongly recommend that you stay with friends for next few days." Sabu calls the number I give him and promises to look after things at the house. As Sabu said, Ronald was organized; even in death he had picked the right person to help with the aftermath of his foul deed.

Carmilla arrives within a few minutes. She takes the suitcase to her car and comes back to support me on the way to the back seat where I can lie down. When we get to her home, she heats up some ham and pea soup and makes me eat a reasonable helping. Then, she gives me a sleeping pill and a hot water bottle and puts me to bed. Carmilla wakes me up the next morning when a policewoman arrives. She tells me that I have been muttering unintelligibly all night. The kindly visitor hands me a photocopy of a letter addressed to me in Ronald's handwriting. The letter was found on top of one of the neat piles on the table. Carmilla snatches it from me. She reads it first to make sure that I can handle the contents. Then she gives it to me and sits down next to me with her hand around my waist.

<h1>3</h1>

"Some inner instinct told me on the morning of our wedding that we were making a mistake. However, I did not have the courage to face up to it and do the right thing. I went along and tried to do my best over the years. I provided for the family as well as I could. I helped in bringing up the kids as much as my business commitments would allow. I tried my best to control my impulsive temperament to suit yours. I gave up my own culture to adopt yours. I supported you whole-heartedly when you decided to go to the business school. I reduced my business load when you started your job with the enthusiasm of a new convert. Yet I could never do enough. You always said that whatever I did was always because I wanted to do it, not because I wanted to help or please you. That maybe true. On the other hand, you felt no need to do things to please me either. Yes, you did not serve me pork because I hate it. I heard of this kindness every time I did something which was not to your satisfaction. I also heard every little detail of my acts that caused you even the slightest inconvenience and the list grew longer with each passing year. I tolerated everything and put up a brave face for you and the world. I felt that our promising young sons needed two parents and it would be very selfish to deprive them of their birthright.

"As you became busier outside the home, I took on more and more of the chores including cooking dinner once or twice during the week.

I hoped against all evidence that you would see a little good in what I did for the family, if not for you. But it was not to be. I became, in your eyes, more evil as the time went on. My shortcomings became more unbearable and my advice on matters of home and hearth were treated with the contempt they deserved, in your opinion anyway. My contributions went unnoticed and you took credit for every job that I did. All mishaps were my fault. I continued to grin and bear it, even though not a day went by when I did not wonder what I was doing at home. Then the time came when I could no longer patiently listen to your tirades, make ample apologies and make up. I started losing my temper and arguing back. You were of course not going to back down and our arguments became more and more fierce. Looking back it is funny in a strange way. The altercations were caused by less and less important issues. The final straw was that day last month. My mind was elsewhere and I did not sympathise with you on some sad news about your colleague I had never met and you were mad. I could not control my frustration and apologise as I always did in the past and left you bubbling in anger to go for a long walk in the rain. You had to go to two parties without me and were probably glad. I walked drenched in the park and considered what I could do.

"Staying together was not an option any more and with the children grown up and gone there was no overriding need. The matters were beyond therapy. Therapy assumes a rational approach from both sides and I knew you too well to expect it from you. On the other hand, separation and living separately would not work either. I have a weakness for female company and within a short while I would fall for some one else and make a hash of it again. Why would the replacement be any better? If I deserved any better I would have received it from you. This left me only one option. The only questions were when and how?

"Jumping out of the third floor window may have broken a lot of bones, it would not have solved my problem. Walking in front of a truck or a train would have put the driver in trouble and this was not acceptable. Driving the car into a concrete post was an option and I gave it a serious thought. With all the safety features in the car there was a possibility of escaping death and ending as an invalid for life. That left only one option – to take a strong poison when no one was going to be around for a while. Once this was decided every thing fell into place.

"I have arranged all my papers in order so you should have minimum inconvenience. I am leaving my retirement fund to our sons because they can use the money and you have plenty for your needs in any foreseeable future. I would prefer not to have any fuss after I am gone, you are at complete liberty to do whatever you wish. It is you, after all, who has to live. Any grief will be short-lived. I know I am not worth grieving about and there are many who will fill much better any space left.

"I do wish you the very best in your life."

4

I had a cremation and memorial service for Ronald in which Sabu paid the tribute and twenty odd friends, most of them mine, showed up and expressed sympathy for us. In view of the circumstances, not much could be said and not much was. The post-service reception was a short and quiet affair. Upset by the offensive tone of the letter, I had not shown it to my sons, Sammy and Juno. They appeared hurt, maybe they felt some guilt as well and did not say much. They were not close to their father and I did not think that their grief, if they had any, would last. The hurt would no doubt remain for a while.

It did not take long to sort out the affairs. Sammy and Juno left with their inheritance without disclosing their plans or showing any interest in my future. A colleague who had lost her husband a few years ago frightened me when she said that she had still not recovered from the loss. To counter this possibility my analyst recommended that I return to normal life as soon as possible and pointed out that this is what Ronald implied in the last line of his letter. I had a life to live and I should do my best to fulfill what he wished.

I returned Ronald's concert and opera tickets and received a donation receipt. Next, I threw all the Mahler and Vaughan Williams records and books in the trash where they belonged. Sabu had his business and family and our paths hardly ever crossed. My theatre and hiking groups helped me recover my bearings by paying me special attention. Jonathan, the assistant manager in my department and a keen fitness enthusiast, was particularly considerate and I reciprocated. I resumed the theatre evenings with Carmilla and hiking and cycling in the countryside on weekends with Jonathan. A few weeks after the event, Jonathan and I were resting on the bank of a lake after having hiked for four hours to get there. We were lying on the soft grass admiring the beautiful bright blue prairie sky with a scattering of odd shaped discs of silver. Jonathan now did something he had never done before. He put one hand to support my head and the other on my tummy. When I did not protest he moved it to my right breast. I loosened my bra to make things easy for us. However, the place was not as private as one would wish. It was time to return to the car anyway. When Jonathan stopped to drop me off I invited him in for dinner. He stayed afterwards and we shared our first night together.

For once Ronald turned out to be right. Jonathan and I were married soon after and Jonathan filled the void much better, literally and metaphorically. I hate to admit it: there are times I feel thankful to my first husband for knowing when to take his leave, even if it required what some people would call the ultimate sacrifice.

5

The seemingly immaculate script Ronald had written for Diane fell apart a week before she was due to leave for England. Diane was white when she came out of the shower, "Feel here, what does it feel like?" she asked Ronald. He felt her right breast halfway down from the nipple, "It is hard, feels like a bone fragment."

"Oh my God, Why are you doing this to me? I am too young to die." She sat down and burst into tears.

Ronald put his arms around her, "Let us not assume the worst. Let us see what the doctor has to say." He called the doctor's office, told the receptionist the details and was booked an appointment the same morning. The doctor examined the lump and arranged a mammogram and a biopsy the following day. As usual Diane was proven right although she wanted to be wrong. It was a tumor and it was malignant. A mastectomy was scheduled for the following week. Her trip was off and Ronald's plan collapsed. Instead of escape from a miserable existence with a demanding wife, he now had to help her recover from a serious illness which could take six months or longer.

Diane was an A type personality who was always on the go. Cancer frightened the life out of her even though the doctors said that it had been detected early and the probability of a recurrence was small. In spite of statistical evidence to the contrary, she chose the tougher chemo to keep the cancer cells at bay. She had a terrible five months during the chemotherapy. Ronald wondered often whether the cure was worse than the disease. She was sick with fright for three days before the chemo injections, extremely tired and nauseated for several days after. In between, because of reduced immunity she was in bed with colds and fevers. She was furious for being bedridden. Carmilla, Jonathan and other friends visited at first, then the visits tapered off, they had other responsibilities too. It was Ronald she was encumbered with. Ronald had no job to go to; he was with her every minute of the day whether she needed him or not. Diane instinctively knew his caring was only for appearances and his heart was not in it. He was only doing it because that is what was expected of him. This sense together with her helplessness made her furious and she was often depressed. She took her frustration out on Ronald. He had done this and that to harm her career and had not done this and that to help her when she needed it and he could easily have done. She asked, "How can I be sure that I will be looked after when I am helpless? What were you doing to be useful when I needed you?"

Ron suppressed his own anger, letting it all wash over, then brought her a cold drink and waited till she calmed down. The irony of fate left him confused as to the future course of action. He did not fight back in consideration of her sickness. Instead, he took to beating his head against the wall when he was upset. Just the way his dad did when he felt helpless. Rather than reducing dad's misery, it may have caused the Alzheimer's he developed soon after his retirement. The thought frightened Ronald, it did not stop him from doing it.

Both of them breathed sighs of relief after the last session of chemo. The oncologist examined Diane and pronounced the treatment a success. However, he warned that the treatment usually affects the hormones and that she should expect mood swings as well as stronger sex urges. It made Ronald smile ruefully; sex was the last thing on his mind after the physical exhaustion of the last five months.

The first week after the last Chemo was harrowing for both of them. Their distress was getting worse by the day with no hope of resolution because Diane's energy level did not improve as she had hoped and her fury did not cool. Almost every day, she told Ronald of some new service that would have made her life tolerable and he had not rendered it. Her life was intolerable and she was making sure his was too. He had reached the end of the rope. They both had. Only he did not have anyone to take his frustration out on.

Just before they reached the breaking point, the hormonal pendulum swung the other way.

6

The clattering of crockery woke Ron up. Diane was coming through the bedroom door with a tray of morning tea. "What is up? She hasn't done this for years," Ron wondered.

Diane was all smiles as she brought him the cup, "Tea just the way you like it, the same shade of brown as the back of your hand."

"What a wonderful surprise! What did I do to deserve this?"

"I had a nightmare last night - I put my arm out and you were not there. I wondered why and all the angry episodes flashed past. I woke up in a shock. I was so relieved to find you here. You have been so kind and understanding even when I was so cruel. I did not realize then what I was doing, I do now. Chemo made my hormones play up so much worse and made me even more unreasonable than I was before. That water is now under the bridge. I am determined to make up to you. I am well now and I will look after you in health as you looked after me in sickness."

For a while Diane was as good as her words. She reduced the travel after returning to her job. Ronald took up cricket again, though only as an umpire and they rejoined the dance club. She insisted on him joining her for dinner and theatre evenings and he did his best to be a good company. They booked a long cruise to the Caribbean to celebrate Diane's recovery and excellent prognosis. So absorbed were they in their social life that neither of them saw the dark cloud hovering above them.

It was Diane's birthday. She settled on a romantic candlelit dinner for two at home. Diane, in a lovely blue dress, sipped sherry and picked cashews from the bowl of mixed nuts while Ronald barbecued the steaks, medium for her and rare for him, baked two large potatoes and tossed the spinach salad. Red wine was the right vintage and the meal was a great success. For dessert, they had pecan pie a la mode washed down with a couple of glasses of fifty-year old port. Ronald blew the candles off and helped a somewhat wobbly Diane to the couch.

They both wanted a great evening of love making. The gods did not. Diane reached close to the climactic point again and again without attaining it. Her frustration mounted with each disappointment and the big release came in a furious explosion. Ronald had never seen her so angry. He felt guilty and apologized but to no avail. The tirade lasted till Diane was exhausted and went upstairs to bed. Ronald slept on the couch.

The following morning Ronald heard movement upstairs. He took Diane a cup of tea as a gesture of reconciliation. Diane's face was puffy; she hadn't slept much. At the sight of her husband the fury returned with full force. "Have your tea yourself, I don't need it." She threw the cup back at him. It hit him full in the face.

7

There was a knock on the door. Come in, Ronald said, hoping it was the pretty young nurse who was always so anxious to please.

"Time to turn off the light. Here is the sleeping pill and some water. You will likely be discharged in the morning after the doctor has examined you. So have a good sleep"

Ronald looked at the pretty face. "How innocent the young can be," he mused and asked, "Will you pass me my jacket from the hook please? I will use it as a comforter."

"I will get you another blanket if you are cold," the sweet girl offered.

"No need to bother with the blanket dear. My jacket is all I need," Ronald insisted.

The nurse spread the jacket on his upper body and turned to leave. Ronald waved saying, "Thank you, dear. Don't work too hard. Even the angels need to look after themselves. Good night."

"Good night," the nurse replied as she closed the door gently behind her.

Ronald fished into the inside pocket of the jacket, took out a small envelope and emptied it in the glass of water. He stared at a few stars twinkling in the narrow patch of sky visible through the window hoping to see what waited beyond the dark world outside the hospital room, the glass shaking a little in his hands. He steadied himself, put the glass to his lips and swallowed the contents in one big gulp.

7. THE DREAM

I

Dreams often recall the past; rarely does a dream project the future.

2

Amit was indeed lying on the couch and he was not flipping the remote and staring blankly at the big screen TV as he often does. He was in that agreeable position in the clinic of Dr. Bliss, a psychoanalyst known all over the continent for his interpretations of dreams. Amit was fortunate to get this appointment quickly. To tell you the truth, his good fortune was in having Sophia for a wife who had many strings to her bow, one of them indirectly hooked to Dr. Bliss.

Sophia had been worried about Amit for a while. There were several reasons and they all had one root; he did not value her and therefore did not pay enough attention to her. Not only did his eyes wander while she was talking, he tapped on the table, clicked his tongue, hummed some strange Indian melody, or made other annoying sounds. The consequence was that he bought meat at the grocery store when she had asked him to buy milk and drove over to the hardware store at the other end of town to buy nails when she wanted him to pick up the mail. He spoke to her facing away as if mumbling in his foreign accent was not bad enough and sulked when she complained. He took over many small chores around the house while disregarding her suggestions on serious issues even when she had the professional expertise and he refused to discuss the issues she had with the children. Sophia's frustration with the situation reached the point that she was losing patience with him every hour of the time they were together and their sex life, never great at the best of times, had now hit a new bottom.

Then came the last straw: the dream. Over the years, Amit had frequent dreams from life at the students' hostel when he was studying engineering in India. In these dreams he was having problems such as an interminable wait for the washroom, the shower running out of water just after he had soaped his body, long line up for meals and the loss of large sums in the games of bridge. He would wake up sweating all over and describe the dream in great detail. Sophia listened patiently and patted him back to sleep as she had done with their sons when they were babies. However, this new dream shook her up. She had read on the internet that older men in early stages of senility start craving for what they were fond of in their childhood and now wish to return permanently to the place they loved then. She wondered if her husband of forty years, in addition to becoming inattentive and partially deaf, was also suffering from some mental disorder. After Amit had gone back to sleep she made a note in her bedside memo pad to investigate the issue. She let it simmer in her head for a couple of days before discussing it with a few of her friends who were knowledgeable in such matters. On their unanimous advice she arranged an appointment for Amit with Dr. Bliss within a month of the nightmare, as she called Amit's dream, although the waiting list of the celebrated analyst was known to be longer than nine months.

3

Dr. Bliss's opening line in the session surprised Amit. "Are you comfortable? Does the headrest need adjustment?" the famous doctor asked.

7.   The Dream

"Thank you for your concern, sir. I am so comfortable that I am afraid I might fall asleep," Amit replied.

"Please don't do that. I might think you are considering a reply to my query and some time will be wasted. My time is precious although I am charging you the special rate of only five dollars a minute. Now let us get down to business. Am I right in thinking that you had a dream recently that has your wife concerned about the soundness of your mind?"

"Yes, that is true although I do not really see it that way. I have often had dreams of my old haunts in India which wake me up because most memories from those days are not all that pleasant. Although this new dream sends me back to earlier days than the other dreams, there is nothing particularly creepy about it."

"Interesting, very interesting. Goes back to earlier days. How early?"

"The frequent dreams are from my late teen years in college. This dream is from preteen days."

"Interesting. Before we go into the dream itself, have you had it again?"

"Yes, several times over the last month. It scares Sophia every time."

"And not you?"

"Not really. It does wake me up and I am happy to realize that it was merely a dream. Unfortunately, Sophia wakes up too and she insists on knowing what disturbed my sleep. I quickly return to slumberland after the episode while Sophia lies awake."

"Interesting. Does it appear again after you have gone back to sleep?"

"No it doesn't. In fact the sleep is unusually sound, no dreams whatever."

"It is like letting the steam out. Once it is gone you can relax."

"I never looked at it this way. This is also true about my scary dreams of college years."

"Interesting. Now you can describe the bad dream, or the nightmare, whatever you call it, in its most usual form?"

"First a preamble. I was born in the foothills of Nilgiris in Southern India in a then small town called Anmora. Tall peaks, white in the winter, grayish blue in the summer, dominated the view in the South. About 30 kilometers away, an hour by bus, is Sensous, the famous resort town where the rich families of the region spend the summer to avoid the scorching heat of the plains. I was never impressed by Sensous even when I was a child. It was too crowded for my liking. The hill town that won me over was Sonagaon, about a hundred kilometers from Anmora on a narrow road with tight switch backs, downhill side so steep you were scared to look over. I was in Sonagaon only twice, for a week each time, when I was eleven and twelve. It was a ride of three hours on a bus that panted up steep slopes spewing out black smoke that made its way into the bus on the higher limb of the switch back. Even the regular passengers were sick by the end of the journey. But what views once you reached there! The glorious sun rising in the East from behind the majestic mountains, the fantastic colours of the sunset across the valley in the West; and yes, the rainbow after the noon drizzle. It was as if the great artist in heaven had taken his pallet and brush and drawn an arc of seven distinct colours on the clear blue sky. It is perfectly possible that time has burnished the memory of what I really saw. In any event, I felt throughout my teens and twenties that I was born to live in Sonagaon. Like a rich man of independent means with maids and servants to attend to my every whim, not like a poor boy that I was then. The strange thing is that the prospective family never made an appearance when I day dreamed of this life – no wife, no children. However, Sonagaon receded from view when I migrated to Canada and married Sophia, only to reappear a month ago."

"Interesting, very interesting. Carry on."

"As I said in the beginning, the dreams of late teenage life at college persisted, mainly reminding me of the struggles in those days. In the dream that Sophia suspects is indicative of approaching senility, I am standing on the balcony of my palatial home on a hilltop looking into the distance. Sometimes I have a glass of red wine in my right hand, sometimes a cup of steaming tea, sometimes nothing. My appearance is similar to what it was in my fifties. Mountain peaks are without doubt those of Sonagaon. I look right; the sun is rising slowly, the sky becoming brighter as more of the white disc comes into view from behind the peaks. Then I turn left and see the sun going down beyond the valley in the West, sky dressed like a Hindu bride in brilliant shades of pink. The sun sets completely and twinkling bright stars cover the velvet black sky. Then a heavy curtain falls on the scene and I wake up."

"Very interesting. The dreams as vivid as yours have some meaning. We have to work together to find out what it could be. One thing it is not. It is not the onset of senility. You said you look in the dream as you did in your fifties. Can you tell me what was happening in your life around that time?"

"Those were the good years. Our two sons were at colleges in Toronto and Montreal. Sophia had her business under control and I had enough spare time on most days for afternoons at the club, golf or bridge, depending on the weather. Perhaps it was the best time of my life."

"How is your life now? How do you get on with Sophia?"

"Sophia has two distinct personalities. She is an angel when she is relaxed, you would not find a better person anywhere. She makes everybody around her feel good. She makes me look like a great father and a good person which in itself is a miracle. Under stress she becomes temperamental and has outbursts worse than a cannon fire. That is why our life together has its ups and downs, more downs than ups in recent years. We are from very different cultures and have never been a homogeneous couple like many of our fortunate friends. We have been growing apart over the last twenty years or so because our interests have been diverging more and more. We do things together on occasions, more to be obliging on the part of one or the other than out of his, or her, personal interest. Sometimes it works, other times it adds to the stresses."

"Interesting. Is this divergence the only source of stress or there are other factors too."

"Illness of a son and the grandson, the marriage break-up of the son and the illness of Sophia have all contributed. The grandson continues to stress Sophia and it adds to difficulties between us because I want to detach myself from situations where I can't help. Sophia grows deep emotional ties and she frets when her suggestions are disregarded."

"How do these stresses impact on you?"

"It is not the events themselves; it is the reaction of Sophia to them. She gets upset with the sons or the daughter-in-law, becomes tense and takes her anger out on me. I understand what is going on but feel pretty depressed all the same. I am not willing or able to stand up to Sophia and fight when she is being unreasonable. I take her snapping and bullying without protest – in fact I try to appease her by taking over housekeeping chores from her. It does hurt and I wonder why I stay in that situation."

"Why do you appease her rather than stand up for yourself?"

"There are several reasons. First, I think her temper tantrums are more extreme due to the effect of drugs prescribed for an almost fatal disease she had five years ago. Second, she was very kind to me in our first few years together. She helped me settle in the West by advising me on how to behave in a different culture than the one I grew up in. Not only that, she uprooted herself and moved away from her family and friends to promote my career. Third, she was an excellent mother to the children and a great role model for them. Fourth, she showed great concern as if her world were falling apart whenever my life was in danger. There is so much gratitude I owe her I wouldn't know where to begin."

"What you are telling me is very different from what I usually hear. In my experience, it is human nature to devalue, if not forget altogether, the kindnesses of the partners and remember vividly their unpleasant actions whether innocent or intended. Over the years the perceived imbalance starts to weigh them down. You present an interesting angle. Nothing you said before gave me the impression that you were sensitive enough to have such feelings."

"I am often told that I need to be sensitive to others and I have been trying. That may be a part of the problem."

"Why is that a problem?"

"In the old days I wouldn't notice Sophia's change of tone. Now her snapping upsets me although I keep it to myself."

"Very interesting. Any thing more to add?"

"I have been thinking of late that there maybe some truth in what she often says when she is angry – she would be better off without me; a butler would be an improvement over me in every way. If that is indeed true, I would be doing her a favour by leaving. If our separation improves her situation it could offset some of the burden of gratitude that I carry."

"Yes, one could look at it that way."

"Then the old American saying: today is the first day of the rest of your life. Should we be making each other's present and future miserable because of the past kindnesses?"

"You have a point. A relationship can be great at one stage of life and a misery at another. While raising the family, most couples work out how they share the load. As they start wilting in mature years, one may start to feel burdened when the other is stressed beyond endurance, or is not able to do her, or his, share."

"What you say is frightening. What happens to the notions of love and understanding in such cases?"

"Love is an abstraction and understanding fleeting. Practicalities and burdens of daily life are always the first consideration."

"Social implications of what you just said are immense. Marriage is for raising children, not for life. After kids have grown up each is on his own."

"Not always. In old days people did not live long and this was rarely an issue. These days many couples adjust to new realities and carry on. Not because they love each other any more, just that adaptation is easier than the complications of a break up. Some struggle and carry on regardless. Separation and new relationships maybe better when both are driving each other mad. Each couple is a different case. No one can tell you where you should stand and what is your best course. That is for you alone to consider. Anything else?"

"I think I have said all there is to say on this issue."

"Then let us move on. Do you have any financial stresses?"

"I wish we did. Then the divergence in temperament and hobbies would probably take the back seat. We have ample funds in our separate businesses to cover all foreseeable needs for the rest of our lives."

"Interesting. Well, I can have you in that couch for several consultations and charge you a bundle. I won't do it because that time will be more helpful to other patients. I will tell you my interpretation of your dreams. After you have given it some thought, we can meet again if you wish.

"Your dreams of the college days are expressing your fears of returning to India and reverting to being single. I am certain you had them after aggravation with Sophia and when you were wondering 'What am I doing here?' Those dreams encouraged you to continue working at pleasing Sophia in spite of mixed results. A month or so ago, you concluded that your relationship with Sophia was beyond repair and your future happiness lies in being single. This is why your dreams carry you to an earlier happy place. They reflect the idea down deep in your mind. Yet, you are not certain what to do. That is why you look to the right and the left and not straight in front at the rainbow. What should you do now? This is a different issue and I am not in the right specialty to help you with that."

"Your interpretations are not far from what I was thinking. How to present them to Sophia is indeed a problem. I need to give that some thought too."

"Sophia is no fool. She had her suspicions and she arranged this visit to confirm them. Tell her the good news that senility has not touched you yet. Then discuss the issues between you. As I indicated I am not qualified to tell you how to do it. I am sorry, my next patient has been waiting for ten minutes and I must say good bye."

Dr. Bliss opened the door with his left hand and offered Amit the right for a handshake. Amit accepted it with a wry smile. He stood still after the door closed behind him, not knowing whether to go to the right or to the left, East or West.

8. A Cliché

I

I know it is not a good form to use a cliché in a conversation, certainly not among literate friends. However, maybe because I learnt English later in life and unusual phrasing has a special appeal, I am tempted to use old sayings at every opportunity, even when I do not remember their correct form. That maybe the case this time too. So please humour me by allowing me to say it and I promise not to repeat the offence. Cliché of the day goes something like this: *the more things change, the more they stay the same.* I do think it applies to Madeleine and Anil although I wish it did not. Being a mere mortal I do not control events, I relate them the way they played out.

Commonwealth Students' Hostel offered lodging and three meals every day of the week for four pounds, the best deal you could get in Leicester in the early sixties. It was located on a quiet street in a rundown area a few blocks from the city centre and within easy bus ride from important educational institutions. Across the street was Thompson Square, a rather unkempt park that had swings and slides for the kids to play on but was rarely used. The hostel was a refurbished Georgian building that had suffered damage during the war. It had creaky floors and a musty smell that every one soon became used to. Single and double rooms in the hostel had large windows opening on the park, or the well maintained back yard and were adequately furnished with single beds, desks, chairs and small wardrobes obtained from 'antique' furniture stores. There was space for fifty young men and women from all over the former British Empire. Most of them were students ranging from younger ones completing A level courses to prepare for the University to some older ones earning professional qualifications in medicine or engineering. A few British young men and women stayed there to help the foreigners settle in an environment strange for them. The deputy warden interviewed each local candidate. Ones she deemed suitable were presented to the warden who gave them a five minute sermon expounding on the virtues of making the foreign guests feel at home.

One evening in early October, the air was unseasonably warm, the sky deep blue and the oak trees that lined Thompson Square, the colour of gold. A breeze whispered an invitation to young and old, men and women, "Come out and enjoy a pleasant stroll." At the Students' Hostel the gong had sounded and the residents were lining up for dinner: overcooked spam with undercooked peas and boiled potatoes covered by thick, tasteless gravy. Anil was perhaps tenth in the line. He was a twenty something student from India who had been a resident for just over a year. He heard the breeze and, without knowing who it was, turned to the person behind him, "It is a beautiful evening. Will you join me for a walk to Chinatown? We can have something good to eat for a change." The person happened to be Madeleine, a new resident who had been there just a few days. She was surprised at the boldness of the invitation from this not unpleasant looking brown man with dark penetrating eyes. She was just about to say "No, thank you, I have to wash my hair," when key point of the warden's lecture crossed her mind – "They can be sensitive. Don't hurt their feelings. Treat them as honoured guests." She looked at him again to make sure his intentions were 'pure' as her anxious mother would have put it, then said, "Well, why not. I will see you at the front door in five minutes."

Madeleine changed into a modest blue dress with green stripes, put on sensible shoes and brushed her light brown shoulder length hair. Anil was waiting for her in front of the dining room. They hit it off straight away. It was mostly uphill to China town but they did not notice the climb. Anil told her that he was doing postgraduate work in electrical engineering on a scholarship with an agreement to return to India after two years of study, he found the people generally friendly and he was enjoying his stay, although he missed home cooking. Madeleine revealed that she had travelled a little in France and Germany, was looking forward to her stay with overseas students and was studying English literature.

"Have you read Thackeray, Kipling or Orwell?" Anil asked.

"I am more into Dickens and Lawrence. Have you read them?"

"I am not much of a reader of literature, not even in my own language. I only know these names because they had connection with India." Anil's honesty was pleasing.

They were ready to eat by the time they saw the sign of a dragon exhaling fire with Far E st Ca tonese Restaurant in gaudy red and green neon lights across it. They were relieved to note an air of affordability when they peeped through the open door. There were fifteen or so bare plastic tables, each with four wooden chairs. The tables were set with cheap cutlery, glasses and paper napkins which were coming into use then. Only two of them were occupied and it turned out that the owner was helping her two children with home work on one of them. A young waiter came out and told them to pick a table. They chose one next to a window. The waiter returned with a jug, filled their glasses with lukewarm water and handed them a bulky menu from a table in the corner.

They had a good laugh when they discovered that neither of them had been to a Chinese restaurant before and each had been hoping that the other knew what to order. Being too young to have the confidence to acknowledge their ignorance, they ordered from the menu everything that caught their fancy; won ton soup, sweet and sour pork, chicken chop suey, mushroom foo yung and mixed vegetables. The waiter calmly took the order and walked away without comment.

Soon a huge bowl of soup arrived with brown bits which looked like pieces of beef at the bottom and what seemed like clouds floating in it. Madeleine looked at it and exclaimed, "Oh my God, half of this bowl will fill me for two days. You will have to eat the other dishes we have ordered."

Anil was staring at the bowl too and having similar thoughts. He took a long minute before responding to Madeleine, "You are right. This bowl will be enough for two meals for both of us. What will we do with all the strange dishes we have ordered?"

They were still pondering the grave issue when the waiter arrived with an enormous basin of rice and a large dish of what he said was sweet and sour polk. "Stop, please stop," both shouted in unison. This unnerved the waiter and he stood transfixed. The owner noticed the commotion, looked at her unfamiliar customers and trundled over. "Is something wrong with the food?" she asked sounding perturbed.

Madeleine took control of the situation, "I am sure that the food is fine although we have not tasted it yet. The problem is that this is our first visit to a Chinese restaurant and we did not know what we were doing. We ordered more food than we can eat in a week."

"No problem. We can pack it and you can take it home. It will last for several days in the fridge," the owner assumed an authoritative tone.

"We live in a hostel and there is no fridge for the students to use. It doesn't help to take it there."

"Well, we do have a problem. Let me see what stage the kitchen is at with your order," the lady said before disappearing behind the bamboo curtain on the far side.

She was back in a jiffy. "I stopped them from cooking anything else. My children and I will eat the pork. You just pay for the soup. Does that suit you?"

Madeleine and Anil could not believe their ears. A great weight was lifted off their shoulders and some otherwise needed money stayed in the wallets. Madeleine spoke for both of them, "Oh, it is so generous of you. We do appreciate your consideration. We will be back again and again to show it."

They enjoyed the soup and left after thanking the owner once more. They returned several times over the next few weeks to taste one by one the other dishes they had ordered. It firmed up their friendship although it did not bloom into romance. Perhaps Anil's intentions remained 'pure' even when Madeleine wished they would not. In any event, at the end of the academic year they went their separate ways and lost touch.

2

Anil returned to India and married a girl his parents had chosen for him in advance. The wedding ceremony lasted a week and there were a thousand guests at the reception held under a huge tent on the cricket ground. Veena was pretty with expressive eyes and shiny black hair down to her waist. She had a college education and came from a 'suitable' family. She brought a dowry appropriate for an engineer trained in England; emerald and diamond jewelry, silk saris with gold-thread borders, imported furniture for their home, a car and fifty thousand rupees. His father-in-law profusely apologized to each member of Anil's family for the car being an Indian make, import of vehicles had been banned three years ago and this is the best he could find.

The country was going through yet another recession and in spite of his qualifications and family connections to high places the only job Anil found was in frozen tundra, a place called Calgary in far off Canada. Veena put her foot down; she was not going to live in the boondocks so far away from her family and friends. In a last ditch effort to persuade her, he borrowed an issue of National Geographic from the public library with a long article extolling the virtues of life in Canada. The pictures of elegantly furnished homes with beautiful gardens and luxurious cars in the driveways softened her and she agreed to go after he promised to pay for her to return at least once every two years. It was on one such visit, tenth or twelfth he had lost count, that the taxi taking her from the airport to her parents' home collided with a truck. His life with Veena had been happy and he only rarely wondered what it would have been like if he had been foolish when he was young and followed his heart rather than his head. After their two sons married and moved away, he thought of Madeleine more often but did nothing to find her whereabouts.

Madeleine went on to study literature at Oxford and became a writer of fiction. Her stories appeared in literary magazines regularly and her novels, although not best sellers, sold enough to keep the publisher interested. She married Thomas, a poet, in a simple civil ceremony and had twin daughters. Other than occasional cheques from publishers for their writing they had no other income and lived hand to mouth. Ironically, soon after a collection of love poems of Thomas scored major success with reviewers and the public, he had a heart attack and died. The girls were in kindergarten then and it was a while before they were over the grief of losing their father. After three years of bringing up the girls by herself, Madeleine fell in love with a newspaper editor and they lived together for ten years till he left her and moved in with an older woman. The twins grew up, went to college, fell in love a few times before settling down and now lived abroad with families of their own. Anil crossed her mind once in a while in the early years, more often during her single periods. She imagined him living the life of an executive in Delhi or Mumbai, looked after by maids and servants attending to his smallest wish and with a dainty Indian woman for a wife who did what he told her to, gave birth to six boys and never asked anything in return except permission for trivial indulgences. Once out of sheer curiosity she googled him. There were 4,798 responses for hundreds of different individuals with the same name.

3

Anil was driving to the club for the morning session of bridge. It was a warm day, the trees on Crowchild Trail were changing colour, the branches swaying gently in the breeze. For some strange reason, he thought of the walk with Madeleine nearly forty years ago and started humming a melancholic song from his teen years, "I have no control over love, please tell me whether I should love you or not." Unbeknown to Anil, the host was interviewing a famous author on the car radio. Something the interviewer said stopped his humming. The celebrity was visiting the city as a stop on North American tour to promote her book which was a sensation in the U.K. It was a novel called "An Ordinary Life" and the author was Madeleine Lewisham. "Could she be Madeleine who was studying literature in Leicester?" he wondered turning into the parking lot.

"Why did you not return my spade lead? They would have been down two. Your stupid diamond play let them make the slam," his partner screamed. He had several occasions to be upset that morning because Anil's mind was on Madeleine and what he missed by being a coward when a little courage might have been all he needed. "All that is water under the bridge. It would be fun, though, to see her and exchange notes on our lives if it can be arranged," he muttered to himself.

"What did you say?" his partner asked, wondering if his partner had lost it and it was time to find a new one.

Anil returned to the table. He had to do something to pacify his mate, "Oh, my mind is elsewhere this morning. I am sorry I am letting you down. To make up I will pick up the tab for both of us."

After the game ended Anil started calling the hotels where Madeleine could be staying. He hit gold dust on the fourth call, "Yes sir, Ms. Lewisham is staying here. I have instructions not to forward calls."

"Can you convey a message? I am an old friend from our college days," Anil asked with all the politeness he could muster.

"I will record your message sir and put it on her phone. What happens next is up to Ms. Lewisham," the operator was in a good mood.

Anil did want to see Madeleine and the message he dictated was detailed and persuasive, "Madeleine, I am Anil Venugopal, your friend of forty years ago. You have most likely forgotten me and our adventure in the Far East in Leicester. I fondly remember you and cherish our friendship. If you have a few spare minutes, it would be a favour to me if you could find time for us to get together and exchange notes on how our lives turned out. My cell – mobile to you – is 403 999 1350. Best wishes."

Not a minute had gone by when the cell played its tune. His face lit up. It was Madeleine's sweet, though authoritative, voice of forty years ago, "So nice to hear from an old friend in a strange town. Can we meet for lunch? I am busy otherwise."

"Yes, of course. For old time's sake we should go to a Chinese restaurant. There is one in the same block as your hotel. It is known all over the world for inventing the dish called onion pork which is now served in every Asian restaurant. They serve excellent dim sum too. I will meet you at your hotel lobby in fifteen minutes, if that suits you."

The lobby was busy when Anil pushed past the revolving door. There were several people standing around admiring the fountain, some sitting on the sofas waiting for the visitors and a few talking to the receptionists. He did not recognize Madeleine among them. Then the door of one of the elevators on his left opened and an older version of the familiar face looked inquiringly in his direction. He waved and walked over. Madeleine wore light make up and a smart blue suit over white blouse. Her hair was still light brown and well coiffed. Both smiled happily as they shook hands vigorously. There were no hugs, let alone kisses, it would have presumed too much familiarity. A short walk on the street buzzing with hungry workers pouring out of office towers took them to the Golden West. There was no waiting at the restaurant and they soon found out why. It was Wednesday, the only day in the week they did not serve dim sum. It didn't bother them though. They remembered what they had ordered at the Far East and Madeleine repeated the dishes verbatim. Changes in the world over two generations were reflected in what was served on the table covered with an immaculately ironed white cloth and a bunch of red roses in a tall vase in the centre. The size of the dishes was much smaller although the price in dollars was what it had been in pennies. It did not matter; they were not hard up now and both were hungry. Not enough was left to take home, although both had access to a fridge.

They talked of many things - about the lives they had lived, happy times in many words and the sorrows in a few; successes with modesty and failures without excuse. They did not discuss what each of them had wanted to – the future they wished in their hearts. Hard to tell whether egos got in the way or their courage failed once more, perhaps head won over heart this time too. Whatever the reason, after the lunch was over they went their separate ways, looking back longingly at what could have been, then and now.

Great and Ordinary

1. In the Shadow of a Giant

I

I lived in his shadow most of my life. He basked in the glow of fame while I composed in almost complete anonymity from what came out of my soul. No one cared for my music except for a few friends who admired what I played and sang, and who played and sang what I wrote for them. Outside this small circle, no one knew Franz Peter Schubert, or his music. They were too busy listening to Ludwig van Beethoven, praising him to the skies, or attacking him as a vain composer who composed incomprehensible unplayable music. Herr van Beethoven could take the praise as nonchalantly as the criticism. He told them, "I put down on paper what my God tells me and God does not care for what a poor fiddler can or cannot play."

Herr van Beethoven came to Vienna to learn composition from the masters. But none could satisfy him. Mozart, Haydn, Salieri, they were in awe of young Ludwig's genius and there was nothing they could teach him. He did not hide his contempt for them, said their art was for the dying eighteenth century, not for the new century waiting in the wings. Music of the nineteenth century shall have emotion and melody of course, it will also have passion and it will be full of surprises. It will be as fresh after years of performing and listening as it would be the first time. Not only will it touch the heart strings, it will raise the spirits, rouse the patriotism of the oppressed and give strength to the weak. Old masters did not understand how music could do this and the young genius did not understand why it would not.

It took a while for young Ludwig to make his mark. And when he did, it was huge. People flocked to his concerts, to listen to him playing his piano sonatas and concertos, his trios, quartets and symphonies and the nobility showered him with commissions and invitations to play his chamber works. When they were paying full attention, not when they were dining as they did for other musicians. Proud Ludwig entered the palaces from the front door not through servants' entrance as Haydn used to and was announced by the butler with his full name with due emphasis on van. He discoursed with the counts as their equal and no one dared to keep him waiting without a reasonable excuse. He was offered commissions from all over Europe and travelers to Vienna made special efforts just to have a glimpse of the great man.

The three years leading to 1809 were difficult in Vienna. Napoleon was the hero of the common folks and many in the arts community adored him. It was rumoured that Herr van Beethoven had composed a special symphony, the longest anyone had ever contemplated, and dedicated it to the French Emperor. However, without any provocation, the French marched into defenseless Vienna. This wanton aggression so angered the composer that he scratched the dedication from the manuscript. When calm had returned to the city, the work was premiered with no dedication. The overflowing hall was stunned by the work in which passion was paramount. The applause after each movement was deafening and so long that it took two hours to finish playing it and some parts of the advertised program had to be omitted. The music gave birth to a new spirit in the Viennese people who felt that the end of their misery was not far off.

As a singer in the Royal Boys' Choir, I heard these and other stories of young Ludwig who soon became Herr van Beethoven. I took every opportunity available to study his eight symphonies, five piano concertos and countless works for solo piano and chamber groups. I was amazed at the novelty of the music, it was so different from the music of Mozart and Haydn we were told to emulate. When I was fifteen, the famous composer and teacher, Antonio Salieri, heard some songs and two symphonies I had composed for the young musicians of the academy. These works were in the traditional style and the master was so impressed that he offered me free lessons in composition. I was grateful and learned much from him. About this time Herr van Beethoven asked Herr Salieri for advice on his opera and disregarded it when it was offered. Naturally my master was upset and I was too when I heard of such intransigence. However, when I had the good fortune of seeing the opera in performance, I fell under the spell of Herr van Beethoven for the second time and this time it was for good.

During my teen years I set numerous songs by Goethe, Klopstock and Heine for me to sing and play with my friends in school and in their homes. Since I was not composing for any temperamental diva, I gave as much prominence to the piano as to the singer which was not customary. We had great fun with everyone standing around me at the piano and singing from the music sheet even before the ink was dry. I also composed pieces for solo piano and loved playing them in private soirees. It never occurred to me that they were worthy of being played in public. I was afraid that they would be compared to the works of Herr van Beethoven and found wanting. However, I did not destroy any music and stored every composition in a steel trunk.

2

1815 was the year when I started my first and only job as an assistant to my father who was a teacher. I was an unprepossessing eighteen years old, shorter and wider than almost everybody. I hated the job from the moment I first walked in front of the students. The boys were noisy and I was too gentle to bring peace to the room by punishing them. I was glad at the end of the day when the boys rushed out to play on the streets. I would sit in the silent room for a while to recover my composure before dragging myself to my tiny apartment. I would open the door and there stood the piano waiting for me. I would sit on the stool, caressing the keys as if they were the body of a young woman. Then a melody would spring in my mind from nowhere. Sometimes it was related to a poem I had read and was moved by, other times it was on its own. I would play it, go with it where it took me and forget the school, the children, the tired limbs. When I had done all that could be done with the melody, I would jot the whole thing down. Many of them stayed there, scribbles on pieces of paper, never to stir the imagination, never to play on the heartstrings, nor to move the spirits and become music.

The next few years were difficult for Herr van Beethoven. He suffered from poor health, lost all of his hearing and had problems with the family on his brother's death. There was a drawn-out legal case before he gained custody of his nephew. It is amazing that in spite of so many problems he did any work at all. He composed a wonderful piano sonata and an amazing mass and let it be known that he was drawing sketches for what would be the greatest symphony of all time. He attended soirees whenever he could and I had the good fortune of watching him from a distance. I was too shy to introduce myself to my hero.

I worked steadily all these years carefully preserving the compositions in my trunk just in case posterity finds one or two of them interesting. I set hundreds of songs to music, composed piano sonatas and lyrical quartets for my friends, sometimes reworking the melodies from the songs. Good old Sylvester. He heard me play the song I called the Trout and immediately commissioned me to write a piano quintet. I didn't even know what to charge him. It took a few weeks to compose and he was very pleased with it. Soon after, the Royal Opera House commissioned me to write a heroic opera. I worked on it for a year. However, the House ran into financial difficulties and it was never performed. Over the next few years I wrote 17 operas, none found any success.

Although the operas failed, it was at this time that my music received notice. My songs, for one or more singers, were in demand, as were my piano works for two, or four, hands. I was even being hailed as the Prince of Song in some circles. At this time, a bizarre thought began taking shape in my head. Vienna will need a musician to look up to if something were to happen to Herr van Beethoven. Why can't he be Franz Schubert? I knew the answer. Great composers write great symphonies, concertos, operas. You are not recognized as great by writing lieder and music for drawing rooms, no matter how artistic it is. To graduate from the Prince of Song to the King of Music I must write successful operas, symphonies, and of course serious artistic chamber music for the violinist Ignaz Schuppanzigh to perform in his concerts, not simple pleasant sounding pieces for amateurs to play in informal gatherings.

These thoughts inspired me to write two symphonic works. They were longer than half an hour each and much better developed than six such pieces I had composed in my teens for the conservatory orchestra. I needed some worthy opinion and after wavering for several weeks I gathered the two symphonies and some piano music and walked over to the home of the greatest symphonist of them all. Unfortunately, Herr van Beethoven was out for a walk and the maid could not say when he would return. I left the symphonies and the piano music with a note signed "Your humble admirer, Franz Schubert" and rushed out breathing only when I had stepped on the street.

3

It must have been January 1823 when I read the poem "The Beautiful Daughter of the Miller" by Wilhelm Muller. I felt the tragedy of the rejected lover of the maid. After all, rejection by the other sex has been my fate too. The poem buzzed in my head day and night. I dreamt of the daughter, of the stream, of the lover. I saw my lifeless body floating in the cold stream and, strangely, felt good about it. I was so occupied by the poem that I couldn't play the piano, did not even eat on many evenings. I walked aimlessly along the Danube, in the Prater, on the streets often colliding with people I did not see. Fortunately, the spell was broken one evening when I was resting on a bench under a linden tree. The gentle perfumed breeze had a calming effect and I must have dozed off. When I woke up, a smile was probably playing on my face. My head was not buzzing with the words; instead it was playing the music to go with them. I sat there till the whole poem was played out in my mind. Then I rushed home and put the music down on paper. I did not need to play it; the perfect match of the music and the words was as clear as the water in a mountain stream. As soon as the last note hit the paper, I felt hungry for the first time in weeks. I picked up a large sausage and sauerkraut from a stall, ate them with relish and had the most refreshing sleep in a long while.

In the spring of the following year Vienna was in a state of great excitement. Herr van Beethoven was preparing for the performance of his latest symphony and had booked the Karntnertor Theatre. It was a huge work, needing a large orchestra and a larger choir with four solo singers. People had a hard time believing it. What was the great man doing, booking the opera house for a concert? Was he putting on an opera or a concert? What is more, he was planning to conduct the vast forces on the stage himself, although he was known to be deaf and had not appeared on the stage for twelve years. Word had leaked out that Schiller's great poem was set to even greater music with all these people on stage ready to bring down the heavens or maybe raise us all to heaven. There were no tickets to be had for love or money. I managed to get one only due to the kindness of Schuppanzigh who was organizing the concert for Herr van Beethoven.

The date of the performance was approaching fast and the rumours of all sorts swirled round the city. It was being said that there were problems in putting together the choirs and orchestra in the numbers demanded by Herr van Beethoven. The whole city breathed a sigh of relief when the performers were engaged even though there was time for only two rehearsals. What Schuppanzigh told me later really shocked me. It became clear to him during the first rehearsal that the deaf maestro could not really hold the orchestra and choir together. With great difficulty he persuaded Herr van Beethoven to let the kapellmeister of the Karntnertor theatre Michael Umlauf share the stage. He then instructed the performers to follow the Kapellmeister during the performance and to ignore Herr van Beethoven altogether.

On May 7 the Karntnerstrasse and the other streets in the area were packed with the carriages of the nobility. Ladies, resplendent in silk gowns and diamond necklaces, had to alight some distance from the hall and walk to the theatre on the arms of their escorts. Every seat was occupied several minutes before the concert was due to start. A loud cheer broke out when it was announced that the performance would start with the Consecration of the House Overture to be followed by the first three parts of another new work, Missa Solemnis, to be followed by a new form of symphony. I noticed the kapellmeister with the music on the lectern in front of him. He was standing among the violins partly hidden from the audience. Suddenly the orchestra stopped practising and an expectant hush settled over the hall. Herr van Beethoven walked to the stage as serious as ever and faced the players. He mumbled something to them and raised his arm.

Many in the audience were familiar with the overture and there was only a mild interest in the performance and a little more than polite applause. The Missa Solemnis received a much better reception and the audience now was impatient for the symphony. Thunderous cheers greeted Vienna's greatest composer when he returned to the stage to conduct it. He could not have heard them, perhaps he felt the vibrations and bowed stiffly a few times. Then he turned to face the orchestra and my heart jumped with the first barely audible notes from the violins and horns. Then the orchestra exploded into a burst of activity. It was as if the creator, after a long period of meditation, had come alive and started the work of creating the universe. For the first three movements the music continued in this vein. Although it seemed repetitious at times, it was always pleasant to the ear and perhaps challenging to the serious listeners. Then the fourth movement began with the recapitulation of first three and the bass telling the audience to forget what has gone on before, the music had to tell us something new. Indeed it did. The drudgery of creation was over; it was time to celebrate the greatness of the human spirit, now and for the eternity to come. The audience jumped up as the last note sounded and the ovation was deafening. The composer who had become a legend stood still facing the performers till the soprano turned him around to face the cheering mass.

The premiere was followed by another performance a few days later. Most of the nobility had left for their summer palaces and the hall was no more than half full. Still, Schuppanzigh told me that it was a great performance and pleased Herr van Beethoven.

4

Vienna gradually returned to normal. I never received a note from Herr van Beethoven regarding the music I had left with the maid. It did not surprise me considering how busy he must have been. One evening I ran into Schuppanzigh on my way to the tavern. He looked unusually cheerful. He shook my hand heartily and asked, "Haven't seen you for a while. What are you working on these days? It is time you moved up to some large scale work."

"The performance inspired me and I agree with you. I have some ideas about a new symphony. I had left two full symphonies and some chamber music with Herr van Beethoven and was hoping his comments would give me some direction," I replied.

"I don't think you should wait for him. He is very busy with some quartets he has been commissioned to write. Dear Franz, if you want to be worshipped in Vienna there are only two ways for a composer of your genius to go. Either create operas like Rossini or orchestral works like Beethoven. You know from your own experience how hard it is to get an impresario to accept a German opera, it doesn't matter how good it is. That leaves great orchestral works; symphonies, concertos, maybe a mass or two. If you put your mind to it, you can do these better than anyone else anywhere, let alone Vienna. I will make you a promise. If you get busy and put enough music together I will arrange a benefit concert of your music. It would acquaint the Viennese with your genius as well as bring in some cash. Think about it. You know how to get hold of me." With that, the celebrated violinist waved goodbye, crossed the street and walked towards the rehearsal room in Karntnertor.

I decided to work on a symphony. To prepare for it I cleared my mind of the clutter of all the ideas for other works. Over the next eighteen months I composed a song cycle from the poems of Muller, an octet, a string quartet, arpeggione sonata and a piano sonata among other works. The symphony was not forgotten though. In the autumn two years after Beethoven's Choral Ninth, ideas gelled for a four movement classical symphony. Counting the ones I wrote at Imperial Seminary and the two I had left with Herr van Beethoven it would be my ninth. It would be melodic, it would have movement, it would be thrilling. What is more, people would hum and whistle the tunes. Over the next six months I wrote the whole work including the orchestration. For a diversion, I wrote a quartet based on the theme from the setting for a song "Death and the Maiden" I had worked on a while back. I liked the symphony. It was in C major. It was melodious; it had excitement and joy oozed out of every note. I made a copy and sent it to the Society of the Friends of Music.

The spring arrived early in Vienna in 1827. Or that is how it seemed to me because the performances of my songs and piano pieces were being received well by the Viennese. Then the bombshell dropped. I heard someone say that Herr van Beethoven was very ill. I made haste to his lodging. There was a crowd of well-wishers in the courtyard and I joined them. I did not think that the last moments of this great man should be wasted on someone like me and did not make any effort to

see him to pay personal homage. It was quite late when the word came
that his condition was stabilizing. The crowd thinned out and I sat
down on a bench with my head in my hands, "What will happen to
music now that the greatest of them all is on his deathbed?" "I should
be able to make a worthwhile contribution, what form should it take
after the greatest of them all?" My thoughts were confused. Then I felt
an arm around my shoulders. It was Anton Schindler. He had a folder
in his hands. I recognized it straight away. It was the one I had left
with the maid for the master. He had tears in his eyes, "For last year
or two Beethoven has been asking, 'What will happen to music after
me, where is the successor?' I called on him one morning last week. He
was shuffling through pages of music looking perplexed. He did not
notice me and continued his study. Then he went to his special piano
and played some notes. He turned around, saw me and a sigh escaped
his lips, 'Schindler, at last a successor.' He instructed me to make sure
that the music was returned to you when he had finished with it. I
don't believe he will look at any music again."

Tears flowed freely from our eyes. When we had collected ourselves I took the folder. It seemed much thinner than I remembered
it to have been. I did not worry about the missing sheets. "At last a
successor," the words of the master were spinning round my head with
a ferocity that made the loss of music irrelevant.

The next day, March 26, 1827, Ludwig van Beethoven, who had
defied authority as a citizen and the convention as a musician, passed
away with raised fist as a gesture of defiance. In spite of the thunder
and lightening, the crowds gathered in the courtyard and on the streets
to pay last respects to their hero. However, there was bright sunshine
when the huge procession followed him to the cemetery three days
later. Perhaps thanks to Schindler, I had the honour of being one of
the pall bearers.

5

Vienna recovered from the loss and the wheel of life resumed its normal pace. I set about composing driven by the urge to live up to the master's words. I was thrilled to hear that the society had accepted my symphony for performance. "My day has arrived at last," I thought. Prematurely, as it turned out. The orchestra rehearsed it and decided that the work was too difficult for them to play. They sent it back to me with regrets suggesting that if I made it easier to perform they would consider it again. I was shocked. My headaches, which had resumed a week earlier, became worse. The whole of my body ached and I felt feverish. I could not eat. I felt weak and my clothes hung loose. There was some good news though. Schuppanzigh sent a note saying that he had booked Theater an der Wien for March 26 for my benefit concert and was gathering the performers. The irony of the date, the first anniversary of the death of the great man hit me straight away. I did not feel well enough to revise the symphony for that day; in any event it would be too expensive to perform without a patron.

The concert was a big success with the public as well as the critics, even without the symphony. This encouraged me. I had a busy summer. I completed the revision of the symphony, set to music two groups of songs, most of them poems of Heine and Muller, and sketched another symphony. The autumn was beautiful. I joined some friends on a walking holiday to Eisenstaedt. However, after we had visited the grave of another master, that unique genius Haydn, the headaches of a couple of years ago returned with great ferocity and I had to cut the visit short. Back in Vienna I developed a fever and lay in bed muttering to my dear brother, "Ferdinand, you are so kind to me. I do hope that the fever will go away as it did last time. If it does not and my life were to end, I would be so sorry I did not live up to my hero's expectations. I am not worried about what will happen to music after my death. After all is said and done, music is greater than an individual, howsoever talented. It is a reflection of human spirit.

Like all true Art, it will prosper as long as the human spirit is alive. Oh Ferdinand! The pain is too much to bear. Oh my head! It is exploding." I closed my eyes tighter. The pain did not go away. Then my whole life passed before my eyes.

2. A MUSICAL TRIANGLE

I

We were not quite like two peas in a pod. Perhaps we were in some ways. Both were born in the same year, both came to Vienna to study music at the Conservatory from distant little towns at the same time, both were uncomfortable in the strange culture of the big city. We were barely sixteen and poorer than church mice. We shared a cold room with no hot water. The kitchen and washing facilities were shared with twenty other residents in the building. If we had one full meal every day we considered ourselves rich. The difference was in our temperaments. Hugo was fiery, challenged every one including the professors, was full of outlandish plans, wanted to be another Wagner when he grew up. He studied composition, nothing but composition, and stinted on food to buy the music sheets. His teachers told him that a good grounding in piano is essential to be a good composer. He thought he knew better. He would rather spend his time in the library studying the score of Lohengrin.

Although not a pushover, those who earned it had my respect. I paid attention to the suggestions from my professors and acted on the useful ones. I studied piano along with the composition. I was told from early childhood that I could be another Liszt if I worked hard. Liszt was my idol. "One day the world will come to hear me play Schumann and Chopin and orchestras will play my innovative compositions," I said to myself several times every day. Somehow it made my hunger go away.

One morning, I don't remember the day though I do remember that it was cold and wet. I was dreaming of a room full of entranced young women in beautiful gowns surrounding a pianist with dark curly shoulder length hair in a smart evening coat and polished shoes with soles without holes. The pleasant dream was cut short by the shouts of "Gustav, wake up, wake up. We are going to be late."

I reluctantly opened my eyes and saw Hugo bending over me ready to grab my shoulders. "What is the matter? What are we going to be late for?" I asked.

"Late for the rehearsal, don't you remember?"

"What rehearsal?"

"Rehearsal of Lohengrin, you idiot. I told you last week Herr Wagner was in town to rehearse the orchestra for the opera. We want to go to the Imperial Hotel to see him and hopefully catch his eye. Why don't you pay attention when I am telling you about the earth shattering events?"

"Sorry, I forgot all about it. Give me five minutes and I will race you to the hotel."

We ran to the hotel and saw an elegant coach with two beautiful Holsteiners, a coachman and a footman on the door. The coachman told us with pride that he was there for Herr Wagner. We sneaked through the door and stood in the corner to wait for our hero to come down and bless us with his glance. Every few minutes we checked the coach to make sure Herr Wagner hadn't left through some other exit. As the clock in the lobby chimed ten we saw a servant come down the majestic steps with a folder and behind him a short, thin man with clipped, dark hair dressed elegantly in a silk shirt and a smart morning dress coat. Two servants followed, one with a baton and another with a silk robe. Hugo came forward, opened the front door, bowed deeply and uttered the inane words, "My deep respects, master." There was no sign that the great man noticed him. The footman held the door open as he entered the coach. The coachman raised his whip and the horses set off at a gallop.

"Come on, come on, what are you staring at?" shouted Hugo and we sprinted at full speed across the park. We reached the Opera House just as the heads of Holsteiners appeared around the corner. Hugo rushed to the door as the coach stopped. He managed to open it after a struggle. Herr Wagner stepped down, looked at the boys, one holding the door and the other standing behind him with his head bowed in respect, smiled and walked away without a word. Hugo banged the door shut and screamed with delight, "I did it. I caught his attention. Hooray. Come on Gustav, let us celebrate."

The best celebration for us was to go to the conservatory and work on our assignments; for him to compose music for some songs and for me to practise Brahm's Sonata No. 3 in F Minor. On our way to the conservatory he hatched an elaborate plan to meet the master in his suite at the hotel. "Leave everything to me. Just get your best music ready to show him," he said when we parted to go to our respective class rooms.

A couple of days later we set off for the Imperial Hotel after our lunch of Wurstel sausage and beef broth. We were dressed in our best clothes, our frayed coats covering holes in our shirts and fresh newspaper as the insole for our shoes. We put our scores in our inside pockets to protect them from the drizzle. A young maid met us at the entrance of the hotel and led us up the stairs. "Herr Wagner is not back yet. Wait at the landing till he returns. I will escort you to him," she commanded as she left to attend to her duties.

We did not need to wait long. The retinue of the master ascended the steps and passed us paying scant attention to our bowed heads. The maid appeared at the tail of the group, rushed past us, bowed deep to the Master and said, "Sir, two young conservatory students are here to pay their respects and to show you their music, if you would be kind enough to oblige."

The master turned around to look at us. A faint whiff of recognition crossed his face, "I am sorry, I am too busy to look at the scores. Maybe the next time we are in Vienna you could play for us your grown up compositions. Work hard in the meantime and learn as much as you can from the learned professors at the Conservatory." With that he resumed his progress to his chamber.

Alas! Herr Wagner was never to bless Vienna with a visit again.

2

Six months went by. Hugo did not take Herr Wagner's advice seriously. He would rather compose than attend classes. He believed that composition was an innate talent, it could not be learnt. I split my time in practising piano pieces under Prof. Epstein's guidance and studying composition. I worked hard to please the professor. Thanks to him I had one or two piano students every day to cover my half of the conservatory fees while the kindly professor paid the other half. Hugo did not have my good fortune and he was always struggling to pay his share of the rent even though we took in Rudolf, another student, to share our cramped room.

Hugo had two distinct personalities. He was boisterous and full of great ideas when he had eaten a good meal, unfortunately not a common occurrence. On other days he was grumpy, ready to scream at anyone around him. We soon learnt to keep out of his sight on these days. We respected him for his talent and knew that one day he would be revered as a great composer while we would most likely be forgotten.

One afternoon we were sitting around the table sharing the food packet my parents had sent me. We could each have three Wurstels and plenty of sauerkraut. Hugo was soon laughing and telling us about some songs he had just set to music that a publisher had promised to publish. Then he dropped a bombshell, "I am going to start work on an opera."

Rudolf asked the question we both had, "Great, what is the opera about?"

"You know the story of the gnome Rubezahl, don't you? I think it will make a great opera. I am hoping to start the work on the libretto in a day or two."

Rudolf's curiosity was not satisfied, "Tell me the brief synopsis. I don't know the story."

Hugo hesitated because his mouth was full. I took the opportunity to add my two-bit worth, "Rubezahl is the king of the underworld. He falls in love with a princess, kidnaps her and assumes the form of a prince. Happy at first, the princess soon gets bored and manages to escape and reunites with her old prince charming. The disappointed Rubezahl reverts to being a gnome and returns to his underworld kingdom."

"I agree that it could make a great opera. How long will it take you to finish?" Rudolf asked Hugo.

"Three to six month for the libretto, about the same for the music. It should be done by Christmas. Herr Wagner, you have competition."

"It would take Herr Wagner six years. He has so many things to distract him," Rudolf replied, thinking it was an encouragement.

Hugo did not think so. He stood up, grabbed Rudolf's shoulders in his two hands and screamed, "No one says rude words about the master in my presence. No one, do you hear?"

He shook Rudolf violently once, then let go. He picked up his tattered coat and ran out.

3

My dear mama used to tell us fairy tales when she wasn't busy cleaning, washing, cooking and all the things she had to do. Rubezahl was her favourite story because the princess escaped her prison which my mother never could and I liked it because the fate of the gnome seemed to me what I would have to suffer as an adult. However, an opera based on the tale had never occurred to me. After Hugo's tantrum I said to Rudolf, "I don't know about a full-blown opera, a one-act comic opera for the conservatory students could work."

Rudolf looked at me strangely, "You are not going to steal Hugo's idea, are you?"

"I won't compose the opera. I don't think I have the ability to do it. All I will do is make some sketches to help Hugo."

"Don't do even that if you value his friendship. He will be most upset and with good reason. Leave Rubezahl to him. There are enough fairy tales for you to compose. Read some of Brothers Grimm."

"My head is buzzing with ideas. I will put them down on paper and that is where they will stay. Hugo will never get wind of it. Your Grimm idea is really interesting. I will follow that too."

I prepared a libretto over the next two days and set it to music over the next two weeks. I showed it to Rudolf. He looked at it and remarked, "It is amazing. And Hugo doesn't have a word on paper. Let me review it over the next few days."

"Take your time," I replied and added, "This is not going anywhere. Hugo has the first right on the story. Just make sure he doesn't get to peep at it. I am going home in the morning for a few days, haven't seen the family for a while."

When I returned a week later the landlady greeted me with the news that my fiery friend had left without giving her the notice. The thought of Hugo seeing my draft crossed my mind and made me uncomfortable. When Rudolf returned his face was drawn. He burst out, "I told you to leave Rubezahl alone. Now Hugo has broken off with me too."

"How did he come to see it?"

"He was looking for some papers he had misplaced. He saw the script on my bed and exploded. He thinks I am in league with you. He kept saying 'it is over, it is over,' as he collected his possessions. I am missing him already."

"I will miss him too. He is a genius and he will write songs that will be performed for eternity. I will go and see him and explain my motivation. It may pacify him."

"How will you find him? He is no more at the conservatory. He had no clue where he was going when he left, not a pfennig in his pocket. No entreaties and explanations helped. He took it as a grave insult. He will run away if you happen to come across him."

Rudolf was right. I did not see Hugo again for twenty years. I did see some of his compositions. I did not get the impression from them that he had lived up to his promise in our student days.

4

After I won the first prize in a piano competition at the conservatory Prof. Epstein, my mentor, thought I had a bright future as a pianist. On the other hand, I wanted to compose symphonies on a scale not yet imagined with orchestra of a hundred or more musicians, a huge choir and several soloists, although all I had to show so far were a quartet and a quintet. To help me decide the direction I should follow I showed Herr Professor my piano quintet and asked whether I had any future in composition. He arranged a performance of the quintet by his students with me at the piano. After the concert, he said to me in presence of many people in the audience, "The quintet is the work of a young and promising talent. But Gustav, piano is where you belong. Practice, practice more and then some more. You have the skill, the ear and the musicality. You have it in you to become another Liszt."

I had a lucky break; the greatest pianist of all times visited Vienna a few months later for a recital. I obtained one of the free tickets available to the conservatory students. The recital consisted of three Liebestraume - Dreams of Love - the maestro had composed some twenty years earlier. I sat there mesmerized from the first lively note of the first dream to the last dying note of the third. I walked to my room in a trance. Rudolf looked at me and asked in an anxious tone, "Gustav, what happened? Are you all right?"

"Yes, I am fine physically though not in spirit. In one sense I am elated and in the other I am depressed. I was at the recital of Herr Franz Liszt. It was uplifting because I never imagined a piano could produce such glorious sound. It was depressing because there will never be another person who can play those divine notes. I will be lucky to create music one tenth – nay, one-hundredth – as sublime as what I heard this evening. Now I know. I will always be dissatisfied with my playing if I take piano as a career. I can't bear the thought of disappointing Herr Epstein but I must. Instead I will devote myself to composition. I hope he will forgive me some day."

"I am confused by your reaction. Maybe you can't be as great as Herr Liszt, you could still be great. What makes you think you will be as good as Beethoven as a composer?"

"I will not compare my work to Beethoven or Wagner or Mozart. I will compose for the modern orchestra with the sensibility of our time. My music will grow from the traditions of great works of the past and I will attempt to reach the pinnacle of music for my time. That is the difference in composition and performance. I will be found wanting when playing Liebestraume because I was not as good as Herr Liszt. No one will compare my symphonies to Beethoven's. They will stand and fall on their own merit."

"I am even more confused. That doesn't matter though. I am convinced that you will be great at whatever you decide to do, in music or in any art form you choose. So it is just as well you have decided on what you will do. Now take some courses and get to work on some fairy tale to enter the Beethoven prize."

I enrolled for courses in harmony and counterpoint and read the tales of Brothers Grimm. One made a deep impression on me. It was the story of two brothers, one noble and the other wicked. The queen announces that she will marry the person who brings her a rare red flower from the forest. The brothers go to look for the flower, the good brother finds it, puts it on his cap and goes to sleep. The wicked brother kills him and takes the flower to the queen. A wandering minstrel finds the bones of the dead brother and makes a flute. When he blows on it the story of the two brothers is played out. The minstrel rushes to the queen and meets the brother who grabs the flute and plays it. The flute tells the sordid tale, the queen faints and the party ends in disaster as the castle collapses.

I worked feverishly and wrote the three parts of the cantata in six months and composed the music in a year in the time I could spare from teaching piano to the children of the rich, and attending the conservatory. The Beethoven prize at the conservatory mentioned by Rudolf carried a cash award of 600 gulden and the public performance of the work. If I won the prize, the performance would make me known and the cash would permit me to compose works which would be welcomed by orchestras. When I showed the piece to Rudolf he was not very encouraging, "Do you know who is on the judging committee?"

"No. Does it matter?"

"How naive are you? Of course it matters. Richter is on the committee. And Brahms. And Hellmesberger. All stuck in the mud. They want something Mozartian or Beethovenian, something old-time Viennese. Your work is Wagnerian. Richter may support it, not others? They will look at it, sure. Award it the prize? Over their dead bodies."

I believed in my work and Rudolf's words did not discourage me. Full of hope I submitted 'Das Klagende Lied' for the consideration of the august body. However, Rudolf proved to be right. Instead of bringing joy, 'The Song of Lament' broke my heart. With the sadness of crushed hopes I went to cry on the shoulder of Prof. Epstein. He was sympathetic, "It is a good piece. It is melodious, it has drama, it shows maturity beyond your years. Of course it can be improved and you will do it in your mature years. I am confident that one day it will be performed by the major orchestras all over Europe."

The venerable Professor paused for breath and continued, "It did not win because its language is too modern for our judges. I understand two of them were on your side. When Brahms called the cantata immature they changed their mind. It is the old Brahms-Wagner rivalry. You can't expect him to appreciate even remotely the Wagnerian music."

"I was hoping that this prize would set me up as a budding composer. Now that is dashed. What do you suggest I do, other than playing piano in a flophouse?"

"Don't put down the pianist in a flophouse. That is how Brahms started in Hamburg. You don't need to do that. You can conduct. There are opera houses all over the country looking for conductors. Start in a small town, learn the ropes and establish a reputation. Time goes fast when you are busy. One day you will be conducting the Imperial Opera."

5

Time did go fast. I started with a small orchestra where I had to be a carpenter, stage hand, singer when the cast members did not show up, and of course prepare and conduct the amateurs in the orchestra. However, my mentor's prediction materialized in a very short period and before ten years had gone by I was conducting the Royal Opera in Budapest. Looking back it feels strange. Directing Wagner operas sung in Hungarian, the language I was not familiar with, was hard and fun too. I had a substantial budget and independence to decide the program. In my third year I presented a new production of Don Giovanni. It was to be the main attraction of the season. I engaged the best singers available and trained them to sing the way Mozart wanted it sung. The problems in the dress rehearsal were small and easily corrected and the whole cast was in high spirits for the opening.

Count Geza von Zichy, the intendant of the Royal Opera, sent me a note on the morning of the performance, "Just to let you know that

2.   A Musical Triangle

Brahms is in Budapest on personal business. He loves Don Giovanni. I am told that he has been disappointed by so many performances that he now studies the score when he wishes to enjoy it. I have invited him to the opening night performance anyway although it is not likely that the great man will accept." So imagine my surprise when a rotund bearded figure entered my dressing room after the first act. "Splendid! Remarkable! Just the way it should be done," I heard the booming voice of the man who had deprived me of my composing career. We shook hands and had a very friendly conversation. I soon realized that he did not remember his role in the misdirection of my destiny. In any event, the glow of the praise from the greatest living composer of the day, renowned for being hard to please, erased the old grudge from my memory too. Count Zichy told me later that his guest was very excited and kept repeating, "That was the best Don Giovanni I ever attended. Not even the Imperial Opera in Vienna can rival it." To say that I was flattered would be a slight understatement.

For the next few years I spent my summers in Steinbach on the Attersee. I was conducting at the Hamburg Municipal opera in those years. After eight months of rehearsing the orchestra and the singers during the day and conducting almost every night, the summer on the beautiful lake in the mountains was most welcome. I woke up early, spent the morning composing in a hut away from the bustle of the house and went on long walks in the mountains for the day. I had been working on a major symphony for several summers. It was unusual – it had five movements, the short fourth movement consisted of a poem and it had a massive chorus in the last movement like Beethoven's great Ninth, Its musical language was novel, so novel that when I played the first movement to a famous musician he exploded, "It makes Tristan and Isolde sound like Haydn." I was so disheartened by this reaction that I put it aside for more than a year. However, once I started again, it was completed in two summers. This summer I was putting the final touches on it. I hoped that its performance would erase the memory of the disastrous premiere of the tone poem.

Herr Brahms spent his summers a few miles away from my cottage. On occasions I took a detour to visit him. The grand old man of music was showing his age and was growing feebler every summer though his mind was as sharp as ever. He treated me with kindness on these visits and we had lively discussions on the music and the musicians. One afternoon I took the score of my symphony to him. He shuffled through the pages for a few minutes. After seeing the whole work, rather cursorily I felt, he asked me to play the third movement. He listened intently and when I finished he stood up, patted me on the back, shook my hand vigorously and said, "This scherzo is the work of a genius." What more could a young composer wish?

The words of an acknowledged genius buzzed in my head constantly. The buzz raised the question, "Is it time to give up the burden of conducting and focus on composing?" Other questions followed, "Will composing earn enough to support my siblings? Will the poverty endured by composers take away my sanity like it did for Hans Rott? Does conducting help composing rather than hinder it?" The answers floated in the air in different hues. I did not open the score for several days. My sister Justi, who looked after the household, was worried, "Are you feeling all right? What is worrying you? Is something wrong with the symphony?" Her concern annoyed me and I screamed, "Leave me alone. It has nothing to do with you. It will soon be over."

It was indeed soon over. In a most unexpected way.

I received a note saying Herr Brahms was returning to Vienna and wanted to see me the same day. In response to my anxious enquiry, the messenger told me "The master was all right, as well as you can expect a man his age to be." I was relieved and walked over to his cottage after lunch. It was a beautiful day. The blue of the languid lake reminded me of the eyes of my last Isolde after we had made love. Not a cloud in the sky except a patch of silver where sky met the water. A cool breeze took away the heat of the brisk walk. I was as close to heaven as one would wish to be without being in it. And I was too young to wish to be in heaven.

Last of the three Bs was sitting in the balcony overlooking the lake with a note pad in his hands. He stood up when he heard my steps and extended his hand. The size of his hand and fingers reminded me of his career as a pianist so admired by his mentor Robert Schumann. "I have been thinking of you and I need to talk to you about an idea that cropped up in this old head. My mind is so taken by it that I haven't made any progress with the songs I promised my publisher," he said without asking how I was, as an old gentleman is apt to do.

"I am sorry, sir, to have taken up so much of your attention."

"You have been away from Vienna for a while. If you keep in touch you would have heard that Jahn is losing his sight and can't really handle the responsibilities of the director of the Imperial Opera. It is no wonder that the quality of the performances has deteriorated to an unacceptable level. I am thinking of suggesting to Prince Montenuovo that Jahn be eased out. I think of your Don Giovanni in Budapest and wonder why you should not be the man to take over."

My heart stopped beating, thankfully just for a moment. "Sir, it has been my ambition since my student days at the conservatory. Perhaps it is a pipe dream of a Jewish boy. In any event I maybe too young for old hands like Richter."

"We will play it gingerly. I will have a word with Hanslick and get him to write some favourable articles. I will ask the Prince to do research on you. Let us get the ball rolling and see where it stops."

"I also have some connections. In due course I will prompt them to push my case. Vienna will answer the other question I have been asking myself."

"What question is that? Do you have other options open to you?"

"Ever since your favourable comment on my symphony I have been wondering whether I should give up opera and become a full time composer."

"Take the advice of this old man. One can't make a living from composing alone these days, never could. Most promising composers are starving unless they have conservatory positions. If you are tired of Hamburg, let us wait and see how Vienna unfolds."

It is amazing. One buzz disappeared and another started, "Imperial Opera; get ready for Gustav Mahler."

6

As I feared, it was hard work changing the tradition of sloth in Vienna. Many established stars had to go and the younger generation took over. The quality of performances improved steadily, we could do Wagner operas without cuts. The salaries of orchestra members were raised and they agreed to stay for the whole performance and not send substitutes when better opportunities turned up. Audiences became more disciplined and attendance improved. My mornings were spent in administration, afternoons in rehearsals and evenings in performance. It was hectic but the results were there for all to see. I often think that old Brahms would have been pleased with the improvements had he not passed away soon after I took over the directorship.

One morning I was reviewing Der Barenhauter – The Sluggard, an opera by Richard Wagner's son Siegfried. His mother was pushing it as the greatest comedy since Die Meistersinger by Richard and I was attracted by its association with a Grimm's tale. Then, without a knock, the door flew open and a man in dirty threadbare clothes and unkempt hair barged in. He had a folder in his hands which he dropped on my desk on top of the score I had been looking at. He pushed his hand with chewed dirty nails towards me, "It has been twenty long years and you don't recognize me. I am Hugo Wolf. Congratulations on your appointment. From what they tell me you are doing a grand job."

I took his hand in mine and shook it heartily. It was good to see a childhood friend even though he seemed to be in straitened circumstances. "It is so delightful to see you. Sit down and tell me what you have been up to."

"I have been composing songs, some orchestral pieces, a symphony or two. They are played all over Germany. I am surprised you have not heard them. My songs are particularly popular and provide me a good living. Not in Vienna though, it is a struggle to get anything accepted here. There is so much opposition to any thing evenly remotely Wagnerian, all the Brahmsians come down hard on it." He paused for a reply. When he did not receive any, I did not know what to say, he continued, "What you have on your desk is my opera, 'Der Corregidor – The Magistrate.' I am sure you will love it and want to stage it. It was premiered in Mannheim last year in a mad rush for some reason. It needs a better production under your capable direction.. I will leave it with you and call in a week to set the date for the performance."

He stood up as he was finishing his sentence, turned around and walked out leaving me with my mouth open. After I recovered from the painful and, thankfully, short interview, I picked up Hugo's folder. As I turned over the sheets I remembered how Brahms had, knowingly, or unconsciously one would never know, recompensed for his earlier action. I wondered if this was my opportunity to do the same for Hugo for the injury I had caused him in his youth by my adolescent prank with Rubezahl. I put the folder in the bag to study it at home after I had recovered my equanimity. The comedy of Wagner junior helped me achieve that before the pangs of hunger led me home for lunch. It also encouraged me to find time to dust off my own version of a Grimms' tale and to prepare it for performance.

True to his word, Hugo was in my office a week later. "Did you look at it? When are you going to put it on stage?" he barked without any pleasantries.

"I have studied it as much as I could in the time you allowed me. I will, with your permission, suggest some minor modifications which will make it more presentable as well as more interesting to the audience."

"Forget the changes. It is a Wolf work and it will be presented as is. I will accept some minor cuts here and there, no alteration to music or words. We don't want to reenact Rubezahl, do we?"

That hurt. I swallowed it and replied, "Let me think about it. We could present it two ways on alternate nights: the untouched original on one, and with changes that I wish to make on the other. They would both be under your name, of course."

"There will only be one version, my version, that will go on stage. This is not a request you understand. This is an order."

"Pray whose order? Even Prince Montenuovo is not allowed to alter my decisions about the operas."

Hugo was now screaming, "Don't you know it? Haven't they told you? The Emperor has terminated you as of this morning and appointed me to direct his opera house. Move over, that is my chair now."

When I stood up to appease him he ran out screaming rather than move to my chair. I learnt of the unfortunate culmination of the incident when I went home for lunch. Justi was very perturbed when she opened the door, "Did you hear what happened?"

"No. Tell me."

"Around noon I heard some screams and then loud banging on the door of the apartment. When I opened it a wild man pushed me aside and rushed in saying, 'The Emperor has replaced Mahler by me, Hugo Wolf. This establishment belongs to me now'. While I tried to reason with him, a small crowd of neighbours gathered in the hall. A few minutes later two gendarmes came in. One bowed to Hugo saying, 'Sir, the Emperor has sent us to escort you to him for an audience. Please come with us.' Hugo left with them. I think they took him to some asylum."

I made enquiries and found his whereabouts. It did not seem wise to visit him and I anonymously helped to improve his circumstances as much as I could. I worked on Die Corregidor and presented two versions the way I had suggested to him. Neither was a success with the audience. Unfortunately, Hugo was too ill to know about the performances.

Hugo never recovered. He died in the asylum a few years later at the age of forty two. The news of his death upset me greatly. As a tribute to his genius, I burnt the manuscript of Rubezahl I had preserved all these years. It was no great loss, nothing compared to what Hugo would have done if his candle had been allowed to shine with brightness it deserved and not snuffed out so cruelly by people who should have known better.

3. THE MAESTRO

I

Perhaps I should have written the story soon after the events happened. I kept postponing it for one reason or the other. A long time has gone by since and many crucial details are now veiled by more mundane memories. It maybe a little too late to do justice to the actors at this late hour, but for some strange reason the urge to write it down has become irresistible. All I can do is to give in, be done with it and hope that the readers, if there are any, will not be disappointed.

Annabel, our only child, born when Arabel and I had given up all hopes of holding a newborn in our arms, is the apple of my eye. She is a pretty girl, slim and tall, hazel eyes, auburn shoulder-length hair, smooth skin. Just like her mother was the first time I saw her. Growing up she was good in school and helpful at home. Two evenings a week she sang in a children's choir of some renown nationally. As one would expect, the director made high demands on her charges to raise the choir to the standard she aspired to. One of her many rules required each chorister to learn a musical instrument of his/her choice and to practise singing as well as playing the instrument, for an hour each on every school day and for two hours on holidays. Many kids chose to play piano as did Annabel. Their reason was efficiency; they could play the piano as the accompaniment for singing, thus saving an hour for school homework and for the chores handed out by their parents. We commended Annabel's choice for our own selfish reason; we already had a piano we had bought as the décor for the front room and did not particularly want to spend hundreds of dollars on an instrument.

Gordon, Arabel's cousin and a music teacher, was visiting for dinner one evening. He asked Annabel what she wanted to do when she grew up. "I want to be an opera singer," Annabel replied without hesitation.

Rather than use much despised clichés like the understatement of our lifetime or being thunderstruck, I will simply state that Arabel and I were surprised, having never before heard any career wish remotely like singing from our angel without wings who played the piano for an accompaniment instead of the harp. Music, particularly singing in a foreign language for hours and hours, had never appealed to us and neither of us had ever been anywhere near an opera; not on stage, not on TV. I was certain that we would spend our time snoring if we ever went to one. As far as I knew, Annabel had never been in an opera hall either. Gordon looked at us, sensed our reaction and followed up on his query anyway, "That is a difficult career to go into. Have you discussed it with your mom and dad?"

"I haven't yet. I know they love me and they will support me in whatever I wish to do", Annabel replied.

Arabel, who had regained a little of her composure by now, perceived her responsibility and spoke for both of us. "We don't know much about opera, or opera singers. If that is what Annabel really wants, we will help her in every way we can", she said.

Arabel began by enrolling Annabel for the private singing lessons at the conservatory and buying three tickets for each of the six operas in the next season. The next step was to befriend the movers and shakers of the opera world, nationally, not only locally. We began this process by joining the Opera Fans club. The fans contributed thousands of dollars every year to the 'sustenance fund' of the opera association and took turns hosting meetings on the first Tuesday of every month. On these evenings, about twenty somewhat older men and women discussed over wine and cheese the operas and stars in the news, listened to selections from the discs picked by the hosts and occasionally met the performers rehearsing the opera to be performed that month. After attending a few of these meetings, it was our turn to host one. This was when we realized we needed a working sound system to keep up to the standards the other fans had set and a number of opera discs to choose the appropriate music from. However, as Arabel pointed out to her rather busy and tight-fisted husband, a few days spent on research in what discs to buy and a couple of thousand dollars for the disc player and speakers was a small price to pay to promote the prospects of our only child's picture being splashed on the billboards in New York, London and Vienna.

It so happened that the month we were due to host coincided with the performance of The Swimming Dane by the great composer of the nineteenth century Johann Schmidt. The opera was to be conducted by the renowned maestro from Munich, Wolfram Telemann who had, in his glory days, mesmerized audiences in the opera houses all over the world. The maestro was persuaded by the president of the club to grace our meeting and say a few words about the opera, its composer and, of course, the art of conducting.

The diminutive, slightly stooped and soft-spoken maestro was a big hit. He mingled with the guests and basked in the undiluted adoration of the music lovers while sipping champagne and nibbling at English crackers loaded with Brie under a fine film of mint jelly. After an hour of social exchanges, the maestro took the stage – the central point of our living room - with thirty spellbound fans around him. The few words spoken in a quaint dialect, a mix of German, French and English, lasted thirty three minutes. After a standing ovation - there was no place to sit for most guests - Arabel persuaded Annabel to sing for the guests. To every one's amazement, the maestro made his way to the piano bench, adjusted its position and asked Annabel what was she going to sing.

"Dawna's aria from The Slave Dancers by Shumacher. We don't have the accompaniment music though," Annabel replied.

"Ah, don't worry girl. Telemann carries the music here," said the maestro tapping his right temple. Annabel assumed the persona of a singer on stage as the maestro played the notes composer had intended to represent the rising sun.

The song was followed by another, and then by popular demand yet another. The maestro praised Annabel for her talent and every one was delighted, no one more than the father who couldn't distinguish A Major from C Minor. The guests started taking their leave soon after without having had the opportunity to admire our brand new sound system. In a fit of extreme generosity, Arabel suggested that I drive the maestro to his hotel while she and the other star of the evening handle what would be a massive job of clean up if left to me. I apologized when the celebrated guest looked distastefully at the sorry state of the messy car and dusted the passenger seat with a portable vacuum while the maestro kissed Arabel and Annabel on both their cheeks with some passion.

On the way to the hotel I thanked the maestro for spending the evening with us. He turned around to look at me and said in a some-what despondent tone, "I am the one who should be thankful. Our lives look glamorous to the audiences but the glamour is superficial. We have standing ovations, bow deep to the cheering masses and then return to our cold dressing rooms. Once we are out of the hall no one gives a hoot who we are. All our days and evenings are spent by ourselves in preparation for the performance, away from our loved ones in functional hotel rooms without the comforts we are used to at home. It is a solitary life and the opportunity to be with real people is such a joy."

The heartfelt response encouraged me to ask whether he had a free evening for dinner with us. He took my card and promised to let me know after checking his calendar. True to his word, he called the next afternoon, suggesting the following evening. I agreed even though I knew Arabel would have to cancel an appointment with her physio-therapist. We dressed with great care, I in my blue suit and a red tie with yellow dots and Arabel in a white blouse, long black skirt, pearl necklace and sapphire earrings. We met the maestro in the lobby of the hotel and made our way to the Trader's, a five diamonds restaurant across the street. It was early and there were only two other tables occupied, each with a couple of elderly gentlemen discussing business affairs in hushed tones. We were guided to a table next to an ornate log-burning fire place which added to the warmth and elegance of the dining room. I pulled a chair for the maestro who did not notice it. He seemed to be in great pain and had his hands pressed on his ears.

"Piano, piano", he said to the maitre d' in a distressed tone.

"I will see what I can do, sir", the maitre d' replied and went to the back of the dining room while we made ourselves comfortable, the maestro still clutching his ears. The maitre d' was back in a minute, "Sir, we don't have any piano music. Will guitar do?"

Arabel and I managed to suppress our laughter with some difficulty while the great conductor looked at the maitre d' as if he were an orchestra member who had played C instead of F. Arabel, as she always does, intervened to sort out the confusion. She explained that piano also means softly and the maestro wanted the music to be at a very low volume.

"That I can do", said the head waiter. Soon the musical fingers were playing the table and we could converse in a normal voice.

"German friends call me Wolfram, English and Americans Wolf, heaven forbid not Will or Bill", the maestro told us. For emphasis he added, "When one sponsor of my concert called me Bill I looked the other way." He regaled us for next three hours with hilarious stories of the follies of famous composers, conductors and other musicians. Many I do not remember and those I do, would be improper to repeat in print. However, one is worth telling, in his words, if only to show what the great conductors are made of.

"I was conducting a concert with my own orchestra and the program included a short piece by a close friend of mine who is now a celebrated composer. After we finished playing it, there was a deadly silence in the hall. I looked around to face the audience and announced, 'You did not enjoy. Perhaps we do not play well. We will try again.' And we repeated the whole thing.

"When we finished the applause was deafening. Perhaps they enjoyed it, perhaps they were making sure we did not play a third time. Maybe some of each.

"Of course it was planned in advance. I anticipated the feeble reaction from the audience and had discussed the repeat with the orchestra during the dress rehearsal. Alas the days are long gone when an orchestra would do whatever the conductor asked. They have unions you know."

After an excellent four-course dinner had been capped with espresso and thirty year old port, I asked for the bill. Wolf's well-known distaste for modern devices, with the exception of the compact discs he had recorded, was confirmed when he offered to pay the bill and pulled out a bundle of notes from his pocket. However, my bronze credit card carried the day.

2

Wolf's agent organized frequent tours of North America for him and he visited our city almost every year. He usually conducted the orchestra in concerts and only once in a while in an opera. He was a gracious guest when we invited him to lunch or dinner, nothing like the ferocious wolf he was known to be to the orchestra members. Arabel was rather tense on the first occasion. She had the piano tuner come the day before and worked on the house; cleaning floors, dusting furniture and polishing silverware to bring it to the standards of a Munchen hausfrau. That morning she made four different soups because three were not good enough. I picked up Wolf around eleven. After coffee he played the piano for Annabel to sing while I set the table and opened two bottles of Italian wines. He liked the mushroom soup that Arabel decided to serve and accepted a second helping of Hungarian Goulash. He praised the crème caramel, an Arabel specialty.

Leaving the messy dining table, we moved to comfortable recliners. I had just poured Kenya coffee when the door bell rang. "It is my friends from school. They want to see how it feels to be in the close presence of a world renowned personality", Annabel said as she headed for the door.

"Oh, that bell! It is out of tune", Wolf said, looking quite serious.

Arabel couldn't suppress a smile and asked, "What note should it be?"

"I don't know what note it should be. It is not quite E, a quarter note off. Perhaps the tuner could fix it next time he comes," the maestro suggested.

Two teenage gangly boys followed Annabel into the room. "Simon and Eddie, they are in my class and in the school band. They want to play for the maestro and to ask him if they have talent to take on music as a career," Annabel said. Simon carried a violin in a well-worn case and Eddie a sparkly trumpet. The boys nervously said hello and sat down on the dining room chairs Annabel pulled for them.

"You can play for me. Let this old man tell you first, it is not only talent. You need to work extremely hard under exceptional teachers; you have to excel, being good is not good enough. It is a very hard profession to succeed in. Thousands of kids work hard, win competitions and do not make it as an orchestra member, let alone become soloists."

After finishing the coffee we had a mini concert with piano, violin, trumpet and song. The audience of two cheered heartily at the end of each piece. It ended when the clock chimed. Apparently the tone did not hurt the sensitive ears of the maestro. He looked at his watch with a dark dial and bright hands, stood up with some effort and said, "Sorry volk, I have to rehearse the orchestra, should we call a cab?"

On my return from the hotel Arabel told me delightedly that the boys did not let her into the kitchen while they loaded the dishwasher, washed and put away the pans and cleaned the counters. They thanked her for an afternoon they said they would remember all their lives.

Arabel called the tuner, told him Wolf's anguish at the bell tone and asked if he could help. The poor man tried every trick of his trade for the whole afternoon. The obdurate bell stuck to its guns. We didn't expect the tone of a new bell to be any better; didn't have the ears to tell the difference anyway. I did remember to turn the bell off on Wolf's future visits.

3

It was two years before Wolf was in town again. He was here this time to conduct a concert featuring Painter's Joyous Symphony, a perennial crowd favourite and a complex piece which, I am told, needs a lot of careful baton work. Arabel asked him to join us for lunch one day. He agreed a little too quickly, I believe he had a soft spot in his heart for the two ladies in my life. Again it was my task to pick him up from the concert hall after the rehearsal. I had the car cleaned inside and out on my way to the concert hall and waited for him in the car near the stage door. The radio was broadcasting the recording of a lovely serenade. I was captivated by the performance. I wondered which of the great orchestras it was, Berlin, Vienna, Amsterdam under the baton of one of the great conductors of the day, Haitink, Rattle, Abbado. The serenade came to an end, much too soon for my liking. The announcer told the listeners that it was an orchestra I had never heard of under the baton of Wolfram Telemann. Talk about coincidence.

The orchestra must have been making too many mistakes, the car radio had nearly finished another concert item when an attendant opened the door and Wolf walked out. Crawled out would be a more correct description, he was dragging his feet while clutching his right shoulder. He was obviously in pain. I helped him get in the passenger seat and clicked the seatbelt for him. He told me that his shoulder had been troubling him for last few days and it would be very hard to conduct a long program the next day unless something was done. "Arabel goes to a very good physiotherapist for her back. I am sure she can get an appointment for you," I assured him. He believed me, he didn't know me well enough, and his facial muscles relaxed. Perhaps it would have made him feel good if I told him then about the music on the radio. In the bustle of his hurt it slipped my mind altogether.

When we reached home, I opened the car door and undid Wolf's seatbelt. He got out gingerly and almost tipped over as his left hand shot up to clutch his shoulder just as his feet touched the driveway. Arabel heard the sorry tale and without wasting time on finding out how it all came about, called the physio. Susan, delighted with the prospect of having a distinguished conductor as her patient, said that she would hurry her next few patients to make room for Maestro Telemann at three.

Arabel had become more comfortable with the idea of entertaining a celebrity and prepared an excellent lunch with many choices and with hardly any evident stress. The bad shoulder precluded the private concert after the meal and we had an hour till the Physio appointment. Annabel suggested a game of Scrabble. Wolf agreed to play if he were given a fifty-point start to compensate for his poor English. I fetched the game and we moved to a different table, leaving the lunch dishes for later. As the game proceeded, Arabel and Annabel set up some high scoring words and Wolf's lead steadily shrank till near the end he had fallen thirty points behind Annabel. "I don't mind losing to such a fine young lady," proclaimed Wolf, staring at his deck as if his life depended on it. He raised his eyes, looked at the board and put down F on the triple word spot in the top centre followed by R on the left of an A that was there. We wondered what was coming next, a word in German, French or Italian. Then Z appeared followed in slow progression by a blank, L, E and to top it all D on the triple word spot on the top right hand corner. He used up all his letters and scored 320 points. A gorgeous smile played on his face when we totted up the scores. He had finished with more points than two of us combined. Arabel complimented him, "Great game. Wonder what you would have scored if English were your mother tongue."

"Fifty points less," replied Wolf.

Arabel drove Wolf to the physio. To her surprise, the reception area was adorned with festoons and the sound system was playing pianissimo the overture of The Swimming Dane. Wolf hummed the no doubt familiar tune while waiting for Susan. She came rushing in, grabbed Wolf's hand and shook it vigorously making his face grimace in pain. "Oh, I am so sorry, I forgot about your shoulder," Susan apologized.

"Don't be sorry, I will survive," Wolf assured her.

"I hope the ambience of the clinic pleased you. We put the decorations up to welcome you and my husband found a recording of Schmidt overtures made by you," Susan informed him.

Wolf's shoulder was hurting too much after the over friendly handshake for him to be happy. He followed Susan leaving Arabel to find an old Maclean's to while away the hour she expected Susan would need. An hour it was, and Arabel was putting the magazine back on the corner table when she heard Susan's laughter. Wolf was smiling, thanking her for the miracle she had performed. While pulling out the wallet he said to Susan, "There will be two tickets waiting for you at the ticket window if you are free tomorrow evening."

"Thank you for the offer but my husband has already ordered the tickets for the performance," Susan replied and added, "I will be watching you closely and if I see any sign of discomfort, I will come to the dressing room and make you better."

4

Arabel rushed in late after having worked an hour longer, with no overtime pay to boot. The phone was ringing when she opened the door of the house. "Who the hell is calling at this hour?" she asked the thin air as she picked up the receiver. "I am here in Rio de Janeiro doing a great program of Brazilian music. I would love for you to come, you will love it, great orchestra, wonderful soloists I chose carefully for the program," the voice said excitedly without an introduction. After a few moments of silence there was what Wolf expected to be the clincher, "I will have seats for you in the same row as the president of Brazil."

Arabel was nonplussed by this invitation straight out of the blue receiver. She could not admit to Wolf that we could not afford the expense of such a trip, she did tell him the other reason we couldn't go, "Wolf, thanks for inviting us. It is so kind of you to think of us and it is so tempting. I am so sorry. Annabel is giving her first public concert at the conservatory and she is so looking forward to us being there."

"Oh, I am so disappointed. I will miss you. Wish Annabel good luck from Uncle Wolf. She has talent. She will do well if she works hard. By the way, I am negotiating the program for a concert with your orchestra next spring."

Arabel's ears perked up when she heard this, "Your keenest fan heard your recording of a string serenade. He will love to hear it live."

"Let me think about it. It has to go well with the other pieces we play. Well, goodbye for now. See you next spring," Wolf said just before the click

Next season's brochure of the orchestra announced in bold letters that maestro Telemann was returning to conduct a program of his all time favourites, including the serenade. Arabel was concerned when she noticed the concert dates and pulled her diary out of the handbag. "We have to go to Scotland for my parents' golden wedding anniversary. They want us there for three weeks which fall around the dates of the concert," she announced in a tone that brooked no opposition.

When we returned from Scotland the answering machine had a message from Wolf, "I am staying at my usual hotel. Please call me to arrange when I can check on the progress of my very dear Annabel." This was the last time we heard from Wolf. Arabel saw Susan a week after our return and received the bad news; Wolf collapsed during the dress rehearsal when, according to the media, the bassoon hit a wrong note. As an aside, Susan remarked that although the wrong note made a nice story, it had nothing to do with the misfortune. She visited Wolf a couple of times during the week he spent in the hospital before he could fly home. The company sponsoring the concert arranged for a nurse to accompany him on the flight.

Wolf never recovered. He was moved to a nursing home where he lived like a lamb for almost a year. It was an unusually silent night when the maestro, creator of wonderful sounds that thrilled the audiences all over the world, passed away in his sleep. It was around then that Annabel was offered her first significant opportunity on stage.

4. Young Lovers

I

Writers are excellent conversationalists who can discuss a variety of issues for hours and hold your interest the whole time. They present their views forcefully while taking interest in other opinions too. They are curious to find what is behind the face others present to the world. For all I know they are searching for material for their next piece even when talking about what may appear trivial at first glance. Perhaps I was naïve in believing that all writers would live up to this exalted image. Now I know better; I spent an hour the other morning with the writer of an acclaimed novel.

I had met him on a beautiful evening; temperature in high twenties and a slight breeze to keep mosquitoes away. Ravina had invited some close friends to a barbecue on her immaculate lawn with roses and rhododendrons in full bloom and warblers and blue jays singing in the aspen and pine trees along the fence. I was surprised to be included because our contact is limited to jogging together when the weather is not inclement. While the other guests were chatting gaily in small groups, I was standing alone, a glass of Chianti in hand, entranced by the beauty around me. The reverie was broken when Ravina came rushing towards me with a stranger in tow. She introduced us, "Daoud, the charming lady is Morag; Morag, the fine gentleman is Daoud. His first novel was published a month ago and has received rave reviews." She paused to recover her breath before saying, "Now do excuse me, I must attend to the dressing for the salad," and hurried off towards the kitchen.

Being a new single, I am interested in meeting men. It is not helpful being particular at the early stages of an acquaintance and I am happy to talk to anyone who is not taken already. Although I have dated a wide variety of prospects; I have not yet found my ideal. Who knows, perhaps my standards are unrealistic. Be that as it may, of the men I have spent many pleasant hours with, quite a few have been celebrated authors. A writer can be short and fat, have a bulbous nose, rabbit ears, double chin, narrow forehead below receding hairline, spotty complexion and a generally withered look, all is forgiven if his work has appeared in print. Here I have inadvertently described Daoud and my initial attraction to him. He looked uncomfortable. Hopefully, I found the right thing to say to put him at ease, "I am so happy to meet a writer. Quite a few of my friends write and publish poems, stories and essays in local media. None of them has written a novel, leave alone having it published and acclaimed."

"I am so glad to meet some one who appreciates my profession. Very few people do." Daoud's speech was heavily accented.

"How long did it take to write it?"

"Not long really. Three years from the first idea to the finish. Not counting a year to get the grant from the Provincial council, six months for editing and another year to locate a publisher."

"Five years and six months; by golly that is a long time. What kept you going?"

"I must admit there were times when I felt like giving up. No other window opened and I had to keep plugging away."

"What is the novel about?"

"It is about the love affair between a poor Jewish girl and the son of a rich Arab merchant who live in Israel. It is a sad tale really."

"Do you know much about life in Israel?"

"Unfortunately, yes. I was born in Jaffa and lived there till six years ago."

"Is the novel your own story?"

"Not really. This is a big topic. We have to discuss it where we won't be disturbed."

"Can I have your email address where I can contact you and invite you and your wife for a get together?"

"No wife, not even a girl friend. Your husband may not like you being with a single man."

"No husband, not even a boy friend. The road is clear for us."

Ravina interrupted our conversation. "I would like you two love birds to meet an interesting couple. They have just returned from an African safari and had many exciting encounters with lions, hippos and even a rhinoceros you can quiz them about." She shoved an elderly couple between us and rushed off leaving the exchange of formalities to us.

2

I arrived at the restaurant just before ten o'clock news on the radio a few minutes before Daoud. It was a modest place, a little bigger than a hole in the wall, without any pretence of elegance. There were wooden chairs without cushions; plastic covers on rickety tables showed lines left by the wiping cloth, the walls cried out for fresh paint and the pictures of snow clad mountains and lush valleys tilted at all angles. All the same, it had a reputation in the community for good brunch served all day and did a roaring trade whatever day of the week it was. While we were waiting for the table Daoud handed me a plastic bag containing a book. It had an attractive cover showing a teenage couple in a tight embrace. The Forbidden Love above the couple in italics and Daoud Islami at the bottom in bold letters and the publisher's logo in the bottom left corner. The gesture moved me as much as the expressions of anticipated doom on the faces on the cover. "Thank you very much. It was so thoughtful of you to bring the book. I must pay you for it. How much is it?"

"Oh no. I am not going to accept payment. It is a gift."

"That is very kind of you. Will you sign it for me?"

"No sooner said than done," He said. He opened the book, scribbled something on the first page and handed it back. Before I could see the writing on the page, the waitress called us and we headed for the table.

I ordered coffee and scrambled eggs, Daoud ordered tea and chef's special, lamb in place of ham. "What brought you to cold Canada from nice and hot Israel?" I asked to open the conversation.

"Oh, it is a long story I will write some day. My father has a chain of grocery stores in Arab communities in Israel. My older brother has a talent for business and is being groomed to take over the family firm. I was assigned to emigrate to the West; partly to provide a place to go to if things blow up at home. The situation of Arab minority is precarious there and all this unrest in Gaza makes it worse. Thanks be to Allah, kind and hospitable Canada accepted my refugee claim before any other country did and here I am."

"How did you come to write the novel?"

"You probably know that there are volunteer organizations that help refugees when they land here. They assigned me to a lady volunteer who asked me what I did at home and what I would like to do. When I told her that I wrote stories at home and my ambition was to be a writer, she helped me enroll in a Creative Writing course at the community college. Towards the end of the term, the teacher asked us to prepare an outline for a novel we would wish to write. She liked my submission so much that she told me about the grants I could apply for and helped with the applications. An agency of the Province kindly granted a monthly stipend so long as I made a reasonable progress. The grant paid my share of the rent and put food on the table. Now I am hoping that the royalties will keep me going till I land a job."

"You said the novel is about the love of a rich Arab merchant with a poor Jewish girl. Are you the Arab merchant?"

"I am and I am not. Writing is a complex affair. You start with a plot and by the time you are finished, the story is nothing like you planned. I don't know what it is, the deep subconscious, Allah working His magic, randomness of words falling on the paper; it rarely is what one thought it would be. The personalities change, the events take different turns, even the conclusion is often different. We can discuss this issue after you have read the book, assuming you would want to have anything to do with me then. All I can say is that real life never makes a good story, not in the hands of a novice like me anyway."

"Very interesting. I promise I will read it and we will get together when I am done. I am not a critic, just an average reader. My opinion shouldn't mean anything to you. Yet, I am curious as to what has been wrought by whosoever makes these changes to the real story."

"Don't put down the average reader. She is the most important person for a writer. She recommends the book to her friends and colleagues. It is the word of mouth that sells the book, not the critics, not the advertising. Your opinion has an added meaning for me; I feel as if I have known you for ages."

He must have known me well because he did not show any interest in me, not even what I did for a living or what kind of books I enjoyed. I had nothing more to ask and we sat in silence. Fortunately, our orders arrived soon and I drove such thoughts out of my mind. I saw three eggs omelet, a lamb chop, heap of fries and four heavily buttered toasts disappear before I had sprayed a little pepper on my scrambled eggs. He looked up from the clean plate and smiled without saying a word. I asked him what he thought about the issue of Global Warming, hoping that he would turn the question around and I could ride my hobby horse. Alas this was not to be. After a sip from the cup he expressed his view in the tone of a scholar, "There is no doubt that humans are responsible for polluting the atmosphere and that is the main source of the climate change as well as of many serious illnesses like cancer. We must reduce the obscene level of consumption in the

West and help the poor countries shift away from coal to renewable energy."

"Do you think human population has any role in combating climate change?" I asked.

"The issue is total consumption, not what little the poor in developing world consume to barely survive. The reduction in the wasteful West can offset the impact of growing population in the East. Do you realize that the cats and dogs in your homes eat better than what many well-off people in the East can afford?"

My disappointment at lack of interest in my views turned into anger by this unfair comment, particularly because Daoud had been taking advantage of all we in the West had to offer. Moreover, I loved my two cats and felt that they were as entitled to nutritious and tasty diet as anyone in the East. The novelist did not notice my reaction and continued, "In any event, our Prophet was very clear on the issue of population. 'Go forth and multiply' he exhorted. We can't go against the Prophet any more than you can go against Christ," Daoud replied.

"Of course not," I said, hopefully in a sarcastic tone.

"I am so glad you agree," Daoud said with a smile.

The restaurant must have needed our table; the waiter arrived with the bill and the credit card gizmo the moment I put my fork down. I gave Daoud an opportunity to make a move. Seeing no reaction, I put my card on the table.

After a limp shake of hands he waddled towards the bus stop and I walked to my car. I dropped the plastic bag on the passenger seat and wondered if I really wanted to read the novel. Then the cover crossed my mind and I realized that the young lovers will not let me live in peace till I had walked their thorny path.

5. An Amateur at a Book Fair

Penny is a busy professional, working with a variety of clients, attending meetings of all sorts, workshops on the weekends too. Her husband, Jonathan, was laid off several years ago for taking things easy and now spends his time writing fiction. After publishing four books during this period he is currently working on a novel, his first. Penny worries in her rare spare moments about the mental state of her husband whom she dearly loves and sometimes feels guilty for not spending more time with him. Reflecting on their situation one afternoon while driving to see a client, her ears popped up when she heard on the radio that some women were organising a book fair on the Saturday two weeks hence when she planned to be away at a workshop. She had an easy decision to make and she made it instantly. Jonathan, whose books have failed to make triple digits in total sales, though not by much, should display his wares at the fair and raise the awareness of his creations to a slightly higher level. However, she realised that she had to do more than just suggest it to her rather reserved husband. She gave it some thought on her way home and settled on the strategy which had worked before. She prepared his favourite dinner, grilled chicken breast with broccoli and baked potatoes and when they had settled comfortably with their coffees she spoke in a soft persuasive tone, "There is nothing wrong with your books. In fact there are some good bits in them although I can't think of any off hand. The problem is that your publishers did not promote them and you don't do anything either. You should learn from me, although it is against a man's honour to ever follow a woman's suggestion, particularly when she is his wife who has only his good in mind. You have seen how I do it; I promote my DVDs wherever I go. I arrange seminars and show clips from it. I advertise in professional magazines and contact the buyers of previous DVDs. That is how I have sold thousands priced at five times your books. You need to get off your butt, go to book fairs like this one in Nomanlands Community Hall and you will see your sales skyrocket. Even if you don't sell many books there, you will gain experience and make new contacts. What is there to lose?"

Jonathan listened attentively. He did not know how to react. Should he admire her modesty for reducing her brilliant creation to the same level as his amateurish works or be flattered by her equating his books to her great success? After a moment of consideration, he did what any good husband would do, he heartily agreed to follow her suggestion and attend the book fair. The internet, the wonderful invention of geeks in a smoke-filled basement (or was it a fumes-filled garage?) helped him locate Val, the organizer. He felt a wave of relief wash over him when Val said that the tables were all claimed already. The audible sigh had barely made a ripple in the air when Val suggested that someone might wish to share his/her table and promised, threatened Jonathan would say if he were to be honest, to ask around. In a couple of hours Val had found a person willing to share his table. All Jonathan needed to do was to pay him a new slippery plastic twenty-dollar bill, half of what he had paid for the table. When Jonathan told Penny the news, bad to him, good to her, she scribbled a list of instructions for him to follow to make the best use of his time and effort at the fair. Jonathan spent most of the next two days crossing items on the list. He put three copies of the book by their daughter Emma in his pile of books for the half table, prepared a poster extolling the awards Emma's book had received, freshened the posters for his commonplace books, found a table cloth of the right size, bought flowers and snacks for the table and washed and ironed the red shirt and blue trousers he was going to wear for the occasion. On the afternoon the Friday before the fair he packed four boxes of books, eighty four copies in all, and one box of ancillary items. He put them in the garage next to the car enough distance from the back wheel so that he wouldn't run over them accidentally or by subconscious design. For last item on the list, Jonathan highlighted the streets on the map to make sure he would not get lost as he almost always does when Penny is not with him. To make doubly sure, he set the location of the Nomanlands Community Hall in the GPS. Penny returned home just as Jonathan was about to sit down to recover his breath. "Oh, I am so tired. It has been a long day," she said and after a moment's pause added, "Do you mind pouring me a glass of Tio Pepe." When he handed her the sherry glass she looked at it with satisfaction, took a sip and announced to the audience of one, "I see that you are well prepared for tomorrow. I am so relieved. I can go to the mountains with no worries about you at the fair."

The doors opened at ten o'clock. The exhibitors had been advised to arrive an hour early and set up shop in plenty of time. This would also leave them time to visit with each other, renew old friendships and make new ones. Jonathan woke up early, around the ungodly hour of five. To tell you the truth, he did not sleep much. The hopes of selling all eighty four books and the dread of not selling any alternated in his mind all night. Sometime during these thoughts, actually many times during the all too frequent wide-awake periods, he promised to himself that he would take Penny out for dinner if he sold ten, twenty, thirty copies, the number increasing steadily over the night.

Jonathan was showered and dressed by six. The weekend edition of the newspaper was done in ten minutes and there were another one hundred and ten minutes to kill before eight when he was to wake Penny up with her morning cup of tea and two digestive biscuits. What better use of time than to review his first book, published seven long years ago, to remind him of what he had written. He glanced through the stories in "Jennifer's Nightmare" for the first time since editing the proofs. He was glad he did because he found out two of the reasons Nightmare did not sell beyond the circle of friends who felt obliged to buy, though not to read, the first book of someone they were close to. First, most of the stories were of a personal nature and would be of no interest to a stranger. Second and perhaps more important, the humour was way over the top and the tragedy much too subtle in the ill-fated love stories.

Although Jonathan took three wrong turns, the GPS eventually guided him to the community centre in good time and his half of the table was ready to greet the horde of curious visitors twenty minutes before the doors were to open. There was a vase with michaelmas daisies in the centre, four copies of each of his four books and three copies of one on cancer by Emma, display blurbs and two bowls of savoury snacks. Extra copies were carefully hidden under the table behind the overhang of red table cloth with an elaborate design in black. The boxes were left open so the sold books could be replaced with minimum fuss.

Jonathan was sharing the table with David who had two books on display. David immigrated from England in the early seventies about the same time Jonathan left that country for Timbuktu. During many slow periods they discussed the timely topic of whether the northern regions of England would be better off joining an independent Scotland. David's self-published books were biographies of two celebrated Albertans. Jonathan found them to be well written and very well presented. One of them, about an Alberta war hero, not remembered now, had won a first prize in an American competition. David had exhibited books many times before and was well prepared with a large poster and a well rehearsed presentation.

For most of the day the organizers were many, the visitors few and far between. Many of the visitors were grandparents taking their charges out on a stroll and dropping by to see what a book fair looked like. It is quite likely that many of them expected to find dusty old books and comics selling for pennies and were disappointed to see new books hot off the presses on sale for twenty or more dollars. A few of the visitors were intent on showing off and couldn't have been less interested in the books or the authors. Genuine book lovers were rare and only one visitor, an Ethiopian immigrant and a journalist, conversed with Jonathan about the art of writing and what motivated him. Another visitor was an engineer Jonathan had vaguely known some twenty years ago. They had a nice chat about changes in construction industry over the years and the welcome and unwelcome trends of the last few years. The other visitors to the stall were exhibitors whose interests varied from promoting themselves to seeing what this hunched bald man was doing in a fair for young people trying to build a future in the world of art and culture. One author was keen to photograph every one in various poses for her Facebook presentation. A poet with six of his collections of poetry on the table in front of him sat on a high stool with an expression of amusement throughout. He was very pleasant to talk to and promised Jonathan that he would soon write a poem on the book fair and send it to him.

Regular yawns began not much after the opening hour. Their frequency increased in the afternoon and reached a fever pitch, whatever fever pitch is for yawns, as the closing hour approached. The books and ancillaries were back in the boxes and the table cloths folded up even before the last visitor had left. Just as the digital clock on the wall changed to 4:00:00 there was a rush for the exit reminding Jonathan of school kids rushing out at the last ring of the bell. There was a difference though, the exhibitors were too loaded with what they had brought in the morning to run screaming with delight and too courteous not to exchange pleasantries as they passed or were passed by. Outside they saw how beautiful fall day it was, trees golden under the bright warm sun and a gentle breeze soothing the skin. The mood quickly became joyful although there must have been a few feeling sorry for having spent the day in a windowless hall when they could have been hiking in the Rockies or cycling in anyone of the numerous parks their city is known for.

Val came over when Jonathan was loading the heaviest box in the trunk while working out in his mind what percentage of his out of pocket expenses were covered by the book sales. She expressed disappointment in the turnout and wondered whether more people would have dropped by if it had been a cold rainy day. "I hope you enjoyed it all the same," she said in a tone of query.

"It was my first time as an exhibitor and it was a good learning experience," Jonathan replied.

Jonathan thanked his lucky stars that Val did not notice the disappointment in his voice. "We will have it again next year and perhaps every year. What we learnt this year will help us next time. We need to showcase our authors to the public and this is a start," Val told him.

"This is a good idea and worth pursuing. However, the basic problem is that in this age of cable, internet and so much instant communication, no one has time, need or interest in reading. And the short attention spans, not much longer than that of a flea, do not help. As an author friend says, 'There are more writers than readers,'" Jonathan repeated his set piece for such conversations.

"You maybe right; there are a lot of writers who self-publish. Many of them are very good and have to take this route because almost all of the small publishers who took on new authors in the good old days have closed shop. It is these authors who need encouragement and who we are hoping to help," Val was either consoling or flattering, Jonathan couldn't tell which.

It must be the suppressed ego that made Jonathan say, "We need a filter to flush out books that are not worth being put in front of the public and publishers provided that. You may want to select exhibitors for the quality of their writing rather than on the first- come basis. It is better to have a small fair with some assurance of quality than a big one with no quality control."

Val had the final word and it put Jonathan in his proper place, "We may do that next year. Perhaps you will have a new book by then which will pass our filter."

6. A Deal in Morocco

Marlene and Deepak arrived in Fes, Morocco, on a pleasant afternoon in utter state of excitement. They had travelled for eighteen
hours on four crowded planes yet they did not feel at all weary. They
had booked a five star hotel in Medina, the oldest walled community
in the world. It was built in the ninth century on the northern fringe
of Sahara desert by Sultan Idris as the foundation of his empire set
to glorify Allah and his prophet Muhammed for centuries to come. A
half hour ride in a Mercedes Diesel, almost as old as the Medina itself
and emitting as many fumes as a couple of hundred thousand humans
burning wood and coal for cooking and heating, delivered them to
the gate of the Medina nearest to the hotel. A young man promptly
appeared out of nowhere, loaded their suitcases on his push cart and
conveyed them to the hotel five-minute walk away. He demanded
the payment almost as much as the cab fare from the airport. It took
several minutes of haggling to get him to agree to release the suitcase
for about half as much, approximately ten dollars. It should have given
the experienced travellers like them a clue of what was to come. It
did not register, hard to tell whether due to the jet lag or the thrill of
new culture.

An hour sipping mint tea and munching spiced cookies in the
majestic courtyard of the hotel was a pleasant introduction to the
luxuries Riad Fes, their hotel, had to offer. A young Arab woman
wearing tight blue jeans and a revealing pink sweater, no hijab (head

scarf) let alone Niqab (veil with a slit for the eyes) explained in reasonable English the amenities in the hotel and made recommendations about a guide and local travel. The couple promptly booked an English speaking guide for the next morning, specifically opting for sightseeing over shopping. The hostess led them to their room on the roof. It was elegantly furnished in the traditional local decor and had a bed big enough for a sheikh and four wives. Instead of the customary chocolate on the bed, there was a plate with a variety of cookies and two bottles of water on a brass side table. The evening was spent absorbing the atmosphere of Arab culture with a lute player briefly interrupted by the dinner of tajine.

Morning arrived soon enough, hastened by the call of the Muezzin from several mosques close by, or were these recorded voices on loud speakers broadcast five times a day slightly out of unison to create the atmosphere unique to the Medina? Deepak left the room, walked over to the edge of the roof and watched the sun rise behind the domed roofs of ancient houses built on the rolling hills within inches of each other. He woke Marlene up and they enjoyed one of the best sunrise views of their lives with their arms around each other.

It might have been the jet lag or the beautiful sight they had just witnessed, perhaps both, they could not go back to sleep. They talked of all the wonderful things they would do, visit the sights in Medina, look at all the traditional shops, a leather factory, carpet warehouses and visit mosques where millions of devotees of Allah have prayed every day reciting the words specified by the scholars of the Quran. On other days they would visit the Atlas mountains, see the caves where families still live like they did thousands of years ago, visit Mecnes, another historic town nearby and roam around new areas of Fes by themselves. A memorable week was on the horizon and they were eager to grasp it.

A leisurely breakfast - not included in the two hundred dollars a day charge for the room, what kind of miser would worry about such details in this lap of luxury - brought the hands of the clock to nine.

6. A Deal in Morocco

A quick brushing of the teeth and they were ready to meet Abdallah, the English-speaking guide and the master of their day, to show them the sights of the Medina and to protect them from aggressive merchants of carpets, leather jackets and local spices they did not need at their age.

A visit to the king's palace, to one of its many entrance gates to be precise, beautifully carved and firmly bolted, was followed by a short drive to the farthest entrance of Medina. Abdallah took his visitors past entrances to several mosques dating back centuries. Unfortunately, Marlene and Deepak could not see them because only the Muslims were allowed entry. How anyone knew that Deepak was not a Muslim is a mystery yet to be resolved. After walking along several narrow streets with only a few local shoppers and even fewer tourists, they entered a porch through a huge gate with the view of an enormous courtyard. The guide asked in an unusually humble tone, "Will you like to visit the cooperative where the world famous Fes wool carpets, made by the widows and orphans, are sold ridiculously cheap?"

Marlene interrupted, "No, we are not interested in buying anything. We are at the stage in our lives when we are reducing our possessions, not adding to them."

Deepak contradicted his wife, "Let's go in. There is no harm in seeing the beautiful articles. No one is forcing us to buy anything."

"He is right, Missus. There is no pressure. It will be nice to rest for a few minutes and sip some mint tea too."

A very respectful elderly gentleman in baggy white cotton pants, calf-length beige tunic and red Fez cap with black tassels came into the porch, bowed deeply and said, looking in the direction of Deepak, "Please bless this establishment with your presence. It is the only government certified coop in Fes. Every carpet, big and small, is made by widows and orphans in their homes and most of what an item is sold for goes to them. You do not have to buy anything. Just look at a few rugs and tell us what you think of them. Your opinion is as valuable to us as your euros or dollars or pounds."

Marlene turned to Deepak and said in a wavering tone, "Let us not fall in this trap. Once we go in we won't come out without parting with more than we can afford."

Deepak was not convinced. He put his left arm around Marlene's waist and said in the sugary voice he used when he wanted her to do something against her better judgment, "Let's go in for a few minutes. No harm can come out of it. It will be interesting to compare them with Indian and Iranian carpets. You know I am up to any tricks they can play on us."

Marlene had her doubts but a gentle push from Deepak soon had her in the courtyard. Before long they were sitting on a divan sipping sweet mint tea. A young man in a grey jacket, blue shirt and brown pants came through the back door, introduced himself as Mohamed and after some small talk solicitously asked them the details of their careers and family. When Deepak told them that they had two sons and a daughter he perked up, "How old is your daughter?"

"She is twenty five," Marlene replied.

"She lives in Canada, I suppose. Is she married?"

"No. She is a career woman. No time to meet men."

"No need to look any further. I am an eligible bachelor. Just the right age, thirty five. I will love to live in Canada where I could ski all year round, not just once a year,"

"Give me a picture. I will show it to her. She will contact you if she likes it," Deepak replied.

"Just consider me your son-in-law. You won't find anyone better anywhere - fluent in three languages, graduate in Islamic architecture from the University of Fes. Who could be more qualified?"

In the meantime, four short and gaunt men were spreading several rolls of carpets on the floor. The carpets were huge, thirty feet long, twenty feet wide, one inch thick. There was a great variety of designs in every colour one could imagine. With each carpet Mohamed named the weaver, how long it took to make it - anything between six months to two years. He informed us that the wool was imported from New

Zealand at special rates for widows and orphans of the Fes Medina.
Carpets kept coming, as did the mint tea and cookies. The clock kept
ticking. Abdallah was oohing and aahing at every carpet. Work of art,
best I have ever seen, will suit any décor, were just some of his comments. Occasionally he would ask Mohamed the price and declare,
"Why so cheap? Don't widows and orphans eat?" Mohamed would
answer, "It is Ramadan. All carpets are reduced to sell, before the new
supplies come in."

Marlene nudged Deepak every few minutes whispering that it
was time to move on; that there was a lot to see before lunch. Deepak
did not pay any attention and examined every carpet in detail asking
questions about the weave, quality of dyes and the expected life of the
carpet. The answers were always followed by detailed elaboration of
the virtues of the carpet. It was now noon and Mohamed was becoming more excited about the quality and price of the carpet adding new
inducements with each passing minute. Because they are made by
the orphans and widows and sold by the cooperative, and Canadians
are so generous, there is no customs duty, shipping by air by DHL is
included in the price, you can sell each of these in art auctions anywhere in America or Europe for ten thousand dollars, buy three of
them, sell two and you will recover the cost of your holiday, buy six
and sell four, you will have a long queue of men wanting to marry your
daughter. The spiel went on, Marlene continued to fidget and Deepak,
entranced, did not budge from the floor with carpets all around him.
He had a gleam in his eyes that alarmed Marlene. Mohamed was
getting impatient as if he had another appointment, "Tell me which
six carpets you like, I give you such a good price that you will thank
Mohamed for ever even if your daughter does not like him." Marlene
went to Deepak, pulled him aside and said quite clearly so every one
could hear, "They are pulling wool over our eyes. Don't be a fool. If
you are so struck by these carpets, select a small one that will fit in
our bedroom." The man in the fez interjected after having been a quiet
observer for two hours. "His price for three is a very good deal. It will

not be so good for only one." Mohamed had his final word, "I can't offer free shipping for one and there may also be customs. If you buy three full size carpets made by widows and orphans for their cooperative, I will throw in these small silk rugs for free. You must decide soon. These poor workers have to break for lunch."

Deepak's resistance, generally solid as a rock, had completely broken. The man who had walked away unscathed from seasoned sellers in Indian, Persian, Turkish and Egyptian markets and haggled in Nieman Marcus in Dallas and Tiffany's in New York selected six of the most expensive carpets bigger than any room in their house. Mohamed ushered them into a windowless office upstairs lighted by one forty-watt bulb and furnished with two dilapidated steel desks, four shaky wooden chairs and an outdated computer where Deepak lamely handed his credit card for the price quoted by wily Mohamed. Fifteen minutes later they came down to the courtyard, Deepak clutching a receipt for twenty-five thousand dollars for six large and three small carpets. There was a group of six European tourists, four elderly rather plump women and two shriveled men canes at their sides, sitting on the divans. Mohamed clapped his hands and announced to them, "My friends from Canada just bought ten big carpets for their home, please cheer for them." The Europeans looked strangely at Deepak and Marlene as they walked towards the gate. Four assistants followed them with heads bowed. "These poor assistants have no salary or commission and deserve a tip," Abdallah said to the floor. Deepak pulled out a five hundred dirham (fifty dollars) note and handed it to the assistant leading the line up. No doubt the guide claimed a hefty share of it too.

At lunch an hour later when they were waiting for lamb couscous, his folly dawned on Deepak and regrets over being mesmerized by a carpet seller in the Fes Medina took hold of him. Marlene did not add fuel to the fire and left him to stew when she attended to emails. The issue was not mentioned again till they were working on their customs declaration at the Calgary Airport.

6. A Deal in Morocco

The carpets were delivered six weeks later after Deepak had paid the customs duty, a high four-figure sum. Small rugs were used in the bedroom and their home office. They are having a hard time in deciding what to do with the large ones. Enquiries about "art auctions" have been inconclusive and carpet dealers have not returned their phone calls. The last time I saw Deepak he was quite depressed and Marlene's efforts to cheer him up have fallen flat so far. However, I have known Deepak for a long time and he has rebounded from calamities before. He will get over this one too and will be bragging one day about how he turned a bad deal in the oldest Medina in the historic city of Fes into a hugely profitable one.

7. A Chicago Holiday

I

Joanna came out of her home office and found me slumped on the living room sofa watching the business news. "Can I interrupt you for a moment?" she asked.

"Go ahead. I am not doing anything important," I replied.

"I have been invited to speak at a conference in the second week of October," Joanna informed me.

"That's great. I am sure they have a lot to learn from you," I complimented her, eyes still on the screen.

"We always enjoy visiting Chicago. Will you join me again?" Joanna asked.

I turned to face Joanna, smiled and answered, "It is almost a year away. Let us think about it."

Joanna knew that her husband of fifty years does not like to travel anymore. I had my fill when I was the sales manager for Kennedy Kleeners Worldwide. The bother of lining up behind smelly passengers, taking shoes off on dirty floors, stripping in cold halls and answering silly questions from security agents does not help. It happened the way she suspected, I hummed and hawed as the year flew by. In the meantime, she had travelled by herself to see our children in the Bahamas and Hawaii, and her siblings in Majorca. She was tired of carrying bags, sleeping alone in king size beds in strange rooms and being woken up by a rude alarm rather than a steaming cup of Darjeeling tea prepared exactly to her taste by her well trained husband. Frustrated by my dithering, she took the matter in her own hands and instructed me to book the flights for both of us and to check what else was on in the city of the great Chicago Symphony Orchestra, the Lyric Opera and the Institute of Art, not to mention the unique mix of old and new architecture, theatres, museums and parks. Happy to be relieved of the chore of decision making, I made a list of plays, operas, concerts and exhibits we could choose from and booked two seats on Hurricane Airlines which offered the cheapest fares albeit at inconvenient times.

Joanna worked long hours to prepare an instructional DVD to inaugurate at the prestigious conference. After many years of collecting the data, several months of selecting and editing the material and working with a noted DVD director for twelve weeks, it was to be ready on the day of the departure. Joanna has a deserved worldwide reputation and the professionals in her field were eagerly anticipating it. She was counting on recovering some of the significant cash outlay in its production from sales at the conference.

Even after travelling several time a year to near and far destinations over five decades, Joanna is still tense when preparing to leave and my rushing her while she puts the final touches to her packing does not help. This time the director was late delivering the DVDs and that added to the stress. At last, the suitcases were ready, the car loaded and we were on our way two-and-a-half hours before the flight was due to take off. My satisfaction with the timely departure turned out to be premature. There were long lines of the vehicles waiting to enter the cheaper parking lots. I disregarded Joanna's advice to join one of them and parked our car in the most expensive building which was also the farthest from the Hurricane counter. There was no trolley to be found and we had to drag our luggage for what seemed like a hundred miles to the check in. Joanna looked exhausted. Thankfully, the immigration and security personnel were brisk and there were many empty chairs in the waiting area when we arrived at the gate. "We have an hour before boarding. Would you care for a cup of coffee?" I asked Joanna.

Joanna settled in a comfortable chair before replying, "I don't feel like coffee. I do need to relax. I would love a good game of Scrabble. I need to avenge my defeat of last Sunday."

"Oh God! I don't know what I was thinking. We even talked about playing it on the flight. And then I go and pack it in the suitcase. How stupid can one be? I am so sorry," I hoped my tone was appropriately sheepish.

Joanna was not appeased. She gave me a look that would have melted a ton of wax, took out a book from her hand bag and buried her face in it. Except for the snack served on the flight, she opened her mouth only after we had collected our case from Carousel 35 and the words that came out were not particularly friendly.

We walked through the maze of underground paths to the train that would take us downtown. The machine dispensing the seven-day transit pass charged for two tickets but printed only one. The inspector could not issue the replacement, he did let us board the train. We got off at our destination a little after ten at night. On the way out we saw a light in the ticket window and a person reading a book. We walked over to him to ask for the ticket we had paid for and had not received. The kindly gentleman was not in the least upset at being disturbed. He listened attentively as I explained the problem in great detail. After talking with his boss on the phone for several minutes, he asked for a photo ID. I presented him my passport. He looked at it more carefully than many immigration officials would have. "You are from Canada," he asked.

"Yes," we replied in unison.

"Your name is Rajneesh Sharma?" he asked me.

"Yes, it is," I replied.

"And you were born in Qazipur?" The interrogation continued.

"Yes, I was. Why do you ask?" I was perplexed.

"My name is also Rajneesh Sharma and I am from Qazipur too," the inspector explained and added, "We lived near the clock tower. My family owns the Sharma Bank. I attended Qazipur Academy."

"What a coincidence. Glad to see you here. We lived in a mohalla and I went to Dayanand Hindu Mission School," I admitted my humble background, if only because I have overcome it and do not have much to be humble about now; in a material sense that is.

The other Rajneesh came out of his cubicle and shook our hands warmly. He handed me the passport and the replacement ticket and wished us a pleasant stay. After thanking him profusely, Joanna and her Rajneesh began what turned out to be a several-block walk in a drizzle. On the way, Joanna asked "What is the probability of meeting someone from your hometown of ten thousand people and with the same name as you in a city ten thousand miles away,"

I tried to think of an answer that would break the ice and came up with, "Not much more than a short, fat brownie from Qazipur marrying an angel from Whitby."

Joanna turned her face the other way though not before I saw that my effort at reconciliation had succeeded. We turned a corner and the hotel entrance came into view. It was well past midnight when our heads hit the well fluffed pillows and we were snoring, after we had exchanged the usual goodnight kiss.

2

The Lyric Opera was doing, "Love Under the Midnight Sun" by Mahner. Neither of us was familiar with the opera although Joanna admires Mahner's symphonic works. However, the available seats cost $300 each. It was a bit rich for us and we decided to skip it and go for a fancy dinner in The Balkan Café which is known for its southern European cuisine served by stiff waiters in elegant surroundings. The wine was excellent, appetizer big and the entrée' bigger. The dessert menu offered a tempting variety. Conscious of her figure, Joanna resisted. I let the waiter persuade me to order what he described as "the exquisite cake made with goat cheese specially imported from a remote Serbian village." My taste buds were not sensitive enough to distinguish it from other cheese cakes I have enjoyed on my travels, I praised it to the waiter all the same. All told the dinner was enjoyable and the bill was less than a quarter of one opera ticket. It was a nice prelude to the rest of the evening.

We went on the mandatory boat ride along the Chicago River and Lake Michigan and admired the skyscrapers which seem to get taller on every visit. There were no symphony concerts because the orchestra was playing in New York. Instead, we saw two plays which were good without being unforgettable. The Art Institute of Chicago was splendid and I visited it on the three days when Joanna was at the convention. The collection of Asian sculptures is outstanding, as are the displays of European art of the last eight hundred years. This art museum is renowned for its Impressionists; Monet, Seurat, Renoir and Gauguin being exceptionally well represented. On my third visit I spent a couple of hours in the modern art wing. I was confused by canvasses with squiggles, splashed paints and dismembered body parts or surfaces in one colour with or without a little dot in a corner. I reconciled myself with the thought that it must be my ignorance of art that, rather than appreciating these works, I think of them as childish pranks. However, I will keep trying to understand the art of the last century and hopefully some day it will mean something to me. I spent the later half of this visit in the gallery of American art, an integrated display of magnificent antique furniture, tapestries, bronzes and marble sculptures and paintings by Sargent, Hassam, Cassatt and O'Keefe, among numerous others. I remembered having rushed through this wing before and I was glad that I could pay it the attention it deserves on this visit.

As for the convention, Joanna was awarded a long overdue Fellowship of the Academy, her presentation was a success, as always, and the DVD was even more popular than expected. The hotel was comfortable and the stay was a good break from our daily grind. The next conference is to be held in Philadelphia, the City of Brotherly Love where we lived in days long gone by. Joanna is planning more DVDs and I am hoping to meet another namesake from Qazipur who would invite us to spiced tea with Indian sweets.

3

On the day of our return, Joanna was up early with her cup of Taylor's Assam tea served by her faithful, if nothing else, husband. She dressed quickly and rushed off for the last session. I lazed around for a while before putting on my jeans and plaid shirt to go to the lobby café for some milk. On the elevator on my way back to the room I met a not-yet middle-aged lady in a rush. 'How is the day?" I asked.

The lady was breathless though not so breathless that she couldn't answer, "It was ok till this moment. First my noble husband forgets his wallet and I have to fetch it. Then he needs a sweater and I have to run up again. This time he doesn't have a raincoat and it is raining. So here I go again."

"Why doesn't he go himself to get them?" I asked.

"We will be here for ever if I left it to him," she said totally exasperated.

I had to say something to console her, "Your husband is just like all others. They pretend to be incompetent so the wives do all the chores. You have to make him do it. After all, he does it all at work."

"Maybe next time," she said rushing out of the elevator.

I emptied the bag of granola we had brought for breakfasts into a plastic bowl and while eating it checked the messages, deleting them all. In between sips of coffee I finished packing my clothes and stacked Joanna's papers and sundry stuff in neat piles. With almost three hours still to kill, I picked up my swimming trunks to head for the 'spa'. Joanna's swimsuit was hanging from the shower rail and it reminded me of the kids' joke about the disparity between their parents. While

180

7. A Chicago Holiday

Joanna loves swimming even in freezing lakes, my aquatic activities are limited to sweating in the Jaccuzi, the hotter the better. "Mom's great grandparents were fish and Dad's, apes," they often said when they were teenagers. If one were to go by the sleek looks of Joanna and my ungainly appearance, there may have been some truth in it.

Two young women joined me in the bubbling water. One of them had dimples, hazel eyes and red hair, much like Joanna. After they had settled down in front of the jets, I asked the dimples, "Are you from U.K?"

"Yes, I still have the accent although I came here as a child," she replied.

"From England?"

"Yes."

"Cheshire?"

"Yes"

"Whitby?"

"Yes."

"And your name is Joanna Faulkner?"

"Yes. How do you know?"

"Believe it or not, on our way to the hotel we met a gentleman from my village in India who has the same name as mine. According to Hindu scriptures, the more unusual an event the more likely it is to repeat itself," I said getting out of the pool on my way to sauna.

I thought I heard giggles and barely managed to resist the impulse to turn around.

8. REUNION WITH OLD FRIENDS

I

"Hurry, hurry. Beth emailed me that the dinner will be ready at seven. It is ten minutes to." Patricia absolutely hated it when the dinner was late, particularly when she hadn't eaten for a few hours. Once again, it was Andrew who got them in this bind. First, he wanted to come to this God forsaken city to attend the festival of plays by that depressive and depressing Eugene O'Neill. Then he persuaded her to accept the invitation from their college friends, Tom and Beth, to stay with them for the week they planned to be in Playland. Patricia had booked a suite in a downtown hotel and intended to take cabs or to use public transport for local travel. When Beth offered Patricia their basement suite her deaf-to-his-wife's-advice husband cancelled the hotel reservation and insisted on renting a car on their arrival in the strange city. They had to take a shuttle to the car rental building, find the agency, haggle about the rates, decline all kinds of insurance offered in such persuasive tones that they felt churlish refusing the kindness being bestowed upon them. Once they settled in the car, the GPS Andrew had brought with him took for ever to set. Then he missed the exit from the expressway and it was several crucial minutes to the next exit. In total frustration Patricia gave up directing. This was the incentive her vain husband needed and they were soon on the elusive 75th Avenue and arrived at the address only thirty seven minutes late, Patricia hungry and angry; Andrew hungry and relieved.

Beth looked relaxed when she opened the door. She greeted them warmly, showed them their bedroom, the bathroom, kitchenette and the lounge. They watched their step to avoid a wide variety of knick-knacks scattered all over the floor, A settee was the only furniture in the lounge. The bed was unmade with no sheets or blankets in view and Patricia noticed that the shelves and the drawers in the bedroom were full of personal items, those in the kitchenette were bare, as was the counter. Beth was very proud of the 'guest apartment' and assured them, "You will be very comfortable here." Andrew and Patricia readily agreed hoping that Beth would now lead them to her dining table. Alas! This was not to be.

"There is still light. I suggest we go to the lake; it has a marvellous view of the downtown. We pass an organic food store where we can pick up something to eat, unless you have eaten already," Beth said. Patricia managed not to show her surprise and accepted the new invitation with alacrity. Pleased with her guests' response Beth added, "Oh yes. Tom asked me to apologize on his behalf, he has a dinner meeting. Do you mind if my seven-year old, Robbie, comes along?" and shouted in the same breath, "Robbie, let's go to the lake."

When Andrew slowed down for a stop sign Beth said pointing to a corner café, "I know the lady who runs that place. She opens at seven and you are sure to enjoy the breakfast she cooks to order." The store was deserted when they walked in. The guests picked bowls of organic tomato and garlic soup and mixed vegetable wraps while the hostess chose chicken dinner for herself and a burger with coke for Robbie. However, like a true lady of the era gone by she did not wish to offend the honour of the only male in the party by paying for her purchase and Andrew gallantly paid the total bill.

They arrived at the lake just before the dark. The view was indeed splendid and the meal pleasant. Ladies talked about their jobs, forthcoming conventions and Patricia's retirement plans. Robbie had a bite of his burger, took a sip of the coke and sat shivering at the edge of the bench. Andrew, after enjoying his organic dinner, walked to the water's edge to enjoy the shimmering reflection of 'the silver barque in the sea of heaven.'

On their return drive Andrew focused his eyes on the road and ears on Patricia and Beth while Robbie huddled close to his mother. "Are you still free for dinner with us on Thursday?" Patricia asked.

Beth replied, "Yes of course. Tom wants to treat you to dinner. We could go to a Fish and fries restaurant nearby. Believe it or not, the owner imports newspapers from London to serve the fries on."

Patricia demurred, "Andrew has been instructed to watch his weight and fries are a no no. Apart from that, we stopped eating seafood after the last mercury scare."

Beth put the ball in Beth's court, "In that case you could choose the place. It is Tom's treat so don't worry about the cost."

Patricia sent the ball back, "We don't know much about places to eat here. You should decide on one that you like. We can worry about whose treat later."

Beth had another idea, "On second thoughts, we really liked local dishes on our vacation in England last summer. You can get a shepherd's pie in many places here, somehow it is never any good. You are British. Maybe you can show me how to bake a genuine shepherd's pie."

Patricia squirmed noticeably but her innate social sense did not let her down, "Thursday is our only free day and shopping for a foreign dish can be tricky. Let us stick to the restaurant. I will email you a recipe when we are back at home."

So, the restaurant of Tom and Beth's choice it would be. It wasn't long when they were on the driveway. Beth led Patricia and Andrew to the door of the apartment and wished them good night. It was at this point that the lonely cell in Andrew's brain spun a little faster and his mouth opened for the first time, "Where would we find the sheets for the bed?"

"Oh, the sheets. And the towels too, I guess. They must be in the dryer. I will be back in a jiffy," Beth responded. She returned with a pile in her arms and handed slightly damp and crumpled sheets and towels to Patricia, smiled triumphantly and said, "There should be everything you need here," turned and disappeared around the corner.

2

Andrew missed the pleasure of serving morning coffee to Patricia as she crossed over the threshold of dreamland to the land of the living. For their morning jolt they had to get dressed and walk over to the café recommended by Beth. The coffee was strong, just what they needed. "Special grind of Columbian," Andrew pronounced as he inhaled the aroma and took the first sip. They ordered the breakfast, two poached eggs sunny side up with hash browns for Patricia, scrambled eggs and ham and dry whole grain toast for Andrew. While waiting they discussed where to sleep for the rest of their trip. Patricia wanted to revert to her plan and move to the hotel she had booked. Andrew suggested waiting another day before making a decision. He felt that moving out without seeing Tom would be rude. Patricia reluctantly agreed.

They drove to the playhouse and spent the day in lectures about the play, Long Day's Journey into Night - its author, director, artists, real meaning of the plot. Morning was taken with the life and works of Eugene O'Neill. Over lunch Patricia pointed out that in her opinion O'Neill's plays were even darker than the late symphonies of Mahler.

Andrew, not to be outdone by his wife, replied, "Mahler symphonies are a little different, they end with hope or reconciliation"

Patricia, not the one to accept defeat easily, retorted, "Sixth doesn't, neither does the Tenth, so there."

Before returning to the hall they bought coffee, cream and paper cups for their wake-up needs the next morning. The afternoon was all about the play; how the Yale University circumvented playwright's instruction by publishing it three years after his death rather than wait for twenty five, the autobiographical nature of the work about four addicts, great performers of the past in the stage and in the movie productions beginning with the premiere in Sweden in Swedish in 1956; the posthumous Pulitzer prize; the author's fourth; the numerous awards for the performances; clues to hidden meanings in the dialogue and the play's impact on future works. Their minds were full when the session ended a little after six. They were ready for the table Patricia had wisely booked in the dining room at the theatre. They had time to relax with a sherry before a really delicious Beef Wellington with Chianti, followed by peach Melba and Irish coffee. They mused over the change in their circumstances since their first date in faraway Carlisle when they had beans on toast in a hole in the wall before rushing to occupy the cheapest seats far back in the cavernous hall where heads almost touched the ceiling and they had to really concentrate to follow the dialogue.

It was quite late when they returned to the apartment. It was still cluttered and the kitchen was still bare. There was a note from Tom regretting he couldn't see them and he looked forward to treating them for dinner. Beth scribbled below the note that she was hoping to get a last minute ticket for The Iceman Cometh and was looking forward to seeing them during the intermission. "Hope she is lucky. It is always sold out days in advance because the play is difficult to stage and it is not often performed," Patricia commented.

"I have never seen it. I read it in preparation for the trip last month and I am worried that the performance won't live up to what I saw in my imagination," Andrew said.

I have seen it on stage once, have not read it. I am looking forward to the discussions and the performance and it will be nice to hear Beth's views on it," Patricia had the last word.

Just as Andrew opened the door for them to head for breakfast the next morning Beth appeared out of nowhere, barefoot, hair disheveled and wearing a flowery dressing gown, looking eager to see them. After an exchange of good mornings she said in her usual happy tone, "I am so sorry I forgot to mention earlier. I promised the apartment to another friend for the week from Thursday. You are welcome to use the couch in the living room; it unfolds into a comfortable double bed."

Patricia was too polite to let out a sigh of relief. Instead she said, "I am sorry, too. We were enjoying our stay. It is not fair to disrupt your living room. We will move out to a hotel near the theatre today. It will give you time to get the place ready for your next guest."

It was Beth's turn to be relieved, "Are you sure it is not too inconvenient. It will give me time to do the sheets, perhaps vacuum the floor too, no doubt about it. Any way, we are going to treat you for dinner as planned. I know the hotel you mean. We will pick you up from there at six thirty tomorrow. Parking can be difficult in that neighbourhood and we will drive together to the restaurant Tom has already booked. He is so looking forward to meeting you both. Make sure you have your camera, the view of the sunset from their deck is something to behold." They took turn shaking Beth's hand and returned to their room to pack.

Patricia was lining up in the ladies' washroom after the end of Act 1 and Andrew was watching an elderly couple in the early twentieth century costumes promenading arm in arm. His amusement was interrupted by someone calling his name. He turned around to see Beth making her way towards him through the crowd. She had been able to buy a ticket from a hustler at twice the normal price and was happy to be there. She had a giant cup in her right hand, enough coffee to keep her awake for the duration of the play. She was telling him about how busy Tom had been of late and how much he was looking forward to taking them out for dinner when she sensed the whiff of an elderly gentleman passing by. "Oh! He is Dr. Everyman. Patricia would surely want to see him. Watch my coffee. I will return with him in a jiffy." Andrew saw her disappear into the crowd, the cup tottering on a bin nearby. Andrew stood there waiting patiently for her to return with the celebrated doctor till the five minutes bell sounded. Not knowing what else to do, Andrew picked the cup and followed the direction Beth had taken. There she was, about twenty feet way, talking to the elderly gentleman. He handed her the cup and she introduced him to Mr. Nobody, clearly a case of mistaken identity. After elementary pleasantries Andrew made his way to his seat wondering how much an absent-minded individual can get away with if she is confident and has a pleasant manner.

Patricia learnt that the hotel served a complimentary buffet till seven on Thursdays. She called Beth to invite her to come to the hotel around six and have dinner there. Beth replied that Tom was keen to take their old friends out and in any event, he could not leave the work any earlier than six. She must have been right on this score; it was a little after seven when they arrived with Robbie. Tom jumped out of the car and hugged them with great delight. He looked hale and hearty; hard work evidently suited him. They made themselves comfortable in the back seat of Tom's luxurious Lincoln on either side of Robbie who nodded without taking his eyes off from his computer game. "Sorry it is a bit late for the sunset. We have loved the food there and you will have a wonderful evening anyway," Beth said from her perch next to Tom.

They found a good parking spot and Andrew gallantly inserted his card to pay for the parking to make a token contribution to the evening's expenses. It was not clear whether the restaurant had given away the table or had misplaced the reservation. The deck was full and they were led to a booth next to the restrooms. "We should order dinner soon, Robbie has school in the morning," Tom muttered as the waiter was taking drink orders. It was an extensive menu with 57 varieties of seafood and not much else as befits a seaside restaurant. Robbie knew what he wanted without looking at the menu, Tom and Beth made suggestions to their guests on what was good in the scanty offering of salads and the ordering formality was soon over. For the next hour Tom entertained them with the stories from his office and his success in achieving a work/family balance while Robbie sat sullenly looking at his burger and Beth stole adoring glances at her hardworking husband.

Tom took the last sip of his cappuccino and waved to the waiter for the check. It landed in front of Andrew if only because he was next to the aisle while Tom was leaning against the wall looking blankly past the waiter with Robbie sandwiched between them. The bill sat there expecting a move from Tom while the waiter fidgeted. There was no reaction from the supposed host; his eyes still fixed where the starry sky met the darkening ocean. After an uncomfortable lapse of time Andrew picked up the bill, added enough tip to round off the total to two hundred and put down his credit card. There was no reaction from either Tom or Beth. Andrew saw a smile on Patricia's face and wondered if she had anticipated the situation.

Every one stood up as soon as Andrew had entered his pin and walked towards the car. Back at the hotel, Patricia and Andrew thanked Tom and Beth for inviting them to stay in their apartment and for a pleasant evening in the restaurant. After saying goodbye to Robbie who mumbled an inaudible response with eyes glued to the screen they turned towards the door of the hotel. Andrew, reviewing the whole experience in his head, said, "It would have made a classic play in the hands of O'Neill."

"There can be nothing gloomy in a renewal of old friendship. Somerset Maugham would have looked at the humour and made a great story out of it," replied Patricia, having the last word as usual.

Twists and Turns

1. My Aging Body

I

Some of my friends drive, or are driven, long distances and wait for hours to see their doctor. I feel sorry for them for all this time wasted. My doctor is located fifteen minutes at leisurely stroll from our home and she sticks to a tight schedule. I am lucky in another way too. I only need to see her once a year for the annual physical. She is a very pleasant and attractive young lady, young compared to me that is, and it would be nice to see her often. Not in her office and not as her patient though. However, with each passing year the body seems to have more parts that scream for attention and before long my visits to her office are likely to become a more frequent affair.

The receptionist called last Friday to remind me of my appointment with the doctor. It was totally unnecessary of course, the date and time were firmly planted in my mind. When the afternoon rolled around on Monday, I was in fine spirits. I had a great lunch of homemade vegetable soup with wonderful crusty bread baked by a neighbour and had made good progress on the story I am working on. The weather was unseasonably warm, the sun was shining and the birds were chirping. Whistling a well-known Sousa march, I put my boots and coat on, picked up the sports section of the daily paper and walked over to the doctor's office. The nurse came over and led me directly to an examination room. On the way my weight and height were checked. I peeped at the sheet and learnt that I had gained ten

pounds and lost an inch in the year since the last check up. Once in the cubby hole, the kind lady said while closing the door behind her, "Strip down to underwear and wait for the knock."

While struggling to take my pants off I noticed a laminated notice beside the examination table. It said something like this: A check up is just that, a check up. The doctor will listen to minor problems that may have a bearing on the examination, to discuss serious issues patients should make a separate appointment; a separate appointment for each issue please. The knock came when I was wondering where my issues lay in the spectrum of seriousness. Dr. Shepherd entered with a file in her right hand. She broke the ice with the big smile of a woman who knows how attractive she is and said, "How have you been? It is thirteen months since we last met."

It had indeed been over a year although the time had gone fast. I acknowledged it readily, "Yes, it is a long time in between visits. I didn't have any thing seriously wrong, just some niggles. I should really set another appointment to discuss those."

Dr. Shepherd was gracious, "Tell me the more important ones and we can decide whether another consultation is necessary. Before you begin, let me tell you that your tests after the last check up were fine and your weight and height patterns are consistent with your age."

I responded, "I assumed that the test results were satisfactory when I did not hear from your office. I do have some problems though. The biggest one is a cough, like a constant stream from an out of tune amateur orchestra. It annoys my wife no end and she has instructed me to do something about it."

Dr. Shepherd had heard it many times before and had her answer ready, "It is caused by the dry air our city is notorious for. I am sorry I can't do much about it. You can try moving to the coast. If the humidity of the sea air doesn't help your problem could be physical. Till then blame the dry air."

Disregarding the notice I presented the next problem, "I don't think moving is practical at this time and I will have to learn to cough softly.

The next issue is that I get tired rather easily; climbing one flight of stairs makes my breath heavy and my knees wobbly."

Again Dr. Shepherd had her answer ready, "That is an issue of age. When we grow old and reach your age, our joints start showing the wear and tear they have suffered through the years. Again, this is something beyond the doctor's control till it gets much worse. For now you have to bear it, preferably with a grin."

I brought up yet another complaint, "The last issue I want to bring to your attention: My right arm and shoulder ache, more like a muscle pain, not a fracture. I used a muscle relaxant cream and the pain disappeared, only to return a couple of days later."

Dr. Shepherd refused to be stumped, "These are maladies of your age too. It is good that a muscle relaxant helps. I do think that you look much younger than you actually are. Unfortunately, the looks are deceptive in situations like yours. The body is aging all the same and joints and muscles are wearing out. Not much one can do. You have to accept aging as a natural process and be happy that you are doing better than some."

I didn't know how to take this. Was she complimenting me for my appearance, or calling me a crysenior? Either way it was clear that she considered my ailments unimportant, not worth the paper prescriptions are written on. She disregarded my confusion, if she noticed it at all, and said, "Lie side ways facing the wall with knees bent."

I turned over, folded my legs and closed my eyes expecting unpleasantness. She conducted the test with no embarrassment whatever and pronounced her satisfaction with what she felt. Once the glove was off, she scribbled a prescription for blood pressure pills.

"Should last till the next check up" she remarked handing me the tiny sheet and added, "You can now dress up," and left closing the door behind her to protect what was left of my modesty.

On my way out I said hello to Dr. Lamb, Dr. Shepherd's partner who was walking towards her office. After exchanging pleasantries, she told me that she was moving office; didn't quite know where to.

"Dr. Shepherd is retiring and this space is more than a lone doctor needs," she added.

I was surprised because Dr. Shepherd had not mentioned it to me. I resisted the temptation of talking to Dr. Shepherd because her partner may have spoken out of turn. I did ask Dr. Lamb whether she would take me as a patient.

"I do have a full practice and I haven't accepted a new patient for years. I will take you, though, so long as you don't go round telling others," she said in the tone of someone bestowing a great kindness, as she indeed was doing and walked into her office.

I trudged home, my eyes firmly fixed on the muddy ground, sorry that I had lost the doctor of thirty years whose office I could walk to when I needed looking after. Finding a new one so easily was not a consolation since who knows how far her new office would be and how much longer I would be able to drive. My noble wife was at home getting ready to cook dinner when I slumped into a chair. She stopped when she saw my sad face, poured me a cup of tea and heard me out. After a pause she said, "I am glad an experienced and compassionate female doctor accepted you. You could have been stuck with a blasé male doctor straight out of school."

The reminder calmed me. It sure took the bitterness out of the second cup of tea.

2

At first the good wife appreciated my hesitation in carrying stuff up and down the stairs, then her patience wore thin. I had to carry the heavy cases first up and then down, irrespective of how much my knees hurt. When I complained she said with some exasperation, "If the knees are so bad why don't you seek some expert advice. Go and see a physiotherapist. There is an experienced group in the shopping plaza.

My Aging Body

After the doctor's brush off, the advice did not make sense; after all it was from a spouse with self-interest who did not want to take over any more housework than she already had. Doesn't matter, I have learnt after fifty years of wedded bliss that it saves unpleasantness to do what I am told. That is why I was in the reception area of Mountain View Physiotherapy. After the mandatory wait of twenty five minutes Phoebe, a not so young lady, walked in exuding competence, greeted me with a well rehearsed smile and led me to a cubbyhole equipped with a raised single bed and two stools. She listened to my troubles with the stairs and asked, "Do your knees hurt when you are coming down as well?"

"Yes they do," I replied.

"Both?"

"The one which is landing. The other leg is O.K."

"About the same, up or down?"

"As I said, it is sporadic. It is not on every step, once in a while and without any warning. That is what makes it so unnerving."

She handed me a pair of khaki shorts and told me to change into them. She was back in fifteen minutes, enough time to read all the notices on the walls about what is expected of the 'clients.' She pressed around my knees and thighs, asked me to lie down on my stomach and felt around my hips. She led me to the hallway and watched me walk. Back in the cubbyhole, she sat on the stool facing me and gave me her diagnosis. "It is just as I suspected," she said. After a pause to add to my suspense she continued, "It is rarely the knees. It is generally the muscles around the hips that grow soft and the pressure they should be bearing is transferred to the knees. I will teach you two exercises which should help. If they work, I will give you two more next week. If my assessment is correct, you will be carrying the globe up and down the stairs."

Although mythology is all Greek to me, Phoebe gave me hope. I paid attention to how the exercises had to be done, repeated them to her satisfaction and noted in my diary – ten each side three times a day. I thanked her profusely, walked over to the receptionist, paid the bill, only $175, and prepared to leave. But I was not done yet. "Do you need another appointment?" The workman-like lady asked.

"Oh yes, next week," I replied, her attention focused on the screen of her computer.

"Phoebe is here on Tuesday, Thursday and Friday. There are some free spots on the first two of these days."

"The afternoon of Thursday will suit me fine," I said. I wanted to cram on as much exercise as possible before seeing Phoebe again.

I added these new exercises to the regimen I already followed to keep the aches and pains of old age at some distance, if not quite as far as the bay. My knees were no better for the first few days, then the pain reduced a little and became marginally less frequent. Phoebe took the good news in her stride, apparently she was used to being right. She gave me two more exercises to add to the previous two. These were to be done twenty times for each knee three times a day. Again, I repeated them till she was satisfied, thanked her and left. The receptionist gave me the receipt and a date three weeks later.

Being an obedient person, as a spouse and as a patient, I did all four twists and turns three times a day. My hip muscles started shouldering their responsibilities and my knees stopped misbehaving. Almost, that is. There were times, not just on the stairs, when they complained. Often bitterly, albeit only once in a rare while. I pointed this out to Phoebe in what turned out to be the last appointment. She asked me what other strenuous activity I did. I said rather proudly that I did three kilometres a day on a stationary bike every morning. "Reduce the tension on the bike and see if it makes any difference," she suggested.

I continued the exercise regimen even though it took a large part of my day. I reduced the tension on the bike too. My knees still had the tendency to ache. Then Dame Fortune intervened.

I had to pick up Asha, our granddaughter, at the airport one morning. I was in too much of a rush to do the bike part of the morning routine. I also had to skip the bike for the three days she was in town. On the way to the airport for the flight to take Asha back home, I realized that my knees had not hurt during her visit. Over dinner that evening I said to my wife, "Thanks for suggesting the physio. It certainly helped."

"I wish you listened to me more often. My suggestions are not made lightly," she replied with a note of grievance.

"You are right, I should pay more attention to you," I acknowledged and added, "After I followed the physio's excellent advice, there was still some occasional pain. It disappeared too when I didn't have time for the bike over the last three days. Do you think I should give up the bike altogether?"

"Stop for a while to see if it helps. I will find you some similarly strenuous jobs in the meantime." As always the wise one knew what her declining husband needed.

2. Mishap on a Business Trip

I

Poor David! He married Diane when they were students, she doing law and he engineering. They settled in a large home in an upscale community suitable for their future station in life. After graduation, she articled with the top legal firm in Windsor and became a star in highly remunerative criminal defense department of the practice. He, on the other hand, applied to every likely employer in the city, with no luck. On the rare occasions he was called for an interview, he was told that he was too academic to work in a practical profession. Two years went by and his frustration reached such a level that he began applying for jobs in Alberta's oil sands. This scared Diane for two reasons. First, she did not want a weekend husband - after working eighteen-hour days it was nice to come home to a bed warmed up by a loving man even though he was unemployed and disgruntled. Second, and even more important, why would an ethical man, particularly the husband of someone in such a noble profession as hers, want to support an industry which was the root-cause of the climate induced catastrophes all over the world?

Then fortune smiled on one not so brave. A colleague informed Diane that a local manufacturer of small parts for the motor vehicle industry had come up for sale. The owner was retiring. His children were happy in their secure government jobs with guaranteed inflation-proof pensions and did not want the headaches of owning a cyclical business. As soon as she arrived home that night Diane told David of the golden opportunity. Pointing her index finger towards him, as she did while addressing a witness in the courtroom, she said, "This is a chance you must grasp with both hands. Go to the owner. Use the skills in your trading family genes to negotiate the deal. Follow up with the banks and see how much they will advance. I think mom can be persuaded to get dad to help if need be."

It was thus that David became a factory owner in partnership with his father-in-law. For a couple of years things went well. Then the recession hit. People stopped buying SUVs and the sales tanked. At first the profits shrank, then the red ink started to spill. Soon the business was barely meeting the payroll. New contracts were needed before the situation became so dire that it had to be disclosed to his father-in-law.

Dame fortune smiled again. David heard of someone across the border who was looking for parts similar to what David's plant made. If investment in new equipment was required, the bank could be persuaded to help once the contract was assured. David had a meeting with his sales manager about the best strategy and they decided that Marilyn should be sent for an exploratory meeting with the prospect. Marilyn was a promising young saleswoman. She was tall and slender, with blue eyes and shoulder length blonde hair in which she took a great pride. She was in her early thirties married to an older man who had lost his fortune in the stock market collapse. Both of them knew that she needed her job just to get by, let alone live in the style of only a few months ago.

David explained to Marilyn her mission, "The purpose of your visit is to find out the size of the project and to impress on the prospect how keen we are to help him, without revealing our desperate situation of course. Not only your job, everyone's in this operation, mine included, depends on us getting this contract. No holds barred; do whatever it takes to impress on him how eager we are to meet his needs."

2. Mishap on a Business Trip

"Did I hear you right? You said 'no holds barred, do whatever it takes!'"

"Yes, that is what I said. I am sure you understand what it means."

"I understand very well," Marilyn said with a smile. David did not notice the sparkle in her eyes. The opportunity to use her charms always excited her.

2

Marilyn crossed the border without much hassle although an orange from Florida and grapes from California were confiscated by the U.S. border guards to prevent whatever bugs they carried from re-entering the Land of the Pure. She arrived at her destination, checked into a three star motel and called the purchasing manager of the prospect. He was very receptive to her suggestion of a meeting and proposed a rendezvous at a bar near her motel at six after he had reviewed the files of possible suppliers.

Marilyn dressed to impress a prospective client: light make- up, hair brushed back to fall on her shoulders, skirt just above the knees, blouse pretending to cover her ample bosom and moderately high heels. She walked over to the bar a few minutes late to avoid an unladylike wait, or the client cooling his heels for too long. As she approached the door a short, rather plump balding man in an ill-fitting blue suit, white shirt and no tie walked over, extended his right hand and said, "Marilyn, good to see you. Call me Harry. I am standing in for the purchasing manager who had a car accident last week and is out of commission for a few months. Let us go in and discuss what we can do for each other over a drink or two."

Marilyn ordered red wine and Harry asked for a gin and tonic. His idea of conversation was to lecture about the general economy, curse governments at every level for high taxes just to support good-for-nothing welfare bums on cocaine and for not supporting with grants the industries that employ workers. "Bad government; that is what caused the stock market collapse," he said hitting the table with his fist. This touched a raw nerve in Marilyn and her countenance became less business like and more like that of a date. For dinner, he chose a twelve-ounce tartar steak with a baked potato; she decided on Moroccan lamb and they shared a bottle of vintage Shiraz. Over the meal Marilyn told Harry what her company could do for him. "We don't really have a satisfactory bid for the job. It seems to be yours, if you frame the proposal right," Harry said looking with glazed eyes through her blouse while rubbing her calf under the table with his. She understood what the right frame of the proposal was. "Let us go to my room and finish off this conversation over a glass of champagne," she said with a smile.

It didn't take long for them to finish the champagne they had picked up from the motel bar and to end up in bed giggling like teenagers. Just when Harry was trying to position himself the lamp on the bedside table tumbled over. Who knocked it, if anyone indeed did, is beside the point. What matters is the mishap. The lamp fell on Marilyn's face, the bulb shattered and shards of glass embedded in her cheeks. As luck would have it, a maid happened to be passing by the room. She heard the clatter and rushed into the room. One look at the bloodied face was enough for her to call 911. Soon Marilyn was on her way to hospital and Harry was answering harsh questions of a police officer.

It was long past midnight when Marilyn returned to the hotel with one cheek covered with bandages and the other swollen. She told the night desk person to tell the manager to call her when he came in the next morning. It was a relief that the maid had cleaned the room and changed the bed linen. She took a sleeping pill and went to bed wondering what had happened to Harry.

The harsh ring of the phone woke Marilyn with a start from the sleep of the drugged. It was the manager apologizing for the accident. The radio clock showed 9:17. "We need to talk, could we meet in the cafeteria at ten," she said in a drowsy voice that did not reveal the anger she felt. Her face hurt although not as much as the disappointment of the contract slipping through her fingers. The manager knew he had a hot potato in his hands and readily agreed. She showered gingerly, put on a business suit and called Harry. He was out and she left him a message to meet her for lunch in the same bar. She postponed calling her husband, or David till after breakfast and took the elevator down to the lobby. A well-dressed middle-aged man came out from an office behind the reception desk and introduced himself, "I am Jack, manager of the hotel." They shook hands and he continued, "I heard about the accident last night and I am very sorry about it. I do hope that the injuries are not as bad as they appear and there will be no scars."

Marilyn did not respond and they walked in silence to the almost empty cafeteria. Jack led her to the plastic table in the far corner that was set with knives, forks and paper napkins for four diners. A young waitress with flowery plastic apron covering her short skirt came over with a steaming pot. Marilyn accepted coffee and ordered two poached eggs on muffins without looking at the menu and Jack asked for green tea. Marilyn now replied to Jack, "Only time will tell how bad it is. It does hurt in many places. They gave me a sleeping pill so I could sleep. I will have to get the bandages replaced before I drive home. Most likely there will be some scars. I will need some medical advice on how to handle those. My lawyer will call you after all the damage has been determined."

If this perturbed Jack, he did not show it. He replied in the friendly tone he had greeted her with, "I have talked to the maid and had housekeeping look at the remnants of the lamp to find what could have gone wrong. They think that the lamp was knocked over in a tussle on the bed. What happens in a room is none of our business and there is no reason for us to mention it to anyone. We are happy to absorb the cost of the lamp and the clean up. We will even discount the room rate to half. However, if further claims are made against the hotel, the owners have told me to make it clear that, sorry though they are for your injuries, circumstances of the accident will have to be revealed in court and they may not reflect well on a happily married woman."

Marilyn knew that she had lost the argument and had to save face, "Whether the case goes to court or is settled amicably is for the lawyers to decide. I am glad we know where we both stand. I do thank you for your time. I have some urgent business. I hope you will let me keep the room till early afternoon."

She went to the room and called her husband. She told him that she slipped and fell while carrying a glass of water in the room and hurt her face. "Nothing to worry now, I have been patched up by the experts," she told him with a laugh. Fortunately for her, the line was poor and he did not suspect the false note.

Next, she called David. She told him all about the conversation with Harry, the good vibes she was getting and the accident. She told him about the injuries, visit to the hospital and the possible scars on her face. "You need to think how I can be compensated for the injuries I have suffered on this trip for you," she warned before putting the phone down.

When Marilyn entered the bar Harry was sharing a joke with another man near the entrance. He was dressed in the same clothes as the previous evening. His laughter turned into anxious look when he saw her bandaged face, "Does it hurt? How many stitches did you need? Will it leave scars? Will you be able to drive home?" The enquiries came thick and fast. She assured him that it looked worse than it was and she would be fine in a few days. He then apologized for not going to the hospital, the police held him back for questioning to make sure there was no criminal intent. Following the doctor's instruction to stay away from alcohol she ordered coffee and Harry did the same. Over lunch he told her that she had a very good chance of landing the contract and expressed the hope that they would see each other again to toast future deals in his apartment.

The good news cheered Marilyn and she hummed gay melodies from Die Fliedermaus all the way to the hospital. There was more good news. The wounds were healing well and the swelling had gone down too. She took a pain-relief pill at the hotel before taking off. The drive home was reasonable even though other drivers annoyed her and the music on the radio was somewhat insipid.

3

The next morning Marilyn told her boss the good news. Then she walked to David's office at the far end of the corridor. He had already heard from Harry and congratulated her heartily on doing a great job. "Sit down and tell me the whole story. First, tell me how you managed to mangle your face and how bad it is," David had a broad smile on his face.

"It doesn't hurt too much; I am taking pain-killers. It will be a week before the bandages are off. I told my husband that I slipped in the room while carrying a glass. That is not true. The truth is, and the manager of the motel, Jack is his name, will confirm if my word is not enough, that clumsy Harry knocked the lamp down when getting over me in bed and the bulb broke on my face. The pain is bad; however, it will be gone in a week. The scars on my face will be there for the rest of my life. I have an appointment with an injury claim lawyer this afternoon. He believes you are responsible for compensation because I was on business," Marilyn's reply wiped the smile off David's face.

"I never said you have to take Harry to bed. I would never expect that from any of my workers. It would be immoral as well as illegal to suggest such a thing," David was obviously upset.

"You said 'no holds barred, do whatever it takes.' It became clear as a bell that going to bed was what Harry needed for you to get the contract. I have delivered. Now it is your turn."

"Look, the company does not carry insurance for liability for bed activities on a business trip. No one in the world would insure that. I am sorry for you and I will work with you to get fair compensation.

This business of lawyers doesn't help. If you go to court, the truth will come out and it will be embarrassing, to say the least."

"What is a fair compensation? How do you work it out? There are medical bills for treatment and for removing the scars after the face is healed. There is pain I am going through. There are weeks I will be away from work. Not to mention the guilt of lying to my husband. How can you compensate for these things with a few filthy dollars?"

"No I can't. It does help to have the medical bills covered and have some cash to go to Las Vegas when you are recovering from the operation. I have an idea for you to consider."

"The best idea will be for you to pay my bills, give me paid medical leave for the time I need and treat my recovery trips to Monaco as a business expense."

"It is not a bad idea. The only problem is that the company is going through hard times. It is much more realistic to apply to the Workers' Compensation Board. After all you were on business and they are much less fussy than insurance companies and just as generous. What do you think?"

"Surely they will not cover the 'bed activities' as you call them. And they will broadcast my name all over the world."

"Perhaps they will. I can talk to the local chief of the board. She is my partner at the bridge club. She would be more sympathetic to your predicament than a man would be. She will help us if she can and tell me off the record if she can't."

"OK, talk to her so long as it is confidential. She will have to know the full details, I suppose. That will be acceptable only if she can hide my name. Better yet, use an assumed name in your initial enquiries."

"Of course. Your name will appear on the final application for the first time and only if she can hide your identity from snoopy eyes. Do we have a deal?"

"Yes we have a deal. If your friend doesn't help we will be back at square one."

"Let us hope she can. I will pray as ardently as I did for your success."

"Hopefully your next prayer will be better for my well being than the last one was."

The prayer worked. David's partner came through and the board compensated Marilyn to her satisfaction. The increase in premiums was insignificant compared to new business. And Marilyn returned with a new bloom every time she went to iron out the details with Harry.

3. THIRD TIME LUCKY

I

A good writer of fiction picks characters from somewhere deep in his psyche and blows life into them before they are presented to the reader. I have done that in my past stories with some success and many failures. For this one, I have selected someone I knew, not intimately but well enough to vouch for the facts. I followed her progress through the years because the events in her life fascinated me, not because I admired her. It seems to me that her life has reached a point where it can be presented to the discerning observers of human frailties and strengths just as she lived it and without elaboration.

Having been brought up in a part of rural Alberta where French influence was still strong, I fell in love with Paris on my first visit. I take every opportunity to go to the city of Louvre, Eiffel Tower, Notre Dame and glorious food in reasonably priced establishments. One of my recent visits was prompted by an invitation from Claude, scion of a prominent Quebec family, who managed the clan's European business. He wished to acquire the movie rights for my story on the tragic love of Hector Berlioz and Harriet Smith that blossomed when the young composer was working on his first symphony. On his suggestion, we met for dinner at the Ritz, a haunt of the rich and famous. Claude adored Berlioz and loved Symphonie Fantastique and the terms of our deal were agreed upon during the aperitif and the soup. We were now discussing nothing in particular while waiting for the main course to arrive. It was early in the evening, the dining room had many empty tables and in spite of a rather good orchestra playing romantic serenades there were no more than three or four couples on the dance floor. Our table had a good view of the dancers and neither of us was averse to admiring beautiful women even though they were in the arms of other men. One particular couple attracted Claude and he discretely directed me to them. "The old gentleman is Count Vishnovski. He owns several vineyards in Alsace and his palace in Strasbourg is renowned for its collection of Monets and Picassos. He has extensive business interests in the U.K. too and divides his time between France and England. He recently lost his wife of forty years to cancer. I don't know the young lady, perhaps one of many who would love to alleviate the grief of the Count."

I looked closely at the partner. The count held her tightly, cheek to cheek and her face was in the shade. "Flaming red hair, hazel eyes, protruding chin, aquiline nose, pink lips, could she be Charlene?" I wondered. Then the couple turned and the face caught the light and I became certain that my suspicion was correct. I told Claude I knew the lady, adding, "An interesting story goes with her. Some day I will set it down and offer you the first rights."

"Tell me the story. I have no other appointment and I suspect you don't have a friend waiting for you either. If it is as good as you say, maybe the lawyers can prepare one contract for both," Claude's interest was piqued.

"I see the waiter heading for our table and the Count leading his lady to one on the other side of the floor. I will collect my thoughts over Coquille St. Jacques and relate the story over brandy without the fear of pricking the ear of my protagonist."

Claude agreed, "Yes, we should enjoy our dinner. The chef of Ritz is acknowledged the best in Europe."

2

Before taking up writing as my main occupation, I was employed by Hardie Engineering, a small company that built roads and bridges in Southern Alberta. The company was owned by Duane Hardie who was a well-respected engineer though he had focused on securing jobs over last several years. The company directly employed four working engineers, four draftspersons, two accountants, an office manager and a secretary and also engaged several subcontractors. As the office manager, I was responsible for the daily operation of the office, hiring junior staff and solving personnel and contract problems. A fair bit of my time was spent listening to the personal grievances of the female staff and helping them cope with them. I hired Charlene soon after she had immigrated from Britain partly because the provincial government helped with her salary for the first year. She could operate a calculator and appeared keen to learn the book keeping. The accountant was desperate for help and agreed to train her after a long interview. Charlene was a quick learner as well as a friendly sort and became quite popular in our small office.

Duane Hardie – call me Duane – was a widower in his sixties. He was a tall, muscular and affable man with dark hair and a tanned complexion. He had six children in their twenties and thirties. Two older sons ran the six hundred hectare farm in Central Alberta which had been in the family for three generations. They grew canola, wheat and barley, and collected royalties from six prolific oil wells on the property. Duane lived alone in a six bedroom mansion in a suburb with the lake access and a view of the mountains. His long time cook and maid had stayed on although there was not much for them to do. There were a couple of boats moored on the lake. Duane enjoyed being on the water to watch the reflection of the sun going down behind the mountains.

Hardie Engineering held a summer barbecue at the owner's beach every year. Usually this was a staid affair. The families of employees and some key clients were invited. The cook barbecued steaks, some rare, many medium and a few well-done. There were hamburgers and hot dogs for the kids. The maid served the drinks - Canadian wines and local beer, which was quite good - for adults and a variety of juices for the kids. There was no hard liquor and only rarely did anyone get tipsy on too much beer. This year turned out to be an exception.

Charlene was the last guest to arrive. She apologized to Duane for being late, the cab driver was new to the area she told him and moved away to introduce herself to the wife of the accountant. Duane couldn't take his eyes off her and for a good reason. Charlene did not strike her colleagues as an exceptional beauty in the office, although her figure was admired by male associates even in the conservative clothes she wore at work. As if to surprise us, she had dressed to kill for the party. She wore a not-too-tight, dark-green dress which displayed the good points of her figure without looking vulgar and high heels even though it was an outdoor event. Her eyebrows were trimmed and not one of her brighter than usual red hairs was out of place. A red sapphire necklace drew attention to her attractive bosom. What captivated us all was the perfection of her make up. She could have been a star at a red carpet extravaganza.

Charlene took a glass of red wine from the silver tray and sipped elegantly while conversing with other guests. I admired her composure and thought that she looked more like the hostess of a party for the nobility than a guest at her employer's outdoor party. Duane was mostly busy with the client guests, still his eyes found Charlene every so often, then moved away with obvious reluctance.

It was about two hours after our arrival when we sat down at picnic tables covered with white cloths embroidered with red roses and green leaves. There was prime Alberta steak done to our taste, baked potato with sour cream and chives, steamed baby carrots and zucchini. Our glasses were filled to the regulation two-thirds. In a break with the tradition of these barbecues Charlene stood up when the dinner was being served, picked up her glass and proposed a toast. "To our host, his continued good health and to his success in all his ventures," she said loud enough for every one to hear and not so loud as to be unpleasant to the ear. Every one shouted, "To our host," and sipped from their glass. Even the children joined in with their juice glasses. Duane said, "Thank you Charlene, thank you all," without standing up.

There was some moving around before the dessert. A client family of four joined me and I was surprised to see Charlene heading for our table. The glass in her hand was shaking and spilling the wine and she held it at a distance from her body. I attributed the unsteady walk to high heels and the lawn, though I soon knew better. "How are you enjoying the party?" she asked the ten-year old boy as she sat down next to him. "Fine," the boy answered gruffly and turned to talk to his mother. Charlene smiled as if that is what she expected from boys that age and we exchanged greetings. She had her glass filled again and skipped the pistachio ice cream, "Perhaps because it clashes with her dress," I thought. To be fair though, the fruit plate with slices of mango and lychees did not really need the garnish.

The parents decided not to wait for coffee, said goodbye to us and left. Most other families departed as well. That left the two of us on the table. Irish coffee was offered which I declined and Charlene accepted. For a few glorious moments I sat still looking at the beams of light reflecting on the water, enjoying the warm evening with a gentle breeze from the lake, chirping of crickets and hum of other conversations which had a rhythm of music from time immemorial. Charlene sipped from her cup, deep in thought. The liquor in the coffee tipped the balance and she lost her normal restraint. After the maid had collected the cup she moved to sit next to me at a respectable distance. "It has been a long drop from Lady Cornflower to a bookkeeper in a two-bit outfit," she said almost in a whisper.

"I am sorry to hear that. You can share it with me, it won't go any further," I encouraged her.

"It is a long story. Stop me when you get bored," Lady Cornflower was being unduly modest.

"You are whipping up my curiosity," I replied.

"It is an unusual story and you may not believe it," she said and related an amazing story.

3

It goes back ten years. In those days in Britain if a university gave you a place, a government grant to cover the living expenses of students from low-income families went with it. Just as well because that was the only way I could do it. My father worked for the Post Office sorting mail and my mother was a homemaker looking after six children. No way could they help. Thanks to good grades in school, I was accepted to study English literature at Swansea.

Swansea is located on the southwest tip of Wales and has a population of about two hundred thousand people. Dylan Thomas was born there and called it an "ugly, lovely town." The first year there was fun. I shared with one other girl a cheap, but clean flat, what you call apartment, in an old, red-brick building within a three-penny bus ride to almost anywhere I wanted to go. The workload was not cumbersome; in fact the assigned reading was mostly what I would have read on my own. Some or other student held a party in their place every Friday evening, often with drugs – usually marijuana and rarely cocaine, nothing serious like LSD. I didn't have much spare cash and escaped becoming addicted although I do enjoy a joint once in a while.

It was in the second year that all hell broke loose. Bryn was a quiet guy, very good looking even in sloppy clothes and could be irresistibly charming when he wished to be. All through the first year, he was very keen on Mathilda, a beauty always dressed elegantly and driven everywhere in a chauffeured Jaguar. In spite of the obvious differences in demeanour, and perhaps means, they were often seen smooching in dark corners at the parties.

On the second day of the second year my roommate came in very excited, "You won't believe what Glenda told me."

"What did you hear?" I asked.

"Mathilda has dumped Bryn."

"Why would she do that? They were such a handsome couple," I asked the obvious question.

"Glenda heard that they went to Mount Snowdon for a weekend. Bryn tried to take advantage of Mathilda in the hotel and she told him where to go."

"Some thing more must have happened behind the scene. I always sensed that Mathilda was inciting Bryn."

"Maybe so. It is over all the same. I wonder who is going to be Mathilda's next victim."

"I am sure there is a queue of boys hoping for a ride in the Jaguar. It is Bryn I am sorry for," I said, pouring hot water in the tea cups.

A few days later, I needed a break after the Medieval English class and went to the cafeteria in the basement. I picked up a slice of apple pie to go with the coffee and walked over to the table where Bryn was sitting alone. "Do you mind if I join you?" I asked.

"Please do, Charlene. How was summer?" He pointed to the chair opposite.

"The summer was relaxing. Helped mother with the gardening, played with the siblings, made a few shillings looking after the neighbours' kids when their parents were busy. Not much happens in our part of the country," I said adding milk to the coffee and asked out of courtesy, "How about you?"

"My summer was interesting too, apart from usual lectures from my mother on how I am expected to appear in public. Went to several summer festivals, spent a fortnight with grandparents and, oh yes, had a disastrous weekend with Mathilda in Snowdon," Bryn told me of his summer.

The way Bryn said it made me think that he had recovered from any hurt he had felt and that he wanted to tell his side of the dispute. "Do you want to share what happened, or keep it bottled up," I asked, perhaps with some scorn.

"There is not much to tell. We met in the car park at the foot of the mountain. It was a fine day, not a cloud to be seen. It was a pleasant four-mile hike up. It is not a difficult hike and we were on top in a little more than two hours. The views of the surrounding countryside on the way up and at top were breathtaking. After a little lovers' stroll with arms around the waist we sat down on a rock and enjoyed the tea and cheese and ham sandwiches I had carried in my backpack. The walk down was easy and we were at the hotel in time for afternoon tea. It was then that I discovered that she had booked only one room and in my name. I was surprised. 'Isn't it a bit premature?' I asked.

"'You have been biting my neck and my lips for a year and now when there is an opportunity to cement our love, you ask if it is premature. Make up your mind. Is it premature? Is it? Answer me!' She asked and the lobby went deadly quiet.

"'It maybe a bit early,' slipped out of my mouth. She picked up her handbag, swung hitting me across the face. Before I had recovered my composure she was gone."

"It is a little different from what.I heard through the rumour mill. I am sorry for you. I am sure you will get over it," I said consolingly.

"Well, I don't worry about what people say. Life will go on," Bryn said philosophically.

Next time I met Bryn he asked me if I would go out to a movie with him. He wanted to see an artsy film by an Indian director with a name neither of us could pronounce. Although that was not quite my interest, I agreed thinking that it would help him recover from his heartbreak, although he tried not to show it. We went for a beer after the movie and parted company with a wave. After the third date he kissed me, with some passion I thought. Apparently he had learnt from his affair with Mathilda; by Christmas we were making love. I missed my period in February, the pregnancy was confirmed the next month and Bryn insisted that we get married at a registry office two weeks later.

3. Third Time Lucky

My parents were almost relieved by the sudden turn of events especially because my wedding did not cost them anything. Bryn's family had a different reaction and for a very good reason. I had thought from his appearance that we were from similar backgrounds; the truth was revealed when the ink on the certificate was still wet. Bryn was the grandson of Lord Cornflower and next in line to inherit the title and the property that went with it. That explained why Mathilda was so keen to tie him down. He was "invited to visit Llangollen at the earliest convenience to provide them the pleasure of meeting the bride." When we arrived at the imposing castle his mother was there too. Bryn explained the circumstances and stated clearly that it was at his insistence that we had married in such a hurry. I must say that they were very kind to me and I was assured that my well-being was in good hands. However, our student days were over. From that day on we were to start preparing for the responsibilities that go with the title.

A maid was hired to attend on me full time. A whole new wardrobe suited for my new station was ordered. A fashion consultant advised me on proper attire for different occasions, appropriate make up and hair styles. One of Bryn's childhood tutors returned to teach me the manners a lady is expected to have, from how to hold a tea cup to how to respond to curtsies. Only my walk in high heels as well as in-house shoes met with general approval. The concentrated effort was not in vain. I was playing the role of the next Lady Cornflower with panache before the waters broke.

My life was a dream for next five years. Bryn was a wonderful husband, his mother and grandparents were reconciled to their daughter-in-law from a lowly working class family and doted on Charles, our son, who the lord wished to be named after Prince of Wales. I did not get much opportunity to see my parents or siblings. To be honest, I did not miss them.

Then the disaster struck. Charles had an accident when he was learning to ride. Bryn did not like my idea of learning on a pony, that was for sissies. His son had to learn on a proper horse. Well, the proper horse bolted, knocked down the trainer and stepped on Charles. The loss of his son unhinged Bryn. Although he defended himself, I think he felt in his heart that he was to be blamed in some way for the death. At first we had minor quarrels. These escalated into arguments about inconsequential matters and then turned into screaming matches. His family took his side and blamed me for behaving like the 'English trash.' When I told Bryn about my decision to leave him, the family solicitor made it clear that although I had no legal claim for support, Bryn would make one thousand pounds available after I had signed the documents renouncing all claims against him and the family.

4

"It is a moving story. Thanks for sharing it with me," I said.

"The fall from a lady to the tramp is greater than the rise from a commoner to the lady was," said Charlene dabbing her eyes. Then she tried to stand up and lost her balance. The host happened to be heading towards us at that moment. He saw the stumble and her wet face, and assumed that she was drunk. As any good host would in these circumstances, he insisted that Charlene stay the night and guided her to the guest room.

Charlene started being late to work on Mondays, arriving at the same time as Duane. Then she started having lunch with him. Six months later she was pregnant. Still the routine of being on time all week except Monday continued. The accountant was worried that Charlene would take his job if she became Mrs. Hardie and others gossiped about the younger Hardies not being pleased with the prospect and placing all sorts of obstructions to the ringing of the wedding bells. I listened to everything others told me without letting out a word about Lady Cornflower or her downfall. Then I received a note from Charlene inviting me for dinner at a modest restaurant on a Thursday evening.

We met at six thirty. Charlene was dressed informally in the clothes she had on at work earlier and had not even refreshed her make up. We ordered a half bottle of red wine between us to go with our dinner of onion soup and haddock and chips. Then she asked me the question I was afraid she would ask since receiving the note, "Duane wants us to get married before the child is born. His kids want their share of the property before I and the child have legal rights to it. I am in a quandary. What do you think I should do?"

It was my turn to be in a quandary. I did not want to lose my job by suggesting something that could upset my employer. I did feel sorry for Charlene, even though the similarity of events leading to her pregnancies had struck me. I hoped the best for her in the circumstances without getting involved myself. The only way was to pass the buck to more qualified hands. "Have you considered hiring a law firm?" I asked after a brief pause.

She sipped from her glass and let the words gel in her mind before answering, "I have not thought of it. I think Duane will be offended if I engage one. He and his kids have separate lawyers representing them and I believe he thinks his lawyer speaks for me too."

"Perhaps he does. However, one representing you alone maybe helpful in fighting off the opposition. You are engaging him to protect you, not to fight Duane," I suggested.

"I will think it over and ask Duane before I see anyone. Do you know a good lawyer who doesn't cost an arm and a leg?" Charlene asked.

"It is a good idea to mention it rather casually if you can do it while emphasizing that it is likely to help him," I repeated my advice in different words. Then I scribbled the name of a legal practice that handled negotiations of a personal nature and handed it to her adding, "If you decide to engage one, their number is in the phone book."

Charlene eventually engaged the firm I had suggested. The wheeling and dealing carried on till two days after her due date. The wedding took place within hours of the documents being signed and Charlene was rushed to hospital halfway through the reception.

Charlene stayed home to look after the baby boy. The accountant kept his job and found a good replacement, an older woman with brown hair and bookkeeping experience. Duane did not suspect my role in the affair and I stayed in his employ for another two years.

5

Charlene had another boy after eighteen months. It was about this time that three of my stories were published in respected journals and attracted the attention of two agents, one in Toronto and the other in London, England. When I showed them some of my unpublished work, both recommended that I worked full time in preparing a collection they could show to publishers. I followed their advice and "Tales from Timbuktu" came out a year later to much acclaim and sold well enough for me to write full time.

I lost touch with Charlene. However, Duane and Charlene often cropped up during conversation in occasional meetings with my former colleagues from Hardie Engineering, I did not believe all I heard and certainly some of it was malicious gossip. It was probably true that both sons had health problems and were a source of great anxiety to parents. You have to wonder how someone would have found out that Duane was no longer able to satisfy Charlene's physical needs and that he looked the other way to her trysts with Rod, son of his long term maid. I also had difficulty in believing that Charlene had persuaded Duane to put on the market his beloved mansion on the lake where he had lived for thirty years and that they were building an even bigger home on a hilltop with an indoor pool, games rooms and an apartment for the nurse who looked after the kids. The palace was to have balconies where they could enjoy the views of the sunset over the Rocky Mountains and, in the winter, of the sunrise behind the towers in the downtown.

A few months ago, after I had been a full-time writer for five years, the publisher planned a reading from my first novel in a conference room at the Central Library. When I walked on the stage I saw that at least two hundred people had gathered there. The audience reacted positively and book sales were brisk. I was surprised, as I always am when my work is accepted by the public. A much bigger surprise was in store for me that afternoon.

I was talking to a few ladies about the state of Canadian Literature when my eyes wandered over to a gaunt man with a familiar face standing a few feet away and watching me. I invited him to join in. He stepped closer and said, "I don't wish to interrupt your conversation on a very interesting topic and I will be brief. You don't recognize me because I have lost a lot of weight and gained several years since we last met. I am Duane Hardie."

I contained my surprise as much as possible. "It has indeed been too long," I said and added, "Let's meet in the Lobby Café of the Four Seasons Hotel across the street in fifteen minutes and exchange notes. We have so much news to share."

Duane was waiting on a sofa with its back to the traffic. He had a glass of clear liquid in his hands and a half empty bottle on the coffee table in front of him when I joined him. "Vodka?" he asked.

"No thanks. I am always hungry after these dos, I need some food," I said picking the menu from the table. A cute girl in a short skirt, tight sweater and brown, shoulder length hair appeared from nowhere. I asked for chicken fingers and fries with a pot of tea. Then I turned to my former boss, "How is Charlene?"

"I don't know. She left me last year and I have only heard from her through the lawyers. I believe she has returned to England and is living in a suburb of London," Duane replied in a subdued voice.

"I would have thought she would stay around for the sake of children. They must miss you, even if she doesn't"

"Children are with me, she didn't want to have anything to do with them. They have health problems and need a lot of attention."

"I thought you were such a wonderful couple. I am so sorry for you both."

Duane paused for a long sip, looked at me as if appealing for sympathy, "We had a good relationship for a while. After the birth of our second child she became very demanding. She couldn't live in the home I had shared with my former wife and we built something like a Welsh castle on a forty-acre plot. Then I couldn't satisfy her in bed and she started sleeping with the maid's son. I looked the other way for a while. It came to a head when she accused me of sleeping with the maid. 'Look in the mirror before accusing me of what you are doing,' I told her with some heat.

,"I won't have an old good for nothing man shouting at me. Calm down and apologize on your knees if you want me to stay with you,' she demanded."

"I was in no mood to give in and at that moment it did not matter whether she left or stayed. She packed her personal items in three suitcases and left the next day. A week later I heard from her lawyer who had represented her in our wedding negotiations. She wanted a divorce and half of Hardie Engineering according to the prenup agreement we had signed," Duane smiled as he said it.

His smile made me curious. I asked, "A company with that kind of revenue must be worth millions. Did you sell it or bring in a partner?"

Duane had expected the question and had the reply ready, "The company ran up a big debt to pay me the dividend I needed to finance the castle and its net worth had shrunk to almost nothing. It took three independent evaluations before her lawyers settled for a hundred thousand. I guess it won't last long in London."

I felt sorry for my old boss who had shown me much kindness. Hopefully Duane did not notice it. We chatted about his castle and my novel and parted company with a warm handshake.

6

"Claude, this is what I know of Charlene. Your friend is her third try. Let us hope it is third time lucky for her," I concluded my story.

Claude was thoughtful for a minute before saying, "The story has potential. We need to work out the ending with the count. I have one I can suggest."

"Let's compare notes and decide how to end it. Tell me how you would conclude?" I asked.

Claude's reply was short. "I am a producer, not a writer. I will say my piece and will be happy if it helps you. I think the Count Vishnovski will see through Charlene and keep her as a companion on his payroll. He is a self-made man who left Russia with barely enough to survive. He is not going to fall for her old tricks."

I had a different spin, "Your ending is good, perhaps that is what will happen. I was taught that fiction is the art of making the impossible look like the only thing that was possible. So my story will go something like this: History will repeat itself for the third time, although with a difference. Sooner rather than later, Charlene will become pregnant."

Claude interrupted, "It will be later than later. The Count is in his seventies."

I continued my story with some irritation, "I said Charlene will become pregnant, not that the Count will be the father. He maybe, he may not. In any event, the old man will be so proud he will accept paternity without question. Then the lawyers will hassle, only this time Charlene will demand payment up front – maybe the deeds to the castle they will buy and ownership of some profitable businesses. The proud count will concede, overriding the advice of his lawyers and complaints from his children. Of course the new countess will have a Bentley of her own. Guess who will be the chauffer?"

"Rod, of course. Chauffer with privileges," Claude said with a smile.

As we stood up to leave I said, "In my final version I will work Rod in at the beginning of the Third Act. And for all intents and purposes the couple will live happily ever after."

4. A Peep into the Future

I

Like many couples of their generation, Brenda and Henry have decided not to grow the family, not for now at any rate. On the other hand, they are unlike many of their friends in one respect: they are very private individuals - no Facebook, Twitter, blogging for them. Both of them would be embarrassed if the reasons became known outside their small circle. So let us just leave these aside and believe that they did not go to sleep till well after midnight and therefore did not wake up till after nine, an hour after their usual time on Saturday. Brenda jumped out of bed, went to the kitchen, had the coffee going and picked up the newspaper from the freezing porch. Soon she was walking into the bedroom with a tray and the bundle of newspaper.

Henry accepted the steaming cup with a smile that lighted up the grey stubble on his tanned chubby face. The aroma of Columbian coffee induced him to remark, "I could not live without you."

Brenda was not surprised. Henry was known for compliments he did not mean. She responded, "You will do very well. All the single men of our acquaintance are as happy as larks."

"I somehow doubt that. Appearances can be deceptive. In any event, who knows how lonely larks feel?" Henry defended himself.

It was too early for Brenda to get into an argument. She slipped under the blanket and opened the news section of the weekend edition of the paper. Henry picked up the arts and books section.

They commented on what they read without listening to what the other said. Brenda finished the news and more importantly her coffee. "What will you like for breakfast?" she asked.

Henry thought for a moment before answering, "Now that you ask, if it is not too much trouble, chopped steamed spinach rolled in buckwheat pancakes and smothered in a spicy cheese sauce would be most welcome. I don't need to remind you, this goes well with half and half."

Brenda chopped the spinach and put it in the steamer, mixed pancake batter, made cheese sauce with black pepper and a dash of paprika that she had picked up on their visit to Marrakesh a year ago. She emptied a mini bottle of Henkel Trocken in a jug and added the same amount of orange juice and placed the jug carefully in the freezer to chill. Knowing her husband's routine, she shouted, "It is ready," before making the pancakes and setting the table.

Henry leisurely folded the newspaper, went to the bathroom, flossed his teeth carefully, brushed them for regulation two minutes and a half, and walked over to the table in a dressing gown. He poured the champagne-orange juice mix into the flutes as Brenda set the warm plate with a golden pancake in front him. He poured the steaming cheese sauce from the jug on the pancake, raised the flute and said, "To the health and longevity of the happy couple."

They finished their breakfast focusing on the food and not saying much. After Henry had licked the cheese sauce from his plate and wiped the jug clean with a piece of pancake, Brenda wiped the table, put everything away, cleaned the pans and loaded the dishwasher. Henry perused the business section learning how a twenty-four-year old investor grows his savings in mutual funds and how a middle-aged couple can change their spending habits to send the kids to college. Out of the blue, he asked Brenda, eyes still glued to the paper, "Can I see the piece on the interview?"

Henry had promised the editor of the community's monthly pamphlet to write a fawning story on a business executive who lived in the area. Although Henry is a poet with some reputation, Brenda is the prose writer in the family and was not surprised when one evening Henry dragged her to a palatial home with a breathtaking view of a lake and the mountains beyond. Brenda made notes in long hand while Henry asked supercilious questions. The write up had to be finalized this weekend. "Give me a few minutes, it is nearly ready" Brenda replied. She found her notes, made a rough draft of the interview, printed a copy and presented it to Henry. After finishing the paper and emptying the jug of the bubbly juice, Henry picked up the printout and a pen. He scribbled several changes and handed it back for preparing the final draft. When Brenda was doing it, he shouted from the door to the garage, "Going to the store to get some paper." Brenda, who was having a hard time deciphering his comments, shouted back, "Ok, Ok," dripping in frustration. She stopped revising and sent the draft to Henry's mail-box with the comment that she had done all she could and the rest was up to him.

2

Brenda was in the mall looking for a birthday gift for Henry when she ran into Gretl. They hadn't seen each other for a while so they strolled over to the food court to exchange notes over a cup of coffee. "How is Wolfgang?" Brenda asked on the way.

"Don't know. He left me three months ago. Haven't you heard?" Gretl replied.

"No I hadn't. I am so sorry. You looked so happy when I saw you last Christmas," Brenda sounded surprised.

"The happiness was a veneer. We were together for six years. We had problems from the beginning. We ignored them rather than face them and solve them. He blamed me for nagging though I did have a lot to complain about. He made much more money in his job than I did and he thought that entitled him to leave all household chores to me. He expected me to get cream out of the fridge for his coffee and run to the store if we were out. If I asked him to do the tiniest bit he protested. For a while I thought it was a good relationship because we had money for whatever we wanted. Then the overload of work at home after a day of teaching unruly kids started jingling my nerves. Yet, it is funny when I think of it. There was more joy and only a few frustrations in the beginning and without any real change in the situation, the pendulum in my mind started to swing and I began complaining with increasing vehemence," said Gretl, opening her heart.

"That is how it is in many relationships," Brenda's tone was consoling.

Gretl continued, "In last year or so, not a day went by when I didn't think how nice it would be to live alone. I looked forward to my visits to my parents in New Orleans although I hate flying. And I enjoyed pottering around in underwear when he was away on business trips. Incidentally, he met his current love on one of these. Some women may find it nice to have him around even if it means slavery, I did not. It could be a happy trade by-and-large to some, it had become grating to me and I was glad when he left."

Brenda felt a knife go through her heart. She replied, "Well, I also go through a lot although we earn about the same. We have been married a long time too. To be honest, it is now beginning to get on my nerves as well. By the time I have finished all the chores after even an average day at the office I have no energy left to do what I always loved. I haven't put paint on paper for years. Perhaps it is time I did something about it."

Gretl disregarded Brenda's response and continued from where she had left off, "Still, I would like to meet someone nice."

"It's an old saw, you can't live with them and you can't live without them," Brenda said a little cynically.

Gretl carried on, "Now I want a man who would be considerate. He would be less demanding, free with money on outings and holidays like Wolfgang was and would do his bit around the house. You know someone I should invite for dinner?"

"If there are such men they are already taken and they are guarded under seven locks," Brenda replied thinking how protective her sisters are of their husbands.

"Well there must be some; widowed or unappreciated – I only need one." Gretl wasn't ready to give up hope.

"You will need to be more practical. I don't know why after your experience you would want a man. Husbands are all the same. With very few exceptions, when a man is around a woman has the work of two, suffers frequent putdowns and breaks her back to satisfy impossible demands. Most wives lower their expectations or learn to live on their own." Brenda hadn't forgotten her morning of the previous day.

"You have a devoted husband and you can say that," said Gretl, offended.

They finished their coffee and went back to their shopping, both regretting the meeting and vowing to look the other way next time. However, Brenda became thoughtful, "There was no point in telling Gretl what I put up with every day though I must do something about it".

3

Brenda returned home later than she expected. As usual, Henry was staring at the ceiling chewing on a pencil with a writing pad on his lap. Brenda could never understand how he could sit idly looking at the same spot rarely putting pencil to paper. The coffee cup and two empty beer cans were on the table beside him. The kitchen was exactly as she had left it; the used pans on the stove, plates and cutlery on the dining table, left over food on the counter. There were scraps on the floor next to his chair. Brenda rushed to him, picked up the pad, snatched the pencil and screamed, "Why can't you do simple things around the house. Would it have been skin off your hands to clean up the kitchen? I spent hours planning, shopping for ingredients and cooking the dinner you did not even thank me for. You did not even set the table. This can not go on. You have to do your share of the work around the house."

"What is the problem? I thought you enjoyed doing these things," Henry looked at her in bewilderment.

"I don't enjoy the chores. I love the cooking on special occasions, not every meal. No one enjoys cleaning up. People do it because it has to be done. And couples I know do it together. If you do not want to share in the work, don't eat. Sleep on the floor, stop using the washrooms. The choice is yours to make."

"OK. I was wrong to think that you enjoyed doing the chores. I agree that I should do more, much more. What chores would you like me to do?" said a conciliatory Henry.

"I don't want you to cook because I like food that is cooked properly. I do want you to clean up after we have eaten; every meal – not just dinner. I will start the washer, you look after drying and folding the clothes. I do the garden, you do the lawn – mowing and watering. While you are watering I will show you how you should water the flower beds." Brenda assigned Henry his responsibilities.

"Fair enough. I am going to start this minute. You relax and do whatever you like: read the paper, watch the boob tube, check your messages, whatever. If what I do is not satisfactory, point out the faults. I will correct them." Henry accepted the division of labour.

"I am going to start the white load of laundry. You follow up on that. The clothes will be ready for the dryer about the time you are done with the kitchen," Brenda said on her way to pick up the clothes hamper.

Brenda approved the washed and dried utensils, recommended a better way to load the dishwasher, pointed out a few stained spots on the counter and showed him the product to wipe them off with. After doing these things Henry went downstairs to transfer clothes to the dryer. Brenda went upstairs to find her easel, paints and paper, wondering how much of her artistic talent had withered away.

4. A Peep into the Future

The new routine was established and a few months passed in relative harmony although Henry was able to add only a few lines to the poem he had been working on before the new structure in his life. It was a cold and dark evening in December when he walked through the front door from his day job as a personnel manager after driving through a heavy snowfall. Brenda did not pay attention to him; she was glaring at the easel, a clutch of brushes in her hands. He went to her, gave her a peck on the cheek and asked softly "How was your day?"

"Nothing unusual," Brenda replied.

"How are you feeling?" Henry was concerned by her tone.

"I am feeling fine. Skip phony inquiries and ask what you are really wondering about. I will save you the trouble and answer the question before you ask it. I am sick of cooking every day. In fact I am sick to death of doing everything in the house. This is your home too. You have to do your share. You have to cook once in a while so I can have some time for my interests. Don't tell me you can't cook. You managed before meeting me. You can prepare dinner for us once in a while. Let us begin today."

"I had a rough day too. Regardless, I do appreciate your point. I will make some spaghetti and tomato sauce and steam some beans. There are two slices of chocolate cake left over from the other day. Will that be OK?" Henry tried to calm the waters.

"It will be fine today. You will have to do better next time. Chianti goes well with spaghetti. I hope we have some," said Brenda, not quite pacified.

"I will check. If not, there is sure to be a bottle of red," Henry said as he turned towards the kitchen.

After serving Brenda a glass of sherry, Henry put some spaghetti in boiling water, beans in the steamer and poured some sauce from the bottle into a bowl, ready to heat in the microwave a little later. He set the table, a knife, two forks, a wine glass and a dinner plate for each of them and serving spoons. He did find a bottle of Chianti and opened it so the wine could 'breathe' for a few minutes. He placed the steaming bowls on the table and called Brenda. They set down in their usual places facing each other. Brenda looked at the table and asked, "Did you forget something?"

"Is something missing? What else should I do?" Henry was all nerves.

"Buns and butter are served with spaghetti. Haven't you noticed?" Brenda confirmed her displeasure.

Henry found the buns in the pantry. He took the butter dish out of the fridge and nuked it for ten seconds. He brought them to the table.

Brenda looked up, "Are you going to give me a side plate, or do I need to get one myself?"

Henry brought two plates and sat down. They helped themselves and ate in silence. Henry served coffee with the cake. After a bite of the cake Brenda picked her cup and turned to her painting.

"Do you want me to do the kitchen too?" Henry asked.

"It is your job. Who else will do it?" Brenda retorted.

Henry looked at Brenda's back in amazement. He expected that she would clean up the kitchen since he had prepared the dinner. "I must pick the time of battle carefully," Henry said under his breath and began clearing the table.

"You may not have noticed, the laundry basket is overflowing. Will you look after that too before the evening is out?" Brenda's tone made it an order rather than a question.

4

It was a Saturday morning. Henry was awake when Brenda turned to face him and opened her mouth, eyes still closed, "I would like some tea, please. I bought a packet of Earl's Grey yesterday. Make a pot, it is easier. Two bags for the full pot. You will like it. If you don't, feel free to brew coffee for yourself."

Henry got out of bed thinking that he was already cooking the dinners, doing the dishes and shopping for groceries. It was a complete role reversal from a year ago, except that he was still repairing the broken appliances, looking after the finances, maintaining the yard, and almost every chore the one-morning-a- week maid did not do. Yet, Brenda was always stressed and he was often coming short.

He had just hung his coat in the wardrobe after work one evening when Brenda asked, "What did you use to wash the clothes?"

Henry was surprised by the question, "Why do you ask?"

"The clothes reek of a strange smell. It must be the soap you used," Brenda explained.

"The store was advertising a new kind of liquid soap. 'Good for environment because you need much less,' they said," Henry explained.

"I knew you would do something like this. The perfume in the soap has given me a migraine. You will have to get the soap we have always used and do the wash again. And I need it done today." Brenda made herself clear.

One evening they were driving to dinner with some old friends. Brenda sat with her fists clenched. "Watch out you are straddling the lanes," she cried.

"What is the problem? I am changing lane for a left turn," Henry said.

"Then why didn't you signal in good time. Your driving is terrible. You will kill us one of these days," cried Brenda, really upset.

Rather than raising the temperature by saying, "Perhaps you should do all the driving: I don't particularly enjoy being the chauffer," Henry absorbed the punch and said nothing. He was not surprised that Brenda headed for the passenger seat on their way home.

Henry was very distant all evening. His mind was on what was going on in their relationship. Brenda never seemed satisfied by what he did; even a poached egg did not meet with her approval. Keeping Brenda satisfied had become a full-time occupation and the constant anxiety caused by the impression that Brenda was taking him for granted was draining him of all vitality. It was as if he was walking a tightrope whenever they were together. The weekends and holidays

were times he had come to dread. He had not written a stanza of
poetry for months. On the other hand, Brenda was enjoying her new
leisure. She had more energy and time and spent many evenings and
most of the weekend either painting or with her friends. She had
shown her work to some galleries and one was including two pieces
in an exhibit of local art. Henry took pride in his wife's success while
resenting not being able to indulge his passion. He consoled himself
that a happy wife was worth some sacrifice – he well remembered
from his childhood how his mother had made both her husbands feel
so small when she was upset.

5

Henry was filling up the tank of his Volvo when over the clicks of
the pump he heard, "How are you doing old man? Haven't seen you
for ages. When is your next collection coming out?"

It was Wolfgang filling up a Pontiac across the aisle. Henry waved
and replied with a fake cheer which could not have fooled Wolfgang,
"Very well, thank you. You are right. It is a long time since our last
get-together. How is Gretl?"

"Oh, didn't you know? Gretl booted me out on a flimsy pretext
soon after I saw you last. I am a single man now. Happy as they come.
No one tells me what to do with my spare time. All sorts of pretty
girls available when I need a hot date. I will never understand why I
stayed in that prison for so long."

After the fill ups they drove around the corner to a coffee shop.
Wolfgang told Henry how being with Gretl started upsetting him,
"She always invented things for me to do. She resented my efforts at
writing and complained about time I spent on the computer – I have
always done all my writing on the computer."

"Most couples have the same problem. They find ways to work
around it," Henry suggested.

"I wanted to do just that till Brenda told me one day it was either her or my computer. I am sure she meant my writing," Henry replied.

"Then what happened?"

I told her, "I am sorry I can't give up writing." Next day when I came home I found my stuff on the front porch. I was upset and it took me a while to settle down."

Wolfgang then regaled Henry with the funny events of his bachelor life. Had he not been preoccupied with his woes, Henry would have noticed a degree of spin in the joviality. This was not all. Wolfgang gave Henry yet another reason to envy him. "I returned to writing after our separation. I completed a two-hundred page novel last month and two publishers are looking at it." Wolfgang told him with gusto.

This hurt and Henry replied a little shamefacedly, "I must be getting old, I doze off the minute I sit down with paper and pen."

"Come on! You are not any older than me. Something deeper is bothering you or it is a writer's block. You must find a way to remove the block," said Wolfgang, twisting the knife.

On their way out, Wolfgang slapped Henry on the back, "We should meet again soon, this time for lunch. It will be my treat."

6

A shock awaited Henry when he opened the door of their home. Brenda was in the kitchen whistling a gay tune, blonde hair tied in a knot, her blue pinafore on, two sauce pans bubbling away and a frying pan sizzling under the extractor fan. "What is up?" he asked.

Brenda lowered the heat under the frying pan before turning to face him. "We need a break from simple meals and you need a change. I am going to take over the cooking for a while and chicken cordon bleu is the start. It does need lots of utensils, surely a great dinner for a few extra pans is a good trade. You can set the table for the main course, a simple dessert and the wine of your choice. Then check the clothes in the dryer. By the time you are finished folding them I will be ready to put the dinner on the table."

After dinner, Brenda went to her easel and Henry cleaned up the kitchen. When he had finished he asked Brenda if she would like to join him for a drink. Brenda hesitated before accepting and they sat down in the living room facing each other, Brenda with a glass of port and Henry with a snifter of brandy. Brenda took a sip, looked at her husband who was relishing the aroma of his drink.

"Thank you for the port," she said.

"Thank you for a wonderful dinner," Henry replied and asked, "What are you working on these days?"

"I am doing a piece for the exhibit at the gallery. Perhaps the cordon blue will give some brilliance to the colours."

"I am sure it will. You were always a great cook and you excelled today. Surely I owe my good fortune to some higher motive?" Henry suspected that there was more to it than the brilliant colours.

"I don't know whether this meal is the harbinger of a better fortune, or the resolution of an unfortunate sequence. When I was stressed and the pressure of being a superwoman was killing me, I realized that I was approaching the breaking point and I asked you to take over some chores. You were gracious about it. Then, some three months ago, you started talking in your sleep. It was gibberish and I couldn't make out what you were saying. Yet, the underlying agitation was clear. I would lie awake for a long time after you had stopped talking, wondering whether it was the insecurity related to your job that was stressing you, or it was me."

"What did you decide?" Henry asked although he thought he knew the answer.

Brenda continued, "I began wondering if all the work around the house was getting to you. Then I heard you mumble something like 'I peeped into the future and the darkness scared me to death.'"

Henry interrupted, "Did I say that? I can't believe it."

Brenda carried on, tears starting to well up, "You are too good a man to say that when you are awake. I am sure you said something similar in your sleep. In any event, it shook me up and I tossed and turned all night. I love you as much as I always have. I don't want to lose you. I now realize what has been bothering you. You have not been able to write and you miss it enormously, the same as I missed painting. We will organize our lives so that we can both work to achieve our goals. They maybe great works, or they may not. In any event, if our art is important to us, that is what matters."

"It is very kind of you to say such nice things. You were good at what you did and that is what brought us together. You have every right, actually an obligation, to use your talent to the utmost. I was not sharing in the housework and you did what you had to do. Now I find that I can't chase my rainbow and stay with you.

"The root cause of the distance between us is not the housework, or lack of time for our art - these are only the symptoms - it is the dying of the flame of love. We did not nourish our love after getting married. We, perhaps I more than you, took the other for granted. Now the flame is extinguished, we can't alight it again. To make the situation hopeless, you are controlling and I am not a fighter. I am sorry it is too late to start afresh."

"What are you telling me?" Brenda's tears had dried up and there was anger in her voice.

Henry noticed the change, and knowing Brenda as he did, it did not surprise him. "I am not telling you what you don't know already. I don't want every free moment of my life directed by you, or anyone else. We have to go our separate ways to make the best of our remaining days, months, years whatever is granted to us. I am going into the darkness to find my way. I may stumble and fall and may never get up. I am prepared to take that chance."

Henry rose, packed his clothes and files of poetry and drove into the night. The sound of the closing garage door stirred Brenda out of her stupor. She went to the easel, angrily snatched the sheet she had been working on, looked at it once, then again with total concentration. It calmed her down. She put the painting back on the easel and picked up her brushes.

5. Clear of the Fire

I

Like most people who have lived this long, I have been a witness to some strange happenings and have written amusing pieces about many of them. Being well aware of my shortcomings as a story-teller I saved the oddest event I ever came across for the day when, having learnt from decades of experience, I would be able to do justice to it. It would be foolish of me to believe that the experience has helped my writing; recent stories are returned without comment, often unread I suspect, by esteemed editors with just as little consideration as the earliest ones were. It hurts my feelings; it does not stop me from writing. In any event, I think it is time I gave my keyboard a chance to recount the few years Manoj spent in Canada. While I do not expect that this work will be accepted by any editor, respectable or otherwise, it may interest some members of my ever shrinking circle of readers.

It was in the early seventies when I joined the ranks of freelance mining consultants. Times were tough and one had to compete for assignments. It was my practice to invite one of the engineers from a company to meet for drinks in a slightly upscale bar to impress on him how I could help his company's efforts without endangering his job. It didn't succeed often, a few times it did was enough to pay all the bar bills and leave enough for my family to live in comfort. Manoj was one of my early guests. He offered hope without delivering much, yet we continued to meet once every few weeks. Then, for some reason

241

that has slipped my mind, we did not meet for a couple of years till I ran into him on the street near his office. Poor Manoj, he was in a bad shape. He was limping and his left arm was in a sling. He looked haggard even though his hair was neatly parted, his blue suit looked as if it had come straight from the dry cleaner and his black shoes reflected the office towers. He tried to look as if he hadn't seen me but I was curious to know what had happened to him. "Hi Manoj; haven't seen you for a while. How have you been? What have you done to yourself?" I bombarded him with questions.

"You don't want to know this tale of misery. There is nothing interesting in it," he replied.

"I do want to know. What is more I want to help if I can," I said with a generosity of spirit I do not usually show.

"Do you want to know in a nutshell or in detail?" it was his turn to ask.

"In a nutshell now, in detail later," I answered.

"I was going down a hill on my bicycle six months ago. The breaks failed, I lost control and had a bad fall. Broke a few bones in my right leg and in the left arm, banged my head real bad. Have been on the disability since. I was told last week by letter and verbally a few minutes ago that my job can't wait for me anymore. I wouldn't be surprised if my wife shows me the door next. That is the story in a few words."

"Didn't you tell me that Indian marriages were for life?" I asked, focusing on the last bit.

"Perhaps I did. My life took a turn after that. One summer when my family was with my in-laws in India I got a girl pregnant. I did what any honorable man would do; I sent my wife back to India and married the damsel in distress. Life with her and the baby was good till the accident. It is very hard to live on disability pay. Now my current wife threatens to leave every other day," Manoj brought his tale of woe to a close.

"I want to hear the chain of events in detail and do whatever I can for you. When can we get together?" I asked.

"You tell me the time and place. Any day is good for me," he was frank.

"Remember the Bear's Den, our old haunt with the understated décor, almost private, comfortable booths, soft classical music and a rather quiet clientele. They now serve light dinners so we don't have to go elsewhere for the meal. Let us meet there this evening at six thirty," I suggested and Manoj agreed.

Manoj was waiting in the reception area when I arrived five minutes early. He had changed into a pale blue shirt with open collar and a rather rumpled grey woollen jacket. It is hard to tell whether it was informal clothes or a restful afternoon, he was less tense than in the morning. It was early for the bar to be busy. We chose the booth in a dim and quiet corner where we could carry on our conversation in low tones. After a couple of beers to lubricate the throat and to get over his inhibitions, if he had any, Manoj related the sad business with only a few interruptions over dinner and coffee

2

Manoj had arrived in Canada from a part of India where the regional majority was campaigning for its own state. There was some violence and a few members of his community had been killed. Manoj did not sympathize with the cause and did the only thing a young man with a wife and a baby could do. He fled to Canada and, thanks to his degree from an elite school, was admitted as a refugee. Mining industry was hitting the crest of the cycle and he was hired by a company developing a coal mine in the interior of British Columbia. Within two years, he was supervising the construction. His professional reputation reached a new high when he was invited to speak at the mining engineers' luncheon on the pitfalls to watch for while developing a coal mine.

The commodity prices were at their peak and the company was reaping huge profits. As a reward to employees, the Christmas party was planned in one of the best hotels in the city. Manoj viewed it as an opportunity to impress the senior executives. However, Seedhi, his wife, told him she would rather not join him. To change her mind he followed the four stages of persuasion, beginning with gentle and culminating in harsh, as recommended by Lord Krishna. He told her how important it was for his career for them to be seen together at the party, promised her a new sari with gold border and a pearl necklace to match, reminded her how sinful it was for a wife not to follow her husband's wishes, and finally threatened to tell her mother how obstinate she had become. Seedhi was a devotee of Rama, not Krishna. She listened patiently and refused to budge. It is hard to tell what was going through Seedhi's mind during her argument with Manoj. Never having met her I can only guess that his words did not find a resting place in between her ears. As for the reason for her stubborn refusal, it could be one or more of many good ones: she had difficulty with the language, she did not want to leave her six month old baby and the three-year-old child with a baby sitter, she did not drink and was a strict vegetarian, or simply she felt uncomfortable in the company of the locals with their strange customs. Whatever the reason, I am certain that if she had an inkling of the consequences of her absence, she would not have been so impervious to her husband's entreaties.

A chandelier of a thousand crystals overhead and the plush red carpet underfoot welcomed Manoj in the lobby of the Bow Plaza Hotel. He was impressed by the elegant surroundings, not awed, thanks to his new dark-blue suit and matching red tie with golden tie pin. The gay chatter directed him to the crowded room with a twelve foot tall Christmas tree with twinkling red, green and blue bulbs. He picked a glass of champagne from the bar and surveyed the guests standing around in small groups. He spotted Robert Gilmour, the chief engineer, talking to a couple he had not met. Robert noticed him as he moved hesitantly towards them, "Hello Manoj, come and join us. How come you are alone?"

"Seedhi has a slight cold and she did not wish to spread it around," Manoj lied.

"Sorry to hear that. Hope she is well soon and the kids don't get it. You might have met this beautiful lady, Helen, from accounting. Her husband Thomas works for the city. This young man is Manoj. And this lady-in-making is my daughter, Rebecca, standing in for her mother who had to go to her company's do."

"And your son is standing in for you?" Manoj asked.

"Ha, ha. He would have if we had one. Gillian has to manage by herself like you have to," Robert replied.

"Rebecca, what courses are you taking at the U?" Manoj turned to the girl. She was modestly dressed in a high-neck red blouse and a green skirt not much above her knees, her shiny blonde hair covered the slender neck. She was looking somewhat bored.

"Oh I have yet to finish school. There is another year of drudge before the U calls," Rebecca replied.

Robert put the things straight, "She has her mother's genes. She looks much older than seventeen and just like her mother she will look much younger when she is fifty."

Manoj moved next to Rebecca and asked her the usual question adults ask younger adults, "What is your favourite subject?"

"Nothing in particular. I like English literature. I love to read. Ms. French, our teacher, is wonderful. She recommends such interesting books."

"With work and little kids at home I don't get much time now. I do like to read. What are you reading these days?"

"I am into Shakespeare right now. I finished the Merchant of Venice last week. Now I am on Hamlet."

"Did you enjoy the Merchant?"

"I loved it. The character of Shylock is cool. His soliloquy on being a Jew is the most amazing thing I have ever read. I am sure there are not many speeches that good."

"I am sure you are right. I read somewhere that great actors fight for the role just to deliver the oration to a full house. Do you have hobbies other than reading?"

"I love skiing in winter and hiking in summer. We all enjoy the outdoors and go out almost every weekend. I am learning to cook from my mum although I don't really like it."

"Seedhi won't let me in the kitchen, not even to do the dishes. I was like a helpless child when she went home to visit her parents."

"How did you manage?"

"Lot of rabbit food, fruits and nuts. Not a balanced diet but I survived. I saw a lot of plays in that month. Some good classical shows were on."

"Great. We do have a common interest, only I am on stage. We are rehearsing Hamlet for the school's annual drama presentation and I am playing Ophelia. The school does a good job of publicity and the performances are usually sold out."

"How wonderful! I envy the young man who plays Hamlet to your Ophelia. When is the performance? I will be there."

"Tuesday to Sunday in the third week of next month. Curtain goes up at seven each night. You can call the school for tickets."

The conversation was ended by the announcement of dinner. Rebecca joined her Dad on the table for senior executives and Manoj found a seat with Helen and Thomas.

3

Manoj went to the play. Again, Seedhi did not join him. "Tell me why I should throw good money for the ticket and leave my kids with a stranger to see this play called Omelet in a language I do not understand?" she asked with some anger. He had no answer and let the matter rest there. He arrived at the school half an hour early to get a front row seat. When the curtain went up, many in the audience cheered to show their appreciation of the simple, yet attractive set with two boys, trying to look like young men, walking towards each other. The play proceeded smoothly with no unduly long breaks between the scenes. Actors remembered their lines most of the time and the delivery was almost faultless. Not of the calibre of the one he had seen on TV, it would be foolish to expect that, the performance had the charm and suspense of a live presentation. After the curtain came down for the last time, the players received a standing ovation from the audience of adoring relatives and friends. Manoj joined the parents and siblings who were waiting in the lobby for the actors to come out. Rebecca saw him first and called him, obviously delighted that he was there. Manoj complimented Rebecca, "It was a really good show. You were wonderful. Perhaps you have found your calling in life."

Rebecca's dimples looked prettier to Manoj when she responded, "Time will tell whether the stage is my calling or not. Jump from a school stage to the professional circuit is huge. I know it is hard work and mum tells me that most actors can't make a living. Thank God I don't have to decide any time soon."

Manoj asked, "Have you considered something else?"

Rebecca replied, "Dad wants me to try office work. I am going to work this summer in his department as an odd jobber – do whatever work the engineers have for me. That may give me some ideas too."

Manoj was delighted. He encouraged her, "You will have fun. Don't tell him I said it, your Dad is a very good boss and working with him is as pleasant as it can be. I will be spending a lot of time in the office this summer. Seedhi is homesick and wants to see her parents and friends. Summer is the mango season and she can eat them by the dozen. She is looking forward to it."

"Why don't you go as well? Surely your parents are dying to see you."

"I would love to. We need to save for the deposit on a small house. Neither of us has lived in an apartment before and we feel cramped. It would be nice to have a yard for the kids to play in when they are a little older.

Rebecca worked with Manoj on his project several times during the summer. Once in a while Rebecca joined the staff for TGIF gatherings in the bar. She stuck to Diet Coke while Manoj nursed a beer through the couple of hours the party lasted. After the party Rebecca went home with her dad and Manoj took a short bus ride to his apartment. The summer went quickly and it was soon Rebecca's last Friday at work. While waiting for the elevator on their way out, Rebecca said to Manoj, "Dad is away and I don't feel comfortable joining the TGIF party. I will say goodbye now. It was very nice working with you. Perhaps we will meet again soon."

"There is no reason to be uncomfortable. The people in the department would like to bid farewell to their colleague who worked so hard, even though she is the boss's daughter. Just come for a few minutes. The train will be less crowded after the worst of rush hour."

"O.K. For a few minutes. Then I go home and begin preparation for my last year in school."

They joined a group of about ten, engineers and the technicians ranging in age from mid twenties to early fifties, sitting around a large rectangular table. Catherine, an engineer in her early thirties and the only female there, made room for Rebecca next to her. It wasn't long before the beer made them boisterous and sedate Rebecca began to feel a little out of place. Catherine noticed her discomfort and asked, "Have you ever tasted beer?"

"A sip long time ago. It tasted horrible and I have stayed away since,' Rebecca replied.

"Your taste buds are more mature now. Taste some of mine, you may like it." Catherine pushed her mug in front of Rebecca.

The conversation around the table stopped and all eyes were focused on one mouth. Rebecca took a small sip, pulled a face as if she did not know what to think, then took a big mouthful and swallowed. Rebecca knew that everyone was waiting for her reaction. She smiled and said, "Not bad. I could learn to like it."

Catherine spoke for many of her colleagues "The moment to begin the learning has arrived." She waved to the waitress and added, "You carry on with that mug and I will order another one."

Rebecca had that one, a refill and then one more for the train home. Manoj noticed her unsteady walk and offered to walk her to the train. "I am feeling very hot. My mind is a jumble of all kinds of thoughts. That beer has done something to me. I think I need to sit down for a while and let the system settle. Should we find a bench somewhere nearby?"

"My apartment is a few minutes away. Must warn you though, it is a mess. The family has been away two months and I have not even put the toys away. If you don't mind the clutter, you can rest on the La Z Boy. A cup of mint tea may help."

"That is kind of you. I will stay only a few minutes, I promise you. I don't want to be late and worry my mother."

At the apartment, Rebecca made herself comfortable while Manoj made the tea. They sipped it in silence. "I am so hot," Rebecca said as she pulled her dress off. Manoj was embarrassed but could not keep his eyes off the bulging bra.

"Aren't you going to help me cool down?" Rebecca said unhooking the bra.

Manoj moved over and did what was needed to take away the heat, gently to begin with, then with gusto.

"Oh, it was so great to do it with someone experienced," Rebecca said putting her clothes back on. She toasted two slices of bread while Manoj heated beans from a can. After eating the sumptuous meal, they walked over to the station.

4

Seedhi returned from India and the life of Manoj returned to its normal routine, busy at work during the day, playing in the evening with the older daughter Niti and helping with the baby who was now a toddler. The evening with Rebecca, an exciting memory at first, receded into the deep background once the family was home. One morning he was staring at the window of his office not really noticing the snowflakes dropping like fairies expelled from heaven when the phone rang. He recognized the voice, it was Rebecca. "Sorry to disturb you. I must see you, where can you meet me privately during your lunch break."

"What is the problem that is so urgent? I have a lunch engagement," Manoj replied.

"Please cancel the engagement and meet me. It is most urgent, for me and for you too. I can't discuss it on the phone. Tell me where to meet you, you alone."

"I will see you at the entrance of Prince's Park soon after noon. I will pick up a sandwich and coffee for both."

"Thank you for being so thoughtful. Cheese and tomato for me, please. Orange juice, if they have it. No coffee. I will wait for you there. Bye for now."

Manoj wondered for a moment, what was making Rebecca so anxious, then returned to the project he had to finish by the end of the month. The rush of colleagues leaving for lunch reminded him of his date. He put on his coat and toque, picked up lunch from the cafeteria on the ground floor and strolled towards the park.

Although the snow had stopped, Rebecca was the only person at the entrance. He noticed that her eyes were not as bright as he remembered them. Her smile when she saw him seemed forced. They found a picnic table under a canopy of trees and Rebecca sat down across from where he was taking the food out of the bag. "No point beating about the bush. I am pregnant," she said in a steady voice.

"Good Heavens. When did you find out?" Manoj blurted.

"This morning. I am coming here straight from the doctor's office," Rebecca's calm surprised Manoj. He didn't know what to say. It was several moments before he said, "What are you going to do?"

The damn broke and Rebecca began to sob. Manoj went over, sat down next to her and put his arm around her waist, "It must have come to you as a big shock. I don't know what to say, let alone what to do. We need to talk over all the issues it raises calmly and come to the right decision. Let me assure you that I will stand by you."

The sobbing lost some of its intensity. Rebecca turned to look at him, her cheeks wet, eyes glistening with tears. "The doctor wanted to discuss abortion. I stopped her. I want the baby and I want to bring it up. Even if I have to go through life as a single mother living on welfare and handouts, my baby will be looked after and will have a good life. You have a family you are responsible for. My mind is made up; you have to decide how you will handle my baby."

"It is my baby too and I will play my role in its life. Give me time, not months, just a few days. When will you discuss it with your parents?"

Manoj handed Rebecca a paper napkin from the sandwich bag. She dried her eyes and face before replying thoughtfully, "It will be better for me to wait till you have decided on your next step. I can keep this to myself for a week or two. You can leave a message on my email and we will meet when you are ready. Does that make sense?"

Her maturity did not surprise Manoj. He showed his agreement by planting a kiss on her cheek. Rebecca held him tightly in her arms, Manoj reciprocated and their lips sealed the agreement they hadn't yet discussed.

5

"My mother began shedding tears the size of footballs two days before we were to leave and may still be crying for all I know. I have not come back to be told that I can be replaced by a whore who sleeps with anyone who offers her a cup of tea. I am going back to where my children are loved and where I am respected," Seedhi screamed. She packed the children's and her clothes in four suitcases and boarded the plane to India the next day.

The scene was not much different at Rebecca's home. "I am shocked. All this sex education, information on birth control and my only child is expecting while still in school. We were looking forward to your great career at a great college and then in a profession. What do we get? A single mother who will struggle to complete school while working in a Jo job to feed our grandson. Who is the father anyway, some ruffian in your school?"

Rebecca had sat down with her mother after learning that Manoj was now free. Gillian's reaction was what Rebecca had expected. Still, her fury derailed Rebecca's thought processes and she needed a few seconds, which seemed like hours to Gillian, before replying, "You won't like it. He is an engineer in dad's office. I fell for him during the summer and this is the result. His wife and children have returned home and he will marry me as soon as the formalities are done."

"Does Robert know what was going on in his department all summer and its consequence?" Gillian asked, her face redder than before.

"I haven't told Dad anything. I don't have the nerve to face him. He will be even more angry than you," Rebecca replied.

"I will talk to him. In the meantime what will happen to you? It may take years for formalities, as you call them, to be completed."

"I will move to his apartment if Dad and you don't want me here. I do hope Dad does not fire Manoj."

"Manoj, what kind of name is that? Where is he from? How old is he?"

"He is from India, came here as a refugee. He looks like someone in early thirties. Very gentle. You will like him once you are over the shock."

"We have no choice. We have to put up with the father of our grandchild. Don't expect me to love someone who destroyed my dreams for my child. You leave your father to me; I know how to handle him."

5.   Clear of the Fire

Gillian told Robert the news and her decision that Rebecca would stay at home, have the baby and finish high school. She can use this time to get to know Manoj rather than rushing into a hasty relationship. Then, if Rebecca still wanted him, they would help them set up their home. Moving in with him now did not strike Gillian as wise. Robert agreed with her, like every loving and loved husband does.

A healthy boy was born on the Easter Saturday. He was named Hardman Robert to honour both parents of the mother. The delivery went so well that Rebecca was back in school after a short maternity break. Gillian came to like Manoj after a while. He refused any financial help towards buying a home and the new family moved into his apartment during the summer. The divorce with Seedhi became official in late summer and Manoj married Rebecca on a glorious autumn day in a simple ceremony with a dozen or so guests.

The newly weds were over the moon for a while. Then the practicalities of every day living with a baby dragged them back to earth. Rebecca began complaining about Manoj not waking up in the night to feed the baby and Manoj resented having to do breakfast and lunch dishes stacked in the sink when he came home from work. They could not afford to eat out often, neither of them cared to cook and their only decent meal was on Sundays when Gillian invited them for a roast. The silver lining in their dark days was the bicycle rides they took almost every evening with Herdy harnessed to Rebecca's back.

It was a beautiful spring evening. Air had been washed by a heavy shower in the afternoon and perfumed by wet foliage. Wild roses were blooming everywhere and a gentle breeze took care of the perspiration. Herdy was cooing happily and Rebecca and Manoj chatted gaily about the internet courses Rebecca was planning to take beginning with one on English literature. They were going down a steep slope, neither of them paying attention; it was only a few hundred feet long and they had ridden it easily in the past. Suddenly, Manoj started picking up speed. Rebecca, alarmed, shouted, "Slow down, why are you going so fast?"

"My breaks are not working, see you at the bottom," Manoj shouted back.

Manoj never made it to the bottom. His front wheel hit a muddy patch, the bike skidded, he fell heavily and was dragged for several feet along the concrete path. Rebecca screamed and soon several people gathered around the crumpled body. Someone called 911 and the ambulance took Manoj to the emergency room. Gillian took over the care of Herdy while Robert drove Rebecca to the hospital. The emergency room doctor had finished his examination and had moved to another casualty. Manoj was drugged unconscious, his face covered in bandages. The nurse was glad to see Rebecca, "Dr. Jamieson examined him thoroughly, bandaged his face and has ordered rest before he attends to the broken bones. Left hand and right leg are in particularly bad shape. He will sleep till the morning. When he wakes up, doctors will decide what is best for him. You can't do much here. It will be better for you to get some sleep. I will leave a note for the nurse on duty in the morning to call you a little before the doctor arrives."

Manoj was in hospital for a month. Gillian and Robert were like angels from heaven, looking after Herdy when Rebecca visited the hospital, consoling her when the stress was too much to bear and generally helping her whenever there was a need. Although the face of Manoj was scarred, his vision and hearing were not impaired and his wit was as sharp as ever. He needed a wheelchair for another few weeks before moving up to crutches and then walked slowly with a heavy limp. His left arm was plastered and in a sling for six months. In many ways this period was tougher for them both than his time in hospital. They were cooped up in a small apartment and Rebecca missed their hikes and bicycle rides. She expected more help with chores and in the caring of Herdy. She wanted him to do some things for himself. Manoj, on the other hand, was, although he did not say it, disappointed in the attention he received from Rebecca. Many things upset him during the day. Most jarring were the simple neglects like the need to ask for a refill of coffee more than once. He would often dream of the care and unstinting devotion he would have received from Seedhi and it made him even more depressed. As well as her workload and the lack of help with it, Rebecca often complained of the financial hardship. This made Manoj feel guilty for having created the situation, which in turn brought his frustration to the surface and he often took it out on Rebecca. The young and exhausted wife understood the situation but fought back all the same.

It was at this stage when Manoj and I ran into each other. He had received a letter the previous week informing him that the company could not wait for him any longer. Robert told him that the file had gone over to the level above him and he could not help. He did set up a meeting with the manager of human resources. Manoj had just met the gentleman who had recently joined the company and was a stranger to him. He dressed formally, spoke gently and clearly and did not dwell on introduction formalities for long. He opened the file with great deliberation, glanced at some papers, looked up without meeting Manoj's eyes and said, "I am sorry, I don't have the words to soften the blow and it is perhaps better to be direct anyway. It is not in my hands. The word has come down from the president. He is under pressure from investors and has to trim the numbers at every level. The company will not review the decision. The separation settlement offered to you is generous and, I am afraid, it can not be improved."

"Your statement does not surprise me. I am disappointed all the same. I had several good years with the company. I do hope my successful projects will be remembered when the company receives a request for the reference from my future employer," Manoj said as they shook hands on his way out.

6

Although I disapproved of the way he had treated Seedhi, I felt sorry for Manoj. I know couples who 'try' for years to have a baby and do not conceive till they have adopted one, Rebecca became pregnant the only time they had sex. Almost every one who has a bicycle break failure gets away with minor scratches; Manoj had to be going down a hill after a storm. I considered how I could help him in what seemed to be a dire situation. I knew he would feel humiliated and refuse any offer of money even if I called it a loan. I had to think fast when he had his eyes fixed on me. "Do you feel up to working a couple of hours a day if I sent the work to your home?" I asked.

"I don't know. I am prepared to give it a try. Who should I talk to?" Manoj did not hide his excitement.

"I have more work than I can handle at the moment. I don't know how long it will last. For now you can help me. I will pay you whatever I bill for your work," I said hoping he did not notice the lie.

"Oh, you are an angel. It will help us so much. When can I start?" He did sound grateful.

"It will take me the rest of the week to organize the work. Expect a package first thing Monday and call me when you have examined it," I replied.

Manoj did even better than I had expected. However, the bickering with Rebecca continued. Perhaps the work was more strain than he acknowledged. Maybe he expected Rebecca to be more considerate now that he was earning again, though much less than she would wish. Humans being what they are, expectations have a way of staying ahead of the means. Their relationship did not improve even though my workload increased as the health of Manoj recovered. Before long, he rented space adjacent to my office and was working almost full time. Yet, I concluded from what he told me that they were like many people who can neither live peacefully with their partners nor without them.

The next development was a total shocker. Manoj had finished the project much to the client's satisfaction. I could hear him all morning whistling the same Bollywood tune while folding maps and putting the report together. A little after lunch he barged into my office, dropped a thick binder in front of me, sat down across the desk, beamed and said, "I have a surprise for you."

"You and Rebecca are getting on well," I guessed.

"Nice try but no cigar. Actually Rebecca gave up on me and moved out last week to live with her parents."

"I am sorry to hear that. I was hoping your relations would improve now that you have recovered physically and financially," I said wishing to console him.

"Thank you. However, her decision is really helpful in the circumstances. I have been discussing a job prospect for a while. I did not mention it to you in case it did not come through. As you know things are hot in India and they are short of experienced engineers. One of my uncles has bought a mine not far from my home town. After a long fruitless search for someone to take over its management, he asked me if I would be interested. He threw in a carrot - he assured me that if I play my cards right Seedhi will take me back. He called yesterday and we settled the terms. More important, he promised to have words with Seedhi. I can't stop pinching myself. What more could I wish?" he dropped the bombshells.

I looked at his happy face till I could believe that what I heard was what he had said. Then the slightly altered cliché slipped out of my mouth "Out of the frying pan and clear of the fire. Indeed, what more can one wish?"

6. The Decline and Fall of the Reuben Empire

I

Reuben called his motley businesses an empire although he knew he wasn't there yet. From his office window he could see the mountains in the west beyond which one of his companies had the rights to explore for gold and silver on a hundred thousand hectares of land. Although he could not see past the trees on the lakeshore in the south, he could visualize ten thousand hectares where he was collecting data to find oil and gas. If he leaned out of the window he could see the towers of downtown in the east; one of these housed two public companies in which he was a significant shareholder and whose management sought his counsel as a valued member of the board of directors. A few kilometers to the north was located the office of Franz, the broker, who looked after his substantial stock portfolio. These were all in addition to Safety First, the company that owned the two-storey, suburban building he looked out of and where twenty professionals and ancillary staff made sure that the consulting operation ran smoothly and the bids, reports, and of course the invoices were submitted on time.

To say that Reuben was proud of what he had achieved entirely on his own would be an understatement. During his early years in the German Democratic Republic, he had gone without meals every so often and wore his clothes till the holes could not be mended to save enough for bribes needed to escape to England. Once in Southampton, he had studied hard to obtain an engineering diploma while working night shifts at the Post Office. He then worked for a construction company for a few years while in the evenings he studied to enhance his qualifications to the level of a full professional consultant. He had just turned thirty when he met Kathleen, a Canadian woman a few years his senior, on the bus. After a few dates she offered to help him move to Canada where his skills would be much in demand. That turned out to be true and here he was, in short ten years, he could say "I am the monarch of all I survey; my right there is none to dispute." There was a sad side in his story that crossed his mind rarely now. In his early years in Canada his relationship with Kathleen became very close. However, his devotion to success created a conflict between them; they separated and eventually lost touch. A tough youth under the hated dictatorship had taught Reuben nothing if not that there is always a positive in misfortunes, if you look hard enough. For him it was being able to focus exclusively on creating out of nothing a sprawling enterprise. He hoped that, if he tended it well and it continued to expand at the rate it had grown recently, it would be a true business empire in a few years.

2

That was fifteen years ago. This morning there were scattered silvery clouds in a blue sky and Reuben's eyes were looking out of his apartment window at the parking lot with rusty old cars and overflowing garbage bins while his brain was otherwise occupied. He had only one business left and he had a crucial decision to make. He was due to meet Franz to review the options available to him. He wished to concentrate on this problem but some devil possessed him and he could only think of his misfortunes. The worst of them was the break with Kathleen although he did not realize it till much later.

Reuben met Kathleen when he was living a bachelor's life in Southampton. One evening after a makeshift dinner in his apartment of two poached eggs and half-baked beans on an almost burnt toast, he stepped on the bus to make his way to a lecture on Communism and Eastern Europe at the University. The only empty seat was next to a well-dressed young woman about his age in the third row behind the driver. He took the seat and noticed the pamphlet for the lecture peeping out of her handbag. Not able to resist his curiosity, he asked, "Are you going to the lecture on East Europe?"

The woman looked at him with amusement and replied, "Yes I am. I am interested because my grandfather was born and brought up in Dresden. I had a free evening and decided it was time I learnt something about the part of the world my ancestors come from."

"I am going there too. I am from the German Democratic Republic and I was drawn to the lecture because the speaker was a big name when I lived there although his career stalled a bit later. It will be interesting to see his take on life there," Reuben, like all people living alone, was glad to find someone to talk to.

"I am Kathleen. I am teaching a course on Canadian literature this term. I will love to talk about the lecture over coffee if you won't mind."

Reuben and Kathleen stayed together for the lecture and went to Wimpy's for coffee and strawberry pie with whipped cream afterwards. Reuben told Kathleen about his life in Leipzig and his poor impression of communism which contrasted with the tone of the lecture. They exchanged phone numbers before they parted at the bus stop where they had met three hours earlier.

It was Kathleen who called Reuben a week later. A friend was sick and she had an extra ticket for a concert. Reuben was free and suggested meeting for dinner at a new German restaurant before the concert. "It will be wonderful. Black forest cake would go well with Schumann and Brahms," Kathleen replied.

Reuben dressed carefully for his first date in years. A light touch of aftershave, a silk shirt in pale blue, a dark suit and red tie, black shoes polished to perfection, hair brushed to enhance his broad forehead. He looked critically in the mirror before setting off on a twenty-minute walk. He had been at the restaurant barely five minutes when Kathleen arrived in a black skirt touching her comfortable black shoes, face lightly powdered - if at all, lips naturally red, blonde hair enhancing almond shaped hazel eyes with perfectly trimmed brows and a white blouse setting off an emerald necklace. It must be fake he thought, real emeralds this size would cost millions. The necklace notwithstanding, Reuben felt that a fairy had crossed the threshold to his heart. His face radiated joy that was suffused all over his entire self as he move forward to greet her. They held hands on their way to a booth in the corner where they sat facing each other, both transported to a new world.

The dinner of pancake soup, beef roulade with cabbage and spaetzel accompanied by Piesporter Gold, all capped by genuine black forest cake with espresso went well with their mood. The concert hall was two short blocks away and they were comfortably in their seats when the orchestra was still tuning up. All German program including the prelude to Tannhauser, Brahm's second Piano Concerto and Schumann's Fourth Symphony was very well performed and received a rousing ovation from the full house. They made their way out arm-in-arm and found a taxi. They had an intimate kiss when they reached Kathleen's home. She waved from the sidewalk, smiling happily when the cabbie drove off.

Reuben's mind raced forward from this memory to a month later when Kathleen suggested that he apply to immigrate to Canada. "The country needs engineers and you will do very well there," she told him. The Canadian High Commission interviewed them both, checked his papers and granted him a temporary work visa which could be made permanent later. Six months after the chance meeting on a red, double-decker bus, they were in a bustling city in Western Canada, slightly smaller than Leipzig and Southampton and a culture very different from both.

6. The Decline and Fall of the Reuben Empire

Rueben found a good position in a consulting firm of engineers and Kathleen was hired to teach in a college that had ambitions to upgrade to a university. They found an apartment next to a park with easy access to the amenities important to them and not too far from their work. They had fun buying a small car and furnishing the apartment with a mix of new and used furniture. Kathleen introduced her 'partner' to old friends and both made new friends easily. If they were not in heaven, they were not far from it.

Rueben moved up quickly in his firm. He worked hard, got along well with the colleagues, completed his projects on time and to the satisfaction of clients. His demeanour impressed the prospective clients and he brought in new work. His particular skill lay in the organization: he showed the president how the company could improve the flow of work among engineers and technicians and speed the billing and collection systems. His extraordinary contribution was noticed. When the president retired four years later, the hedge fund that owned most of the shares offered Reuben the chance to buy the company in return for a loan that he could pay off over five years. Rueben accepted the offer without consulting Kathleen and this started the downward spiral in their relationship.

A year after he had taken over the ownership of the company, Reuben bought a condo on the thirtieth floor of a tower in an affluent suburb and Kathleen furnished it with the elegance it deserved. The view from the living room was the envy of their friends: snow-capped mountains in the West and downtown towers in the north. Aware of the outstanding loans on Safety First and the mortgage on the condo, Reuben was working harder and longer than ever before and had little time for Kathleen. Barely a year had gone by since the move, when after Saturday breakfast Kathleen asked him, "Do you have time to talk about something that is important to me before you rush off to the office?"

"Only if it is very important and won't take long," Reuben replied.

"It is crucial for my future. I want to know where our relationship stands in your plans."

"Right on top. Why do you ask?"

"I ask because you only think of one thing, your business. We hardly talk to each other. Our relationship is perhaps important to you at some level, to me we are like two ships crossing in the ocean. I have a deep sense that my clock is running out. If we are going to have a family, the time is now. I want us to get married and start a family right away."

"Safety First is at a critical point and needs my full attention. I won't be able to help you in raising the family anytime soon and being an engaged father is very important to me. Please let us wait a few years. We will have a wonderful family when the time is ripe. Let us give it some thought."

"I have given it a lot of thought and I have decided that I don't have the luxury of time at my age. If you have other priorities, that is your decision. I am sorry I have my priorities too. I can no longer stay in this relationship."

The tears rolled down Kathleen's cheeks. When Reuben tried to comfort her she pushed him away.

Reuben's ambition to achieve great success in business and the hard work it entailed brought their short experiment in blissful harmony to a close.

3

His luxurious condo is now gone along with the companies. First to go was the Safety First, his consulting business. The provincial economy took a nosedive, much as the previous owners had anticipated, net immigration became net emigration and most of the planned construction projects were put on hold. The client companies had to cut cost. They pensioned off the senior highly paid professionals to reduce the payroll. The young guys who took over key positions liked to do the work themselves and whatever had to be farmed out went to their friends. Reuben, hoping it was merely a blip, ignored the decline in his consulting business. In a few months the billings dropped to a level where they could not even meet the payroll, let alone finance his dream projects. The erstwhile busy staff spent their days on FaceBook, or tweeting how boring it was to be doing nothing in a dingy office when the ski hills beckoned. It was heart wrenching to see yawning colleagues, not to mention the red ink on the ledger. Reuben had to decide whether to keep a skeleton staff and wait for the good times to return or to close the shop for good. With the fingers of both hands crossed, he chose the later. Now the building was too large for his other ventures and the mortgage and maintenance expenses were hard to justify. It had to be sold in a down market at a price below what was owed on the mortgage. The bank agreed to add the difference to his balance on the condo at a higher rate of interest. Around the same time both public companies asked him to resign from their boards, presumably because he was not spending enough time on their affairs. It would have rubbed salt in the wounds of a sensitive soul, not Reuben though. He was made differently; he disregarded the snubs. None of this was serious. He still had two great prospects with really bright future and his stock-market investments were riding high. The empire was still on the horizon, only a little more distant.

The devil occupying his head guided his thoughts to the oil and gas prospects. There was some urgency in the situation at that time because the exploration rights were due to expire in three years. His knowledge of the oil business was rudimentary and he went into this business by accident in the glory days of Safety First. A client could not pay for the consultation services Safety First had provided for a project that failed to attract investors. In exchange, he offered Reuben the parcel of land and some data he had acquired to look for oil in an area the geologists had pronounced to have great potential. After checking with his contacts he accepted the deal. To manage the exploration work, Reuben lured Willard, a geologist with a great reputation, from a major company with a big signing bonus. Willard advised him to buy land in other prospective areas to spread the risk and Rueben used the spare cash in Safety First, not only to buy exploration rights, also to acquire additional seismic data.

Willard and the consultants he hired analyzed masses of data and made stacks of maps to show where the wells should be drilled to find gushers. Willard recommended that the project needed a partner with experience in drilling and production and that Reuben should offer to share it with one of the larger companies with expertise in this field. The two set meetings with major oil companies to entice them to drill the wells. For reasons only known to the companies, and not comprehensible to Reuben and Willard, there were no takers. Reuben lowered his sights to second-tier companies, then to the small operators. There was only one offer and Reuben was not so desperate as to give up all interest in his land after so much exploratory work for a miniscule share of eventual profits.

Willard advised Reuben to engage an investment broker to find investors in the projects and he would find the consultants to help with the drilling and production. They flew to Toronto and travelled all over Ontario and Quebec. In one week they visited twelve big and small towns wining and dining the brokers and their clients for lunches and dinners in expensive restaurants. When it came to eating out, Reuben had simple tastes and preferred, except for special occasions, hole-in-the-wall family eateries that served ethnic dishes straight from the oven. The stress of entertaining strangers in unfamiliar surroundings was intense and maybe the reason they failed in their mission and returned empty handed. After tallying the expenses the accountant told Reuben that the tour had cost $20,199.27, a paltry sum had he found an investor, a significant dent in his investment portfolio in the circumstances.

A break, which seemed lucky at the time, came to pass when Reuben picked up a message on his phone, "I am David Middleman; your buddy at the Southampton Post Office. I am in town for a couple of days. Let us get together for a drink or two. I am staying at the Knight's Inn." They met in the hotel lobby and walked over to the Last Mug, a café known for a superb selection of coffees and home made pastries. "Rob Holly invited me to visit. You know Rob, he worked for four years at the P.O. during the Christmas rush to pay for his trip home. Very friendly chap; we came to know each other well and kept in touch. I caught the travel bug, became a travel writer and later diversified into business reporting. Rob wants me to write a blurb promoting his company. What are you up to?"

Reuben told him about his businesses and his predicament about the oil prospect.

"I have just the ticket for you. Rob's company I am here to write about is in the oil business. You should talk to him. The company is very successful. Lots of people have made their fortunes by investing in it and appropriately it is called the Fast Buck. Give him a jingle. There is nothing to lose." David seemed excited at the prospect of helping a friend from forgettable days.

Reuben googled Fast Buck on his return to the office. The web site was impressive. It described all the successful wells the company had drilled and showed a graph with the stock price climbing exponentially. There was no mention of the success ratio of the drilling and the balance sheet was fuzzy about debt. Reuben was desperate and did not hear the alarm bells. He called Rob Holly who seemed to vaguely remember his name. They briefly described to the other what their companies were about and agreed to meet the next day. After an informal lunch in the Petroleum Club they joined Willard and the senior executives of Rob formally around a massive rosewood table in the elegant boardroom of Fast Buck Hydrocarbon Enterprises. Willard amicably discussed the technical aspects with the geologists of Fast Buck for about an hour. In the meantime, Reuben explained to Rob the tax losses available to a merger partner.

Rob returned to the boardroom after getting a report from his exploration manager. He came straight to the point, "First, we like the location of your project, it complements the holdings of Fast Buck and your people have done excellent work. Second, the losses in your books will offset some of our recent gains, our bean counters will like that. Although I would be happy to add your locations to the inventory of drilling projects of Fast Buck, there are two problems for you to consider. The deal must be consummated within six weeks to maximize tax benefits and the payment would have to be in Fast Buck shares which have to be held for six months after the deal is approved."

Reuben did not like the time restriction on shares. However, he knew that the regulations of stock exchange demanded it. Moreover, he had come to the end of his patience. He had neglected his other venture much too long and it was time to focus on it. They negotiated the number of shares he would get, the lawyers spun out the work as they always do and the deal was signed on the Friday afternoon of the sixth week. A week later Reuben received an unexpected bill; his share of the legal cost of the merger, a sum of $9,025.97.

Fast Buck drilled three deep and expensive wells on their prospects in the following year. Each showed the presence of hydrocarbons in non-commercial quantities. Investors want production; technical success does not satisfy the bean counters. The stock price plunged to a few pennies before Reuben could cash his holding. Rob was disturbed by what he considered a wholly unjustified overreaction. He called several influential market analysts to assure them that he had other even better prospects and funds available to drill them. It was duly reported in the business sections of the media the next day and the stock price stabilized at a couple of dimes. Reuben suggested drilling one of his prospects. The Fast Buck staff overruled him and recommended a surefire location offsetting known production on three sides. Rob secured the approval of the budget of nearly a million dollars from the partners. Unfortunately, even the last drop of Fast Buck's luck had leaked out. The drill got stuck in the well a mile below the surface. There was a fatal accident in trying to retrieve it and the costs escalated, exceeding the budget by almost half as much.

The partners blamed the incompetence of Fast Buck for the mishap and refused to pay their share. Fast Buck breathed its last leaving the shareholders stuck in the hole.

Reuben still had one shot left and it was a big one - exploration rights on nearly a hundred-thousand hectares in the boondocks. A born optimist, he focused all his energies on finding gold there. Precious metal exploration is expensive and the remote location multiplied the costs several fold. His consultant estimated that it would run close to a million dollars for test drilling and data analysis for the next summer. The first step was to raise the seed money and it was achieved by the sale of his condo. The real-estate market was hot and a Bulgarian oligarch liked the location. Rueben received a sum of nearly six figures after paying the mortgage. He found an apartment with a small room for the office of his mining prospect that he called Prosperity Gold and Silver Corporation and set about raising the million he needed for the company to live up to its name.

4

Reuben met Franz in an upscale coffeehouse called Moondoe's, located across the street from a popular franchise at close to midpoint between them. He had asked his trusted friend the best way to proceed. After formal enquiries about each other's health and ordering the Columbian and chocolate donuts they settled on comfortable lounge chairs in a quiet corner overlooking the trees in full bloom along the side street. Franz was a stickler for details and he had to see the whole picture before Reuben could get a word out of him. He looked at his friend's worried face and asked, "You know nothing about mines or minerals. You studied engineering, not Geology. Why are you involved in a mining prospect?"

Reuben answered with a wry smile, "It is a long story, I will make it short. Andrew, a very good client, went to Yukon every summer for a week or two with a friend on what he called gold panning expedition. The summer days are long that far north. No matter, they sat from sunrise till dark by the riverbank, collecting sediments in their pans and shaking them till the dirt had dropped out. Once in a while one or two minute grains of gold were left. They never sold the gold. After a decade each of them had a few grams in a bag adorning their coffee tables. One summer the friend could not join Andrew for some unknown reason. Perhaps his wife had had enough of solitary summers and forbade him his one pleasure. In any event, Andrew asked me to join him and I agreed because one has to keep the client happy."

Franz was perplexed, "How did you go from a summer lark to this huge project?"

"Don't be impatient, I am coming to it," Robin said after a long sip and continued, "Andrew is an amateur geologist. He explained that there must be one or more veins of gold in the rocks upstream which are being washed by the river or its tributaries. The veins have been supplying the gold bugs for centuries and must be loaded. With all these fancy tools geologists have developed recently, it should be fairly easy to locate them."

Reuben called for refill and carried on with the story, "I was easily persuaded because Safety First had a huge backlog of lucrative contracts and I was looking for places to put the money in. Six months earlier, I had acquired oil leases from a client who couldn't pay my bill and thought that a mining prospect would be a good diversification strategy along with the oil exploration and engineering services. Andrew knew of a local dealer who could help me if I were ever to be interested. I contacted him and we exchanged phone numbers"

Franz was bitten by a sense of envy. He interrupted Reuben, "All sorts of exciting things happen to you, and poor me, I sit in front of a silly computer all day long. We all have our lines on the palms, not much we can do about what comes our way. Did you check up on your gold-bug client's tale?"

Reuben put the cup down, "Yes I did. I called a leading group of mining geologists who confirmed the possibility Andrew had pointed out to me. They also outlined the risks in such ventures and the great deal of money they can absorb. I suppose I was hooked. The dealer called a month later. He had a large parcel, not far from where we were panning, and it came with excellent survey reports. The company had decided to get out of Canada and was selling it cheap. Safety First had just signed a big contract and I bought it sight unseen at the price the dealer had mentioned. I set up a company to explore this land and called it Prosperity Gold and Silver Corporation. Next summer, I hired Jamey, a geologist, for detailing the work of previous owners. I took two weeks off from work and joined him in the boondocks."

Franz raised a finger to stop him, "Was that the time you were in the media all over the country?"

"Yes, it was. It was most unfortunate. Jamey was taking the surface samples – chipping a piece of rock, numbering it and placing it in a plastic bag. I was his mule, carrying the rock bits in my backpack. He was a big guy and amazingly nimble. We were on a steep ridge. He handed me the sample and literally ran down the slope. I was not so steady on my feet and took a while to negotiate the cliff. When I reached the relatively flat ground, Jamey was nowhere to be seen – not that I could see more than a few feet in any direction in the dense forest. When I screamed for Jamey, all I heard was the echo. I realized the seriousness of my situation straight away. I was totally unprepared to be alone in the forest. Jamey had the compass, water, snacks and hammer and I had rocks – on my back and perhaps in my head too. I gave up on Jamey and started walking in the direction I thought would lead me to our tent about five kilometers away. Soon it became dark and I had to stop and prepare myself to spend the night with bears and cougars."

"You were missing a long time if I remember it right," Franz said.

"For two nights and three days it rained non stop. With the clouds and the dense trees I could not see very far or judge the direction. I slept under dripping trees and walked very carefully so as not to slip on wet ground and sprain an ankle. I avoided any clearing where I might meet a bear. After forty-eight hours a forestry road appeared out of nowhere and I screamed with delight. A truck came by before I had gone very far. The driver had heard of the missing miner on the radio and he went out of his way to drop me at the nearest police station. They contacted Jamey who literally flew over, apologized with, perhaps, a little too much drama and took me to the hospital for a check up. I spent the night there undergoing numerous tests. I was cleared by the doctors in the morning and made my way home leaving Jamey to complete the summer's program."

Although Franz wanted to pursue this sad experience, Reuben did not delve into it in any depth. However, he did add, "That mishap had a negative impact on exploration. Jamey refused to go back there after the summer and the next geologist had to repeat some of Jamey's work. For a while I lost interest and gave priority to the oil venture which you know all about. Now Prosperity is my last hope and I am going to put all I have in making it a success."

The stage was set for Reuben to detail his plans for Prosperity and the funds it needed. Franz listened attentively, paused for some thought, then asked, "How much can you raise from your friends?"

Reuben was frank, "I have a few friends who are aware of my recent misfortunes. I doubt that they would take the risk irrespective of how good the chances of multiplying their investment maybe. I need outside sources for this venture."

Franz was buried in thought and the only sound was hum of traffic on the road. At last he put his cup down very gently, looked straight at Reuben and said, "The only real option is to raise funds by issuing shares of Prosperity to the public. I am in that business and I can help you along in the long process. You were on the board of public companies. You know what is involved in operating a public company."

Reuben replied, "I have some idea of operation requirements, I know nothing about setting one up." After a pause he asked, "Will the brokers help in taking the company public? Can you suggest the brokers I should see?"

Franz smiled, "Don't be in such a hurry. Before you see a broker, you will have to engage a firm of corporate lawyers to take your company public, in the parlance of those guys. They will charge you at their standard rate of five hundred dollars an hour. Approval of the application to the exchange can take several months."

"Is there something else before I see the broker?" Reuben was impatient.

Franz resisted a grin lest it offended Reuben, "Yes there is. This is only the first hurdle. Next, you will have to hire a reputable mining consultant to evaluate the prospects, things like how much exploration is needed to find how much ore and what are the probabilities of different levels of success. These companies usually charge a thousand dollars a day and it could take a month to complete the study and report."

"That was the second step. What is the third?" Reuben asked.

"You take the consultant's report to a brokerage group that deals with start ups like yours. I will give you the name of companies looking for work when you are at this stage. They will study the report and make their own analysis. After a month or so, they will tell you if they can lead a group of brokers to sell Prosperity to the public or not. If they agree they will set a price for the offering, heavily discounted from the real value of course, otherwise why would anyone buy it? They will get together with your lawyer, prepare a prospectus and send it to the exchange for approval. The broker will charge you in advance for these services, usually a fixed fee of twenty to fifty grand. In addition, they will take a percentage, usually ten percent of the proceeds from whatever they sell even if the money raised is only a fraction of what you had hoped for. They will also want an option to buy more shares for their own account at a heavy discount from what public bought them for. This process alone can take from three months if you are exceptionally lucky, to over a year if you have to jump over higher than usual hurdles." Franz was not holding back any punches.

Reuben's response was a soft murmur, "It could be two years and cost a hundred grand before I see a new penny."

Franz was moved by his friend's obvious disappointment. However, honesty is the best, in fact only, policy for someone in his profession. He said, "You are in the ball park about the time line, perhaps a little optimistic on the dollar figure. These things are not cheap and good professionals produce results. Unfortunately, they don't value their services lightly."

Reuben was now counting the coffee grinds at the bottom of the cup, "What do you suggest I do?"

Franz picked up the bill and stood up, "You have to decide whether the project is worth risking a large portion of your current assets. If you find gold after the first shot, assuming you get that far, you will have no problem raising money for more exploration. If the holes are poor, the project is dead for all practical purposes. From what I have seen, it could be ten years before you see an ounce of gold. Of course, you can also try to get a large company interested in your land position. One thing I would advise against is to liquidate your portfolio; you don't want to work night shift again and it won't generate enough cash anyway."

The friends shook hands and went their separate ways. Franz was sorry he could not be more encouraging. As for Reuben, he had to decide whether to wake up or dream a little longer. And there was no mentor to guide him.

5

After the collapse of his last venture, Reuben decided that he had some great stories to tell about his life in East Germany and he should write a semi-fictionalised account of the more interesting ones. To add spice to the solitary life of a writer, he could take over the portfolio management from Franz and see if he could stretch it out to last till the book was finished and the royalties started pouring in. He had enough modesty to realize that he had to learn the basic skills of both these professions. Before picking up the pen, he attended two Creative Writing courses at local colleges. He also started reading the business section of the newspaper carefully and borrowed from the library the books frequently referred to by the columnists. After a year of hard work, he was ready to go on his own. He met Franz at Moondoe's one last time and told him with some firmness, "I appreciate all you have done for my savings over the years. I now have enough time to spare and enough knowledge picked up from four books on investment management and the Business Post articles. So, if you don't mind, from now on I will decide what to buy and sell, and you can execute the orders. I hope to have some fun even if the saving in management fees is offset by commissions for trades."

Franz could not hide his disappointment, "I am sorry to lose an account I nourished as my own. Two percent annual return in the tough market of these years is due to the hard work I put in managing your funds. However, it is your money, you should do with it what you are comfortable with. I do have one bit of advice. If you want to manage the account you should switch to a discount broker. Commissions are minimal, service is in some ways better, you can place orders and watch the execution on your computer and have 24/7 access to your account. I suggest Rapid Growth Brokerage and if you agree I will arrange to open an account there and transfer your portfolios. Their representative will call you when it is done, perhaps within a week."

A new life was set for Reuben. The old Prosperity office was now his writing and investment bunker and his hope of a new prosperity. "Although it will be hard work and it may take some time, the success is assured," Reuben told himself over and over again. His first piece was a story built round the dialogue when a Stasi informer asked him, "Why are you learning English? Wouldn't Russian be better?"

"It would be great to have major speeches of our glorious leaders Ulbricht and Honecker available to those ignoramuses in England and America," Reuben replied.

With a somewhat exaggerated description of hard life in the Democratic Republic, goodness of the general population, depressing state of the cities and the natural beauty of countryside, the dialogue expanded into a 3,000-word story. With the confidence of a novice, he sent it to a national magazine. The editor accepted it and paid him one hundred dollars. Reuben couldn't believe how easy the whole process was. He now spent all the time he was not working on investments on writing. There was so much in his mind that needed to be told before North Americans lost even the little interest they had in a country once called the German Democratic Republic. He planned to write and publish individual anecdotes and arrange them in a book form when there were enough of them.

Reuben wrote tales based on his experiences and those of his acquaintances. His writing process had nothing complicated about it. When he decided to write about an event, he would think for a few days to let it take a form in his mind. Then he would let his subconscious refine it by putting it out of his mind for a week or so. Now he was ready to sit down at his computer and let the words fall where they may without a break, not even for a coffee, till his back ached. He was so focused on writing that he did not notice the kettle boiling dry and the potatoes burning down to cinders. This 'free fall' writing session produced the first draft. Over the next few days he edited again and again, reading critically each time, till he reached the point at which he did not have to make a change. He spent the following couple of days thinking about how he could improve the first and the last sentences. His Creative Writing tutors had drilled into his head that they were the critical elements for a reader and deserved utmost attention. When the piece was done, he read it to find the most appropriate title. Once the title went on top in bold letters, the article was ready to be mailed to the editors of respected journals.

Reuben's luck ran out after his first story. The editors hardly ever responded to his submissions and the rare response was a disheartening refusal even though at first glance it was expressed in words full of kindness. He soon realized that these words were the standard form of a refusal letter. However, the realization did not prevent him from sending his works to other magazines he found on the internet. A couple of years after the publication of his story, he had fifty more in digital form in the computer and in print in the pile of rejected manuscripts in one corner of his office. After six rejections of his fiftieth story, Reuben decided that the collective impression of all the stories combined was more likely to persuade the editors than a story by itself. He felt that all he had to do was to arrange the stories in an appropriate order and the publishers would compete for publication rights.

Reuben spent the next three weeks grouping the stories by similarity of content into chapters. Then he read each chapter carefully and made alterations to enhance the continuity. While doing this he found many repetitions and made appropriate modifications. He noticed inconsistencies in writing style in some stories and rectified these as well. He showed the manuscript to one of his Creative Writing tutors who offered to edit it for a special ex-student rate of two dollars a page. She made many suggestions, no page was left unchanged. Reviewing the edits and the recommended rewrites took several months. At last, after hard and solitary work of more than three years, the book was ready. The friendly editor gave it a cursory glance, advised him on how to prepare the material for publishers and suggested three names he could send it to. She also warned him not to be impatient, never to contact the publisher; just wait for the reply. If he received a reply in less than six months it would be bad news, a reply after a year or more may still not be what he was hoping for.

Rueben made three copies of the manuscript, double spaced, single side, one inch margin on all sides, the title on the top left hand corner of each page and page numbers at the bottom right. He prepared a covering letter which included a short description of the book, high-lighted his publication of three and a half years ago and mentioned the creative writing courses he had attended. He prepared three packages containing the covering letter, manuscript, stamps to cover the postage in the unlikely event the manuscript had to be declined and a self-addressed postcard for the acknowledgement of receipt. He sent one each to three leading publishers in the country. All he had to do now was to wait for the advance on royalties. "No bargaining, first acceptance gets to publish it," he said to himself when charging the three-figure postage to his credit card.

If Reuben was worried about his shrinking investment portfolio, his actions did not show it. He had developed a trading style based on the books he had studied, free lectures he had attended, and advice columns he had read. He bought a stock that jumped and sold the one that dropped sharply without looking into the reasons behind the rise or fall. The system worked like a charm for a few months and firmed up his faith in himself and the technique he had developed. However, the pendulum swung the other way and the portfolio had by now declined to a level where many brokers would have asked him to take his business elsewhere. In addition to the dropping value, he had to withdraw funds for modest living expenses: rent on his small apartment, simple organic food which he cooked himself and two or three bottles of brandy, Courvoisier Gold, and Havana cigars – only the best when it came to the only luxury he allowed himself. He had no trouble justifying the hours he spent after dinner stretched out on the sofa with the lights dimmed, a Havana in his right hand and the drink on the side table in easy reach. That is when he had his best ideas, not only on investments, for writing as well. What if the account was down to low five digits? It would be foolish to worry, he said to himself. The stock market has its ups and downs; after a steady down for last three years it was time for an up. In any event, the advance from the publisher would be in before the money ran out.

Two weeks had not gone by yet when one of his packets was returned with a curt note. The company accepted the submissions only from the qualified agents; a list of their names and addresses was enclosed. Reuben took this as a positive sign. He looked at the list, picked a name that sounded most impressive and sent the package to that address, with an appropriate covering letter of course. Reuben was not a person who twiddled his thumbs when he was waiting. He still had to look after his shrunken investments, if only because his livelihood depended on them. Not all the time though, not someone like Reuben anyway. He needed to do something creative to feel useful. Therefore, he continued writing stories, editing them carefully and sending them to the magazines. "If the prospective publisher sees my work in a magazine, he may feel more inclined to look at my book seriously," he thought.

It was the twentieth anniversary of the day Reuben had landed in Canada, years of unimagined ups followed by a steady downward slide in his fortunes. The echo of the eleventh chime of the clock was still in the air when the phone rang. He didn't mind the interruption; in fact he welcomed it. He had been staring on the screen looking at his portfolio, whatever little there was, wondering whether to take out all that was left to pay the credit card bill or incur interest for another month in the hope of a recovery. The call was from an editor to whom he had sent an essay on the integration of West and East Germany. He had discussed at length how the social services and the individual rights in the former socialist state called the German Democratic Republic had improved with increasing prosperity while the cultural industry there had declined because citizens had access to popular programs on modern television sets. This must have appealed to the editor, he also had the problem of declining sales because readers could get what he was offering on the internet. He told Reuben that he would be happy to publish the essay if Reuben did not expect any cash payment for it. Reuben did not know whether to be glad that an essay was being accepted after three years of trying, or to cry because he could no longer afford to give away the fruit of his labours. The editor took his long silence to mean an agreement. "Your essay will appear in the next issue and I will send you four copies at no charge," he said before the click.

"Might just as well have a coffee and check the mail before going back to the lousy stocks," Reuben muttered. He had developed this habit of talking to himself lately, perhaps a sign that the solitary life and the anxiety were more than he could handle. He plugged the kettle without checking the water and went out to collect the mail. It was a thick bundle held together by a rubber band. There were the flyers from Tears and Attlee Bay, thick envelopes from charities although he hadn't been able to donate for a long while, a statement from the discount broker, a thick envelope from an unknown bank that looked like a credit card application and an envelope that made his heart rate jump. It was from the agent that he had sent the book to, and from the looks of it, contained more than one sheet. "I will make the coffee before I open you," he told the envelope and turned towards the hissing kettle.

About the Author

Sudhir Jain is a retired oil industry consultant. Born and brought up in India, he has lived and worked for extended periods in England, Libya, the United States and Canada. In his previous profession, he published more than forty technical papers and won national and international awards. He has been passionate about literature and classical music since early teens. In addition to four books, stories and essays, several hundreds of his Letters to the Editor have been published in the North American newspapers and magazines. He lives in Calgary with his wife of fifty one years.

Other books by the author

Isolde's Dream and Other Stories
Couldn't Shut Up
Pages From an Immigrant's Diary
Princess of Aminabad: An Ordinary Life

About this book

East or West is a worldly, eclectic collection of linked short fiction. In these pages are stories that explore themes like the clash of cultures of east and west, the small instances that shape great lives, starting over, and more.

A new holy site arises in the east: an ashram . . . for atheists, but is it all that it seems? A young British girl struggles against her new boyfriend's fundamentalist religious culture. A musician in the 1800s strives to gain recognition while under the shadow of one of the greatest composers of all time. A business tycoon has one last chance at happiness after his hubris has cost him his fortune. A debut author seeks success at a local book fair. A young executive tries to close a deal that could save her struggling company.

East or West contains more than twenty stories that radiate intelligence, pathos, and humour in a reading experience for all ages.